THE SWITCH POINT

A. D. CHILDERS

To Faith -
Thank you for
your support!
I hope you enjoy!

A.D. Childers

To the Childers line, whose love of reading and writing has been passed on to me. Thank you for such a precious gift.

TRANSCRIPT FROM

AUGUST 27TH, 2017, RECORDING

Kennen: Every little town has its stories, its legends. People think they want to know the truth, but sometimes the truth is disappointing. Or it doesn't have as much meaning as the story.

[Glances over shoulder]

I'm just going to tell you what I know. The facts as I know them now. Things I ignored back then. And then you can decide.

MAY 2017

The loud cheer filled the entire soundstage. Marty Gilwick popped the cork on the champagne, gold bubbling out and dripping to the floor. Glasses were poured and passed, a few more bottles less ceremoniously opened so everyone would have a sip.

A cheer of "Speech! Speech! Speech!" erupted and Marty glanced at Kennen.

Kennen smiled, shaking his head. "This one is all you, Marty."

Marty nodded and started to the front, then paused and looked back at Kennen, serious. "Don't run off. We need to talk about something." As he turned, Marty plastered a smile back on his face.

Marty apparently gave a stirring speech, because the gaggle of crew members broke out into cheers whenever he paused for a sip, but Kennen heard none of it. He was busy eyeing the crowd. Was someone missing? Had something horrible befallen a crew member? Short of death, Kennen couldn't imagine anything dimming Marty's enthusiasm. They were celebrating; the fourth season of their investigative docudrama, *Truth from the Shadows*, was ranked first in the nation. When they first received the news Marty glowed like a proud new father. Kennen looked for his assistant, Gemma Jones. She gave him a flicker of her warm brown eyes then returned her focus to Marty. She was smiling and cheering. Clearly, if there was bad news, she was in the dark as well.

As Marty finished his speech, Kennen stepped over to the refreshment table which held trays of fruit, meat, and cheese. Greg Totmeier, the head cameraman, was loading up a plate, and Cora Tombs, the head sound tech, shook her head with a smile. "Leave some for Kennen," she said.

Greg turned and gave Kennen his big jolly smile and a light elbow. "Eat up! They got the good stuff!"

Kennen started to reach for a plate when Marty caught his eye. "I'll catch back up with you in a few," he said, refilling his empty glass with red wine from a box.

"In trouble already?" Greg called after him with a good-humored chuckle.

Marty said nothing as Kennen approached, but instead headed back to his office. They seldom used the soundstage space; most of their footage was taken on-site, but Marty worked out of a small windowless office to the back when not on location. He held the door for Kennen and then went behind his desk, but he didn't sit down. He bent over and pulled out a bottle of Scotch from his desk. He tilted it towards Kennen, who lifted his red wine and shook his head with a smile. As he poured, Kennen sat down into one of Marty's overstuffed leather chairs. He started to cross his legs but then had to stand and move aside as Marty came around, trying to squeeze by in the tiny space to the other leather chair that sat opposite the desk. Both men settled back into their chairs, though Kennen felt anything but comfortable.

Marty sat his Scotch on the desk and rolled up both sleeves of his button-down. His skin glistened slightly; it seemed the alcohol had warmed him up. Kennen sipped his red wine. It was pretty terrible, but the earlier glasses of champagne kept him from suffering too acutely from its shortcomings.

Marty retrieved his glass and lifted it with a smile toward Kennen. Kennen tapped his wine glass lightly against Marty's tumbler. Both men smiled and drank, and as the sour bite of the wine dried out his mouth, Kennen hid a grimace that had more to do with Marty's smile than the drink. The joviality from the stage floor was gone from Marty's red face; this expression was contrived.

"Okay, so what is wrong?" Kennen asked. "Did something happen with the Connelly case?"

The season premiere of *Truth* focused on the story of Ben Connelly, a child that had gone missing in the late 80s in Jersey. Connelly's case had gone unsolved and, over time, became another chapter in the mythology of the Jersey Devil. That was until the show's researchers had picked it up. The show focused on unsolved cases that suffered from being trivialized by supernatural explanations. Their investigations had revealed not a devil, but a child molester who was already in jail for other crimes. He disclosed where he had hidden the body, and the Connelly family was finally able to put their young man to rest. That is what the show did; it cut through the bullshit. It made these cases real again and made the real monsters pay, not the mythical ones.

"No, no. No issues there. We're still the heroes and all." Marty chuckled halfheartedly.

Kennen waited silently while Marty took another sip of scotch.

"Do you remember when we started? People joked about us being grown-up Scooby-Doo. But there are no jokes now. Top series in the *nation*, Kennen."

Kennen still waited, not sure what to say. He dug through his memories of the last few weeks, wondering if he had done or said something to upset Marty. He came up empty.

"You've never mentioned a ghost story from your hometown." Marty made this statement to the far corner of the room.

"Well, Marty, that's because I'm not aware of one," Kennen

answered honestly after a pause. He tried to think. Was there a well-worn story that he had forgotten about? Taken for granted? Every town had one, sure, but what was Marty on about?

Marty sighed. "Well, I've recently heard differently."

"So, what have you heard about Chicago?" Kennen asked.

"Well, on some lists, it is in the top ten of the most haunted cities," Marty said. "But I'm not talking about Chicago. I'm talking about Ashter."

Ashter was a small suburb of Chicago and not what Kennen considered his hometown. He had lived in Chicago until high school. His mother had died and his stepfather had moved them out to Ashter. As soon as he was done with high school, he got the hell out of there. He had no interest in returning.

"What do you remember about Ashter?" Marty asked.

"No ghost stories," Kennen said firmly. Maybe what Marty had heard had traveled along the grapevine and got so twisted that it was ready to rot right off. Maybe it was the shit in his wineglass right now. Maybe he could get away from this just as easily as pouring it down the drain. "I don't know what you've heard from some dark hole on the internet."

"The research team has already talked to the producers. They want something huge for season five. What better than a story from the host's hometown?"

"I only lived there for a few years."

"All the same. When you were there, you ever hear about a girl named Leonie Tilden?"

"What have you heard?" Kennen wiped his face blank before looking squarely at Marty.

Marty took a sip of his scotch. "What I've been told so far was that she was murdered, there were issues with the arrest, so her case never actually came to trial, and, this is the part where the producers perked up too, that she might have been running from a ghost. A wailing woman."

"I have to tell you, I hadn't heard that about the case."

"But you have heard about the case then?"

"Marty, Leonie was a good friend of mine."

"Shit." Marty paused to take a long sip. "I was afraid of something like that."

"Well, now you know." Kennen stood, retrieving his wine and heading for the door.

"Kennen, wait. I'm so sorry."

Kennen turned and gave a half-smile to Marty. "You couldn't have known, Marty. We'll just forget about it."

"What do you mean forget about it?"

"Well, I mean, they'll have to find another story. Another investigation."

Marty sat still, looking stonily at Kennen.

"Well, come on, Marty. We can't have me investigate that. It would be completely unprofessional for me to investigate something I have a history with."

"I told the producers we should talk to you first. You know what they said?"

"What?"

"They said it didn't matter."

"What?! How could it not matter? And anyway, there isn't anything to solve. They know who they think did it."

"That's the issue. They only think they know. Without a trial—"

"Then I'll just say no. Hell, I'll break contract. What will they do then?" Kennen knew there was no reason to raise his voice at Marty, but he couldn't seem to swallow it back down. The wine glass shook in his hand.

"Kennen, I don't think the producers are going to back off on this. You walk away on this? The scandal and attention will pay for itself. They'll just see more dollar signs." Marty looked like he was about to fall apart. He opened his mouth, shook his head again, then closed his mouth again, looking away. "I can't ask you to stay in this situation. I won't stand in your way if that's what you want to do. But understand, they will do it with or without you. If you want to have your say…"

Kennen wanted to throw his glass. To dash it across Marty's desk, letting the glass and wine break into one. But Marty was right. Kennen started to feel the room closing in on him. He could walk, but the producers had the scent of blood; this story was not going to disappear. He could walk away, try to look like he stood on a pedestal of professionalism. But he would know it would truly be built on cowardice. Or he could stay and sacrifice himself to his past ghosts. Both choices were untenable.

"It's your call, Kennen. I'll understand either way."

"I have to warn you, Marty."

Marty turned his face slowly up to Kennen.

"These ghosts might be real."

Marty gave a nod and raised his glass to Kennen.

JULY 2017

Kennen stood at the window of his Ashter Regal Hotel room and looked out at the old street. The new old street. The buildings were the same, but the names were different from what he remembered. What used to be a hip bar called 673 was now The Red Dragon Chinese Restaurant. The dark and mysterious Weller's Bookshop was now a thrift store, well-lit by fluorescent bulbs with a number of tattered stuffed toys sitting in the window. The corner store, which before had simply been known as The Drugstore, was now a Dollar General. Its main entrance had been moved to sit parallel with the street, and the original doorway that had faced the corner was bricked up. A busker sat in front of the lost doorway on a metal folding chair, playing his saxophone, case open and littered with a few coins.

There was a soft knock at the door. Kennen opened it to find Gemma there, a leather bag of files hanging from her shoulder and a laptop cradled in her other arm. A pen was tucked behind her ear, disappearing into her glossy black curls. She was wearing her glasses, the brown frames a shade lighter than her eyes, which usually meant she was ready for research work. Kennen stood aside for her to enter the room. She went straight to the meager table that was part of the amenities offered in the suites of the Regal. Once she set down her laptop and dug out a few files the table was pretty much full. She sighed.

"I see Marty has come through with his normal level of luxury," she said. The show could afford better accommodations, but Marty always wanted the crew to be in contact with anything that would help them break down the barrier of years between the present and the case they were investigating. This meant that if there was a hotel, restaurant, store, or anything still existing from the time of the case, that place became a new haunt for the crew. All the better if it was also the haunt for the long-time locals. Marty sent them out two weeks before any of the real recording work would start. Gemma and Kennen would make contact with possible leads, but they wouldn't start interviews yet.

Gemma could go out like the rest of the background team, which currently consisted of Greg, Cora, and a few crew hands. They would get the scent of the place, looking for people that would be good extras or characters that would add flavor. Marty always brought in ringer actors from the agencies in New York for the scripted shots, but otherwise, he wanted authenticity. *The flaws of reality make for the perfect documentary,* he would say.

It was trickier for Kennen to be out, being the face of the show. They weren't there to cause waves at first, just to observe, but that could fall apart if word got around town that Kennen Clarke from *Truth from the Shadows* was spotted having a milkshake at the local burger joint. Kennen had discovered that growing out his facial hair (since he hosted clean-shaven) and sticking to sunglasses usually took care of things, but then he had never investigated in a place where he'd formerly lived.

Gemma walked over to the mini coffee machine and held up the comically tiny coffee pot, throwing Kennen her unmistakable you-gotta-be-fucking-kidding-me look. Kennen snorted a laugh and just nodded. She grinned back at him and started filling the pot. Kennen started toward the table, but the notes from the busker snuck into his room through the drafty window, catching him by the ear and pulling him back to the glass. He didn't know the name of the tune, but it seemed familiar. Not so much the melody, but the feeling. Whatever this song was, it sounded like Ashter, or at least the Ashter Kennen had spent his high school years in. Lonely. Solemn. Going nowhere.

Gemma joined him at the window. "He's not half-bad," she said. The busker finished his tune and lifted his flat hat in thanks to the man who threw a few coins in his case, revealing a mostly bald head with a few wisps of gray. Kennen realized the guy who had thrown the coins was cameraman Greg, already out trying to get to know the locals.

"You gotta love street musicians," Gemma said, heading back to the table. "They don't need a stage or a recording studio. They just put their music out there where they're at. There's something inspiring about that. Alright now—" She cut herself off and sat in one of the wooden chairs, typing away at her laptop. Right back to work. "I've got a list of people to call and I have reached a few already. Kennen?"

Kennen was not back to work. Kennen was at the window. Waiting, hoping that the busker would continue playing, but it didn't look promising. What at first looked like a reed adjustment turned into a complete dismantling of the mouthpiece.

"I'm sorry," Gemma said.

This pulled Kennen's attention back to the room. "What?"

"Really, Kennen, I'm acting like this is business as normal, and it's not."

Kennen came and sat at the table. "No. You're right. We need to get to work."

Gemma pulled the pen from behind her ear, laid it on the table, then leaned back. "I really don't think you have any business with this. I can't imagine what you are feeling. You know, if you changed your mind, everyone on the crew would understand."

Kennen thought about making a joke about Gemma just trying to get his spot in front of the camera, but that didn't feel right. And it would be insincere. He knew that all the crew felt the way Gemma did right now. He had seen it in their glances, heard it in the words they didn't say. He was damn lucky to have them all. The least he could do was be honest with Gemma.

"You know what this feels like?"

Gemma waited for him to continue, raising her brow slightly.

"Penance."

Both were silent as the word settled down on the table between them, like a cat. A soft thing with claws. Finally, Gemma swallowed and opened her mouth, taking a moment before she spoke.

"Bullshit."

"What?" Kennen asked.

"That's bullshit. This isn't ... this shouldn't be a punishment."

"Well, that's not exactly what—"

"You were a teenager, right? We all know what that means. No one is going to judge you for that."

"That doesn't mean I am absolved of what I did, or didn't do."

"Listen, we aren't here to dig into your past, we are looking at Leonie Tilden, and only the parts of your life that intersect with her will be investigated. As long as we don't find out that you are the one who pushed her, I don't think it will be as bad as you think." Gemma offered a smile.

Kennen was silent. Gemma was right. She always was. But her words did nothing to the shadow that he felt creeping up in his mind. Her words passed right through it, and why not? It was immaterial; it had no substance. You can't push away something you can't touch.

"I guess maybe this is just karma or something."

"Listen, it's getting late. Let's just leave this until tomorrow," she said, starting to clean up the table. "Really, there was only one thing I needed to run by you tonight anyway."

"And that is?"

"I got hold of this one guy, a retired police chief. Apparently, he was one of the two detectives on the case at the time. He did agree to talk with us off-camera. You know, the regular thing about cops not wanting their faces all over television. I get it. But the thing is, he said he would only talk to you. Named you specifically, but I guess you are kind of a household name now." She stood and flashed him a little smile before packing up her laptop.

"You've got some other leads, right?"

"Yeah. I've got a teacher and a counselor. No dice on Tilden's parents yet, but I got Medina's uncle lined up as well."

Kennen focused on sitting still, trying not to cringe at the name Medina.

"Uncle? What about his mother?"

"She's not doing well. May not have long left. But he agreed to talk in her place."

"I don't think we should approach him quite yet," Kennen said.

"The uncle?"

"No, the retired detective. I know him from before. Let me have a little time to warm him up. In the meantime, let's work with the current chief. He's the one with access to the files now. And you said there was another detective, right? What about him?"

"Died ten years ago. Some sort of drug deal that went south as far as I can find. There isn't much about it really. Kinda swept under the rug. Makes me wonder about the guy's involvement. He didn't have a spotless record. But, yeah, that is a dead end."

Kennen sighed. "Figures."

Gemma left and Kennen went back to the window. He pulled out a faded picture from his wallet. An old picture of two people, one young, one a bit older than Kennen was now. He sighed and shook his head. "Not yet," he muttered and tucked the picture away again.

TRANSCRIPT FROM

AUGUST 27TH, 2017, RECORDING CONT.

Kennen: I first met Leonie Tilden in September of 1994 and I still remember that moment vividly. I had just transferred to Ashter High School, which had started its fall session about two weeks before. It was built out of dusty brown bricks with few windows, hardly inviting. I was standing at the curb, squinting in the morning sun when this girl came up to me. She had this curly honey-colored hair that looked like it was fighting to get out of the braids she had wrangled it into, and freckles viciously peppered over her nose and cheekbones. And her green eyes were ... beautiful in concept but terrifying in execution. [laughs]

She said, "Hey, you!" and I stood there like some idiot statue. I think I was kind of afraid she wanted to fight me for some reason. She sighed and everything about her just softened. "Kennen," she said in this completely different voice. It was kind. Well, cajoling actually, like I was a frightened child. I suppose I wasn't the first person to be intimidated by her.

When I finally got enough balls together to nod my head she told me she was there to show me to my classes. One of the counselors had asked her to help me out because we had a lot of classes together. It was easy for her to pick me out because there were only about 75 kids in the freshman class, most of which had been going to school together since kindergarten. Also, there was the fact that most kids were waving and meeting friends before first hour started, and I was the only person standing outside hanging out with the fire hydrant.

"Come on, I'll show you around," she said. She seemed in no way irritated to have been assigned an apparently mute stranger to help out. She took care of me from the start. She always had my back. I suppose that is why I felt so lost after she was gone.

SEPTEMBER 1994

Ironically enough, Kennen was headed to the drugstore downtown to grab some Tylenol and bandaids when the Jefferson Gang jumped him the first time. Kennen's new house was a faded old thing that sat on the edge of Ashter where Main Street swung south and crossed the train tracks. The saying "from the wrong side of the tracks" definitely applied in Ashter, and Kennen was only spared the label by about 100 yards. His backyard sat against the thin woods that served as insulation between the town and the tracks, and he found that if he cut through them, he saved himself about ten minutes when headed downtown.

Kennen was taking this shortcut and could almost see where 2nd Street hit a dead end at the woods ahead when three guys came up on his left. Two white guys and a Latino. One of the white guys looked like a student that sat in the back of Kennen's English class, but Kennen was pretty sure he wasn't a freshman like the rest of the clientele in that hour. The guy always wore an oversized black and red plaid jacket, even though it was still summertime warm.

"Hey, what're you doing walking out here?" This was from the guy in the middle. The huge dude. Kennen hadn't seen him at school and had a hard time believing he would have missed a guy of such ridiculous dimensions walking down the hallways. The Latino guy was closer in size to the English repeater but skinnier. He had long black hair that he regularly swept out of his eyes.

"Hey, I've seen you. You're the new kid, right? Clark Kent or something?" English repeater said.

"What, like Superman or some shit?" the Latino kid asked, which got all three of them laughing.

"Um, it's Kennen," he said softly, "I'm Kennen Clarke. I think we have English together." Maybe if he played it cool, it would be cool.

"Oh, wait, I've heard about you," the giant said, and the laughing stopped. "And your dad."

Well, shit.

The Latino kid looked at the massive dude. "Wait, Clarke, that's the guy who picked you up last week, right?"

"Shut up," the big dude said, giving the guy a shove.

The big guy started toward Kennen and the other two followed. They cut off his path to the street ahead. He backed up a little, but he didn't want to turn his back on these guys.

"He's prolly not goin' to want to be friends with us, huh, Jeffie?" English repeater said to the big guy.

"Don't think so." Jeffie shook his head. "Too bad."

"I mean, I might. I haven't even got to know you guys yet," Kennen said with a forced chuckle. His survival instinct was somewhere in his mind, facepalming itself.

"That's true," the English repeater said, sliding up to Kennen's side and throwing an arm around him. "Let me introduce you around. I'm Mike, this here is Jefferson, Jeffie to his friends, and this is Tino." Both Jeffie and Tino gave big smiles, though Jeffie's seemed more like a sneer.

Kennen managed to get out, "Um, hi," before Mike slugged him in the stomach and shoved him forward. He caught himself with one arm while the other cradled his stomach. Jeffie was on him in a second, knocking him down on his side. Then Jeffie was on top of him, straddling Kennen's stomach and trapping his arms at his sides.

"Check 'im," Jeffie ordered and Tino slid into view. Kennen felt skinny fingers reaching in his pockets. Luckily, his wallet was in his back pocket, and currently inaccessible due to the hundreds of pounds of Jeffie pinning him to the ground. Maybe his stepdad had been right; those trendy wallet chains did just make it easier to get robbed.

Tino came up with only lint. "Got nothing," Tino said.

"Too bad," Jeffie said. Kennen was finding it hard to breathe. Jeffie held out his hand just past where Kennen could see. He tried to wiggle, but Jeffie just relaxed more weight on him. When Jeffie's hand came back, it was clear Mike was standing nearby.

And had handed Jeffie a butterfly knife.

Kennen tried again to twist and wrench himself free, but he was utterly helpless against Jeffie's weight and strength. Jeffie put a meaty hand on Kennen's chin and pushed his head back, exposing his throat. Kennen tried to cry out, but Jeffie forced his mouth shut. Only pathetic little muffled sounds came out. Tears stung Kennen's eyes.

"Don't worry, Superman, I'm not going to kill you, just give you a little reminder."

Kennen felt the cool blade touch his neck just under his ear. Jeffie leaned forward, which allowed Kennen to get in some much-needed air. Jeffie waited for him to meet his eyes.

"It'll just be a little scar, but if you ever go telling Daddy about us, this little scar will turn into a brand new big red smile right under your chin." As Jeffie talked, Kennen felt the blade trace along his throat to his other ear.

"Hey!" a girl's voice rang through the trees.

"What stupid bitch is—" but Jeffie cut off as soon as he spotted whomever it was coming out of the trees. He folded the knife closed as he scrambled off the top of Kennen. Kennen rolled to his side, coughing. One of them spit on his forehead, and then they were gone, running off back into the woods.

Then there was Leonie, kneeling over him. He pushed himself away and tried to stand, tottery and shaking. Leonie held her hands up ready to catch but let him right himself. He tried to wipe the spit from his forehead and hoped she wouldn't catch him wiping his tears as well.

"You okay?" she asked, using that soft, cajoling voice.

"I'm fine," Kennen growled, trying to avoid her gaze.

"You're bleeding." The cajoling voice was gone. This was just matter-of-fact. Kennen's hand slapped a tickle he felt on his neck. Apparently, Jeffie had nicked him.

"Let me see," Leonie said.

"It's fine," Kennen argued, but Leonie ignored him, peeling his hand back and examining the cut from a few different angles.

"You're right. You'll just need a bandage. If you're headed to town we can stop by The Drugstore and grab you some."

Kennen snorted but didn't argue. He just started walking, checking every so often that blood wasn't running down his throat. He was kind of hoping Leonie would get the hint and leave him alone, but she seemed perfectly comfortable walking along in silence, like he had accepted her invitation.

"Those guys suck," she said once they crossed the boundary where the loose dirt of the woods fell over the low curb of the dead end.

Kennen looked over at her. She was on the short side, and though she was thin she didn't strike him as overly athletic. And she was attractive by Kennen's standards, but she wasn't some beauty queen.

"Why were those guys scared of you?"

"I think they are more afraid of my father than me. He's the only lawyer in town, and half the town treats him like he is going to sue them and take away what little they have."

"And the other half?"

Leonie smiled at the question. "I'm sure you get it, with your dad who he is and all. They probably won't mess with you again; they just wanted to scare you a bit."

"So, everyone is talking about us moving here? We're the big news in town?"

"Fresh meat," she replied, shrugging.

"Well, he's not my dad. He's just my stepdad."

"Hmm," Leonie said, with a curious smile.

"What?"

"Everyone in town always thinks they know everything that is going on. But they always miss some detail, don't they?" She turned and kept walking.

Kennen shrugged to himself and followed after her.

JULY 2017

Kennen rubbed the itchy scruff on his face. He had a pile of notes on his lap and the beige phone in his hotel room stared at him, its benign normality irritating. Usually, interviews were no big deal. Of course, there were interviewees he had liked and disliked, but it didn't really matter as long as he got the information he needed. He didn't even mind the ones he didn't trust; they just provided another layer of challenge. Not a challenge like this though.

As Gemma had said, she had tracked down a teacher and counselor that had connections to both Leonie Tilden and her accused murderer, Alex Medina. Neither the teacher nor the counselor had connected with Kennen in any particularly strong way, so that wasn't an issue. They were neutral territory. But that wasn't true for all of the potential interviews, one in particular.

The crew had been on the ground for three days now, which meant Marty would be looking for an update soon. At which point Kennen would have to admit to Marty, as well as to himself, that they were going to have to talk to that retired police chief. The other detective, as well as the suspect, Medina, were dead. Yes, they had Medina's uncle, but that wasn't going to be nearly enough. As far as Kennen was aware, the uncle didn't even live in Ashter when it all went down.

Kennen was usually the go-to guy when it came to dealing with the police. It was a careful line to tread; he had to make sure to foster a cooperative relationship. The show was about debunking fanciful stories that got in the way of solving crimes, not investigating how cops did their job however many years ago, but sometimes it looked dangerously similar. Kennen knew a lot about working with police officers, though. His stepfather had been a cop. Who had gone on to be a detective. Who had gone on to be the Chief of Police.

In Ashter.

When Kennen had left Ashter for college, he didn't look back. Everything in the rearview mirror was bleeding or dead anyway. His mother had died in a car accident just before he started high school and that left him with Jim, his stepfather. Kennen's biological father had never been around. After Kennen's mother passed, Jim took a job in Ashter as an officer. As an adult, Kennen could see all kinds of reasons why that had been a good choice. There were fewer violent crimes in a small city, and neither he nor Jim needed any more carnage in their lives. The job was a little more flexible for Jim to be a single father, and there was less competition for the better positions like detective. Teenage Kennen had only seen it as a trap. His mother was gone and now the rest of his life was being taken away and Jim was the one doing it, taking them to some small hick town. A town with no hope, the last thing Kennen had to lose.

Kennen had not spoken to Jim after leaving for college. He wasn't even sure Jim still lived in Ashter until Gemma told him.

Kennen stood up and threw the files on the table. He snagged a hat and some sunglasses and headed for the door. It was a cool night for July and Kennen took a deep breath. It didn't even smell the same. It seemed Ashter had decided to not look back either. Urban sprawl had closed the gap between this little town and Chicago. What used to be a clearly defined demarcation between the two, a forty-five minute drive through farmland, was now littered with houses, both places reaching for each other creation-of-Adam style.

Kennen found the changes strangely comforting. It helped him feel like he had some distance from the nightmare. His stride became longer and more relaxed. He lowered his shoulders. Stretched his neck as he walked. Let the threat of having to face his stepfather fall away for now. Instead, he focused on the evening air, the moon peeking out behind full trees. It was working, just being in the here and now.

A few kids, maybe eleven or twelve years old, were riding their bikes down the sidewalk. Another kid, maybe seven, was struggling to keep up on a purple bike with training wheels. Despite this measure, the kid managed to steer directly into a large hole of missing sidewalk and tip over, falling forward onto the concrete. He cried out, and before the two older boys could come to a stop, he was wailing at the top of his lungs. The shorter of the two older boys turned back wide-eyed, then the taller one sighed heavily.

"Joey, how do you manage to fall down with training wheels on? That shouldn't even be possible," the taller boy said.

The little kid was trying to pull it together, but sobs kept breaking through. He leaned back to show a bloody knee.

"That was a pretty nasty fall." Kennen walked past the older boys to the younger one. All three of them froze. Kennen squatted down near the little kid and pulled a white hanky out of his pocket. "Here, this will at least cover it until you get home."

Joey just looked at the ground.

"Sorry, mister. Mom's told him not to talk to strangers." The taller kid stepped off of his bike and let it fall to the ground. The other boy followed suit. The taller kid took the hanky and then looked at the still-bowed head of little Joey, his crown of silky blond hair shining in the dying sun. "What's wrong with you? He's just helping out," the taller kid scolded as he kneeled to bandage his brother's knee. Joey loosened up a bit, leaning back, and kicking out his leg so his brother could wrap and tie his wound.

"Mom says there are three rules I got to remember when I'm out with Johnny," Joey said, suddenly brave and talkative now that he could no longer see his bloody knee.

"Oh, yeah, what are those?" Kennen asked.

"One is to always stay with Johnny. Two is to not talk to strangers. And three is not to play anywhere dangerous."

Kennen nodded and stood. "Those sound like pretty smart rules to me. Your mom must be a pretty smart lady."

"She is," Joey responded.

"I don't know about that," Johnny muttered under his breath as he stood up. "Okay, come on. Get up."

Joey stood, but now that he had broken rule number two, there seemed to be no stopping him. "Dangerous places are, like, parking lots, the street, or the railroad tracks."

Kennen covered a flinch at the mention of the railroad tracks by putting his hands on his hips. "You're right," Kennen said, "all of those places are dangerous places to play. You could get hit."

"And the railroad tracks are haunted," Joey offered.

"Oh, shut up, Joey!" Johnny said.

"Is that so?" Kennen asked, leaning forward slightly.

"That's what everyone says," Joey said, righting his bike.

"Everyone?"

"Yup. Well, I guess just all the kids. Big people don't talk about it."

"The little kids think that," Johnny said. "We don't believe that." Johnny indicated his friend with a quick flick of his thumb, and the third kid just shook his head.

"Why do people think it's haunted?" Kennen asked.

"There's supposed to be this lady—" Joey started.

"They just do!" Johnny interrupted his brother. "Come on, we're going to be late, and Mom's going to be mad enough about you skinning your leg. Thanks, mister." All three boys hopped back on their bikes and were off.

"Sure thing," Kennen called after them.

He sighed and continued on his walk. His mind was on railroad revenants when his feet betrayed him and took him near the old Baptist Church. He couldn't see the parking lot that sat on the far side, but he knew it was there. Accessible only off a gravel strip that wrapped to the backside of the church. Cutting into the woods. Content to wait all these years for him to remember. He turned and headed back to the hotel.

OCTOBER 1997

There had been a freak ice storm on a Thursday in October and school was canceled for the following day. Kennen spent most of the morning bumming around the house in his pjs. Jim had headed in early to help with the large number of calls that always came after an ice storm. At around 10:00 am Kennen got tired of watching the morning kiddie cartoons and game shows, so he shuffled over to the computer. He was on for about five minutes, deleting some emails, when he saw a message come through over Yahoo Messenger from Leonie. They chatted nonchalantly about the snow day and boredom for a few minutes before Leonie went quiet on her end.

Kennen: Hey, you still there?

Leonie: Yeah, sorry. I just got a message from Brittany. Sounds like a whole bunch of people are getting together in the church parking lot in about half an hour. You wanna go?

Kennen: I don't know. It's really cold.

Leonie: I can pick you up. You don't have to walk. It'll be fun.

The lot was an ice rink when they got there. There were five other cars in the lot. Teenagers decorated the hoods and trunks or leaned against doors, puffs of laughter frozen in the air.

Leonie slid into a spot near the other cars. The lines that defined the parking stalls were buried under a layer of ice and snow, but this lot was always a hangout for wayward teens; they didn't need to see the lines to know where they were. Leonie got out and leaned against her door, shouting greetings to the other cars while Kennen penguin-walked around to her side.

"Watch this!" rang out and, heeding the famous call of teenage recklessness, everyone turned to see.

It was Dylan Whitacre, another kid from their class, a scrawny white kid with thin stringy blond hair. He was of the opinion that he was a badass, but he toed the line of being too annoying about it, so no one had bothered correcting him. He bore the dismissive title of "mostly harmless."

Dylan took a small run and then started sliding, trying to hold his balance as he glided across the parking lot. He made it most of the way before hitting a bump that threw him down on his side. His thick coat protected him from any real damage and his momentum kept pushing him along until he bumped into a cement parking block. Half of the crowd broke out in laughter, the other half started to try it out for themselves.

Leonie stepped around Kennen for a better view and slipped. Her hands went up as she started to tumble backward. Kennen reacted without thinking, grabbing her under her arm and righting her. He was surprised to find them both standing. He lowered his hand down her arm to her hand to make sure she had steadied herself. She grasped his leather-gloved hand in her wooly one... and didn't let go.

Kennen felt like his chest had an internal hiccup—everything on the inside jumped, but luckily nothing on the outside did.

He was trying to play it as cool as possible.

But Leonie was smiling, laughing, and holding his hand.

A smile just started across his lips when, from inside the

rumble of teenagers, Alex Medina came flying out. He only took a few quick steps and then he was sliding across the parking lot. Partway across he pivoted around, as graceful as a professional ice skater, finishing the distance sliding backward and bowing to cheers. Leonie dropped Kennen's hand to clap and cheer. Alex flashed her a smile.

JULY 2017

Kennen was locked in an epic battle with the card reader on his hotel door. Swipe the card fast. Angry blinking red light. Swipe the card slow. Angry blinking red light. Swipe the card medium speed.

Angry. Blinking. Red. Expletive. Light.

Kennen started hatching a plan to pry the thing off the door when a hand landed on his shoulder. He let out a high-pitched shriek he was not proud of and turned around to find Greg standing there, hands raised.

"Sorry, Kenny, man, I didn't mean to scare you." Greg was a head shorter than Kennen and was committed to a wardrobe comprised entirely of khaki pants and plaid button-downs. His black hair and beard grayed at the edges, but his hazel eyes didn't look a day over sixteen.

"No, I'm sorry, Greg. I've been having a rather heated interaction with my door lock here."

Greg stepped by him and took the key card from Kennen's hand. One swipe. Happy green light. Kennen sighed but smiled and pushed open the door, gesturing for Greg to go first.

"Have you updated Marty lately?"

"No," Kennen sighed, "not yet. Gotta get on that soon. Coffee? Water?"

"Nah, I'm fine, thanks. Well, I'm glad you haven't talked with Marty yet, because I've got something big." Greg slumped into a chair by the table and took out the small notepad he always carried in his breast pocket. "Something," he said, pausing to slap his notebook on the table, "huge."

Kennen smiled and rolled his eyes as was expected for his part in this. Kennen had always found Greg's theatrical displays corny but endearing. He walked over and sat down in the chair across from Greg.

"So, I was down at the dive bar just south of the tracks. Real hole-in-the-wall place," Greg started.

"The Bear Den? Was there a big carved wooden bear in the corner?"

"Well, it's called The Ring currently, but I bet we're talking about the same place. Bear was there, but he's got some boxing gloves tied on him. Anyway, I hit it at lunch and there are these two good ol' boys sitting in the corner. I go up to the bar and order a beer and the greasiest onion rings in the world." Greg sat back, thumping his chest with the side of his fist. "The things I do for this job."

Kennen gave a snort of a laugh.

"Anyway, I bide my time, and when their conversation dies down, I tell them I'm in from outta town. Just passing through really, but my old Chevy is making one hell of a rattle. Where can I take it that won't bend me over the tailgate?"

"Did they actually buy that stereotype-ridden bullshit?" Kennen asked.

"You're missing the point. I gave them an opportunity to gossip. And boy did they. When the bartender brought over another round, she accused them both of being worse than a knitting club."

"You said you had something important—"

"I'm getting there! So one of them gets on about this one

mechanic that was just a legend, so I lean in, get this faraway look in my eye," Greg said, demonstrating his technique, "and I say, *That's what I love about small towns. The legends. There's no tale that comes out of those big cities that can stand up to a small town yarn.*"

"You've got to be kidding me." Kennen chuckled and rolled his eyes again.

"Hey, don't knock it if it works," Greg said with a smile. "So they tell me about some real legends. Ghost legends."

Now it was Kennen's turn to lean in. He picked up a pen from the table and found an empty space on a page.

"Apparently, back when... well, your friend..." Greg stumbled. An unusual event for him.

"Yes, back when the case happened," Kennen offered.

"Yeah, at the time of the case, there were reports of a wailing woman seen along the tracks."

Kennen leaned back. So, the kids had been wrong; the adults did talk about it, just probably not in front of the young ones. But he had never heard this tale. Of course, it was within a couple of months of Leonie's death when he left Ashter for good, and he didn't talk with much of anyone during that time. He just hadn't felt up to it.

"Kenny, buddy, what's wrong?"

"It's just ... well, a wailing woman is so generic. Every small town from here to Laredo has a tale about a wailing woman. It's not enough to go on. What the hell are we doing here? I'm not seeing a ghost story connected with this case. It's just—" Kennen managed to bite off the last word, but it rang through his head. ME! Kennen rubbed his forehead and looked at the carpet.

"Well, she was seen at the tracks which is where Tilden..." Greg trailed off, looking slightly uncomfortable again. "But there is more, Kenny. There have been more sightings. Just in the last few weeks."

"Oh, let me guess," Kennen said, harsher than he wanted to sound with Greg, but unable to control it. "Someone has seen a wailing woman at the tracks, and it's Leonie, back from the grave, trying to point us to her killer."

"You'd think that, but actually, no," Greg said.

Kennen shifted his body towards Greg, but his eyes stayed down on the rough carpet.

Greg continued. "It's not Leonie that has been spotted. Not even a white woman. Latino. Male."

Kennen blinked, surprised.

"You mean, they think they are seeing—"

"Yeah. Medina."

OCTOBER 1997

Kennen walked up the ramp to the bleachers. He hated football games. It was the mix of the hero worship poured on to teenage boys and the barely-masked bloodlust that put him off the game. Generally, Leonie and he had been on the same page for this. But she wanted to go for half-time tonight because it was the Homecoming game.

"I thought you thought the whole high school royalty scheme was stupid," he had said.

"It is stupid, but this year it's our classmates, our friends. Royalty is stupid, but the people aren't."

Kennen wasn't sure that that was true, but in the end, he had caved. He spotted her at the end of a row in the student section. She slid over and Kennen sat beside her.

"Hey."

"Hey! You almost missed it." Leonie nodded towards the scoreboard. The game started at 7:00. Kennen had arrived at 7:15, saw there was still a line to get in, and decided to wait so he didn't look like a sad sack who was going to the game by himself. But now there were only two minutes left in the second quarter. And the score was 21 to 0, Ashter in the lead.

"Neither side is calling many timeouts. No reason to draw

out the massacre," Leonie said. They were playing Hampshire, which was a tiny town that was even poorer than Ashter, and that was saying something. It wasn't like Ashter had a great team either; a good season for them meant three wins. But Hampshire was always one of those wins. It wasn't a coincidence that this was the game picked to be Homecoming.

The crowd was rowdy. The kids at the front of the student section were standing with arms around each other or throwing up high-fives, cheering and laughing. There were plenty of adults farther up that were acting even more raucous. Kennen wondered how some of them had got their drunk asses up in the stands. Leonie had picked a relatively calm area just across from the band, who were starting to look bored. The drummers were twirling their sticks and watching the clock. Another first down to Ashter.

Two minutes before half-time, the king and queen candidates walked down onto the track in pairs and nestled in next to the cheerleaders' bags.

"Aaaannd the token spic." This comment came from a barrel-chested boy to Leonie's right. His cronies laughed and Kennen looked back at the candidates. Alex Medina stood with two other white boys and three white girls. He wore a black suit and a deep red tie. The last king candidate was already on the field, kicking Hampshire's ass, and the final queen candidate was cheering them on with her glittery poms.

"What did you say?" Leonie asked.

Kennen's shoulders tightened.

"Jealous you're not down there, Bobby?" Leonie continued.

"Bitch, you aren't down there either."

"There'll be more chances. I'm holding off for prom," she said with a smile and turned her attention back to the field where the teams were leaving after the halftime whistle. Kennen looked down at his hands. Leonie wasn't sporty, but that didn't really matter. Royalty nominations went to the preppy kids as much as the athletes. Last year's prom king had been the lead in the school musical. And even though Leonie might not act like a prep, she was rich, popular, and pretty. The next time she asked him to watch one of these, would it be to watch her being crowned and escorted by some dude five times smarter, ten times cuter, and twenty times richer than Kennen?

"Hey, you okay?" She kneed him while the list of accomplishments for the first king and queen candidates was read. No high schooler had any business being that successful already.

"Yeah, of course," Kennen said, shrugging. "I was just thinking that it might really be you for Prom." He tried to put on a smile, like he liked the idea.

Leonie laughed and leaned in close. "No way. I was just kidding. Not me."

"It could happen."

"You always get the right to refuse the nomination. Then it just goes to the next person with the most votes."

Before Kennen could reply to this, she broke into a loud cheer for Medina. Bobby glared at her but didn't say anything. Soon all eight candidates were out on the field, and last year's winners were walking out, ready to crown their replacements.

"Your 1997 Homecoming Queen is Kelsie Lockland!" The announcer paused for the cheers to die down. Kennen noticed Leonie had her fingers crossed.

"And your 1997 Homecoming King is Alex Medina!" The announcement roared over the loudspeaker.

Leonie jumped up, clapping and cheering. She flashed a quick smile Bobby's way then turned back to Kennen. "Let's go get some hotdogs."

Kennen stood and started to step out into the aisle when he was nearly knocked down by a man flying down the stairs two at a time. Kennen pulled back out of the way, Leonie catching him at the elbows. The man turned to glare and grunt at Kennen before continuing to career down the steps.

"What's his problem?" Kennen asked.

"That's Sam Travers." Leonie's voice was near his ear, low

and with a tinge of concern. "He tends to be of the same enlightened thinking as Bobby over there. And the king candidate down there wearing number 14 is his son, Calvin. Just stay out of his way."

Kennen nodded, surprised by the sudden turn in Leonie. All of the bite she had had for Bobby was replaced with a rabbit-like timidity.

"Ok," he said. He looked carefully both ways before sliding into the aisle again. When they headed toward the concession stand, Travers was leaving through the gate, headed into the parking lot. Kennen quickly forgot him.

He was busy wondering how Leonie knew that candidates could refuse the nomination.

TRANSCRIPT FROM

AUGUST 27TH, 2017, RECORDING CONT.

Kennen: Alex Medina was a good kid. I wasn't his biggest fan at first, because I saw him as competition for a girl.

[pause]

For Leonie. But that was just stupid teenage romance bullshit. I still knew he was a great guy. He was friendly, smart, fun. Going places. Like me, he had been fresh meat for Ashter. Both of us had moved out here from Chicago. Both of us had a parent that was hoping things might be better for us there. If I had thought about it, I would have realized we had all kinds of reasons to be friends right off the bat.

He came in 1996 with roughly a month left of school. He didn't end up being assigned a little lookout like I had, and I remember thinking about that and adding that to my list of things to be pissed at him for. I read that as meaning he was so good he didn't need help adapting. Leonie saw what was going on though. She noticed that he was nowhere to be seen that last month of sophomore year. No helper assigned to him, he was tucked away in the ELL English class and remedial math. That was so stupid; he'd spoken English all his life. But he must have proven himself, because, at the beginning of the next year, he was sitting front row and center in all of the advanced classes. I didn't think much about the change, but Leonie noticed.

He was an amazing young man.

He didn't deserve what happened to him. No one deserves that.

NOVEMBER 1997

Kennen was seriously starting to wonder what he was doing in Calculus. This was both literal and figurative. He was not a math guy, but Leonie had convinced him it would do his transcript good to get a few more high-level courses on there. Specifically, it would look good to scholarship boards, and he was going to need scholarships if he was going to be able to attend NYU like her next year. She was lucky; having a dad who was a lawyer meant money, which meant her dream of studying film at NYU was pretty much guaranteed. Jim didn't make bad money, but not NYU money. Kennen dreamt of studying journalism, which, yes, he could have done closer to home, and therefore considerably cheaper. But once Leonie announced she was interested in NYU, he decided that was right for him too. He started putting away all of his meager paychecks from his part-time job. He even put aside the dream of getting a clunker of a car, though with the shoes he went through walking everywhere, he wondered if he really was saving money with that decision.

Leonie never questioned his interest in the university, which was a good thing, because his interest lay more with the fact that she would be attending than the actual school. So here he was, sitting in Calc for appearances, but there was an upside. He knew since Leonie had talked him into it, she would not let him fail. This had resulted in a number of one-on-one study sessions, which Kennen saw as a definite bonus. And they were working. By the end of a unit, Kennen would usually start getting the hang of things. Gain some confidence.

Then they would start a new unit, like today.

And suddenly it was back to the teacher speaking gibberish and Kennen trying to capture every scribble from the chalkboard for Leonie to translate later. Kennen slid his glance sideways at Leonie, who was sitting next to him. Her eyes weren't even on the board, though. If Kennen just felt jealous about the fact that Leonie could do Calc with her eyes closed, he could have handled it. But when he followed her gaze, he realized why her eyes weren't on the board. They were on the back of Alex Medina.

Medina. The dude with perfect shiny black hair, clear skin, and that killer smile. The dude that could always answer the questions posed by the Calc teacher then turn around and be the all-star pitcher on the baseball team. The dude with poise and confidence. Why was there always one of those dudes around? They should round them all up and put them in their own perfect-dude school. Let guys like Kennen at least have a fighting chance.

The bell rang and Leonie turned to Kennen. "What do you think of inviting Alex to our study group?"

Kennen sat there, mouth open. He made a sound that was supposed to be an "uh" but Leonie must have taken it as "yuh." Her eyes lit up. She slammed her books into her bag and before Kennen could argue she was up front, right next to Alex. And then they were smiling and giggling and sending glances to Kennen.

He felt sick to his stomach.

JULY 2017

Kennen filled Marty in on Greg's findings, and also passed along a suggestion from Gemma that Marty heartily approved of: a railroad stakeout. Normally, Kennen would be out there with them, but Gemma made it clear that she, Greg, and Cora had it covered. No need for Kennen to be out at the tracks at night. Kennen knew this was probably a measure to protect him, since it was at the tracks that Leonie was killed, but it still irritated him. He had another task facing him anyway. Marty wanted Kennen's feedback on actor selections. Not something Marty usually did. But then again, he didn't usually have someone on the team that had personally known the people.

At 10:00 pm Kennen waved the trio off and went back to his room. He set up on the bed, pillow across his legs to prop up his laptop. He opened an email from Marty and downloaded three large folders, each labeled. One for Leonie. One for Medina.

And one for Kennen.

He started with the Medina folder. Marty had cut it down to three candidates and it turned out to be a pretty easy choice for Kennen. The first and third were both good contenders, but too soft around the edges. Medina's angles had been perfect; there was no need to round them off. Kennen pretty much had his mind made from just the headshots, but he went ahead and watched the short clips Marty had attached. The first guy did have a closer voice as far as pitch and diction, but not enough to overthrow the overall effect of the second one.

Kennen noted his selection and moved on to his own folder. He snorted to himself. There were five options here. He didn't blame Marty for not doing more to narrow down this choice. So much of this was awkward enough on its own. Kennen dropped one and four just from the headshots: number one gave off too much of a punk vibe and number four looked too preppy. Kennen watched the clips of the other three, listing the pros and cons. After enough cons landed on number three and Kennen was down to two contenders, he went and stood in front of the mirror for a bit. It was strange, trying to peel away the years, like rings from a tree, and find the teenager underneath. It wasn't just pounds and facial hair that needed to go. It was a hardness in his eyes, a turned-down edge of his lip. He returned to the bed and jotted down number five, the less complimentary of the two remaining contenders, and therefore, Kennen felt, the most honest choice.

He was down to Leonie. He looked at the clock. 10:45. The team planned to stay out until at least 1:00 am even though the spottings were reportedly at midnight. Another clue that there wasn't actually a ghost: only humans would follow such clichés. Kennen turned on the television for a while, flipped through the few channels offered, and found nothing that could hold his interest. Finally, he gave up and took the laptop to the table. He then went over to his suitcase and dug out the small flask he always took with him. Kennen wasn't a regular drinker, but during his time on the job he had occasionally uncovered things that required a swig of whiskey to get down. He took one long draw, looked at the flask for a moment, and took one more quick drink before putting it back in his case and forcing himself to sit at the table.

There were only two for Leonie. One or two. A or B. He could do this. He looked at the headshot of the first one. She was okay. She looked kind of like Leonie, but there were enough differences that Kennen still felt comfortable looking at her. He watched her clip. Again, she would be fine, but she didn't have Leonie's fire. There wasn't the strength he remembered being in her voice. The brightness in her eyes. Those beautiful parts of Leonie that used to be there, until near the end, at least.

He opened the files on the second actress. He had to look away and collect himself after seeing the headshot. It wasn't right. There shouldn't be another woman out walking around with Leonie's face. Kennen suddenly felt a wave of anger engulf him. That girl had no right to that smile. That was Leonie's and just because Leonie wasn't here didn't mean...

Kennen put his face in his hands. This wasn't him. Not who he thought he was. Who was this illogical, overly emotional monster that was taking over? It was that shadow that he had felt lurking in the background of his mind recently. But it was becoming stronger. Not just a shadow anymore. It was black lightning.

Kennen pulled it back together enough to hit play on the video clip. He watched out of the corner of his eye, like he was watching a horror film, waiting for something to jump out, instead of a shot of some young lady introducing herself. He let it run twelve seconds before he hit pause. He could pick the first one, the one he could handle. No one would ever know he had rejected the perfect Leonie doppelganger. But he would know. And that had been the problem since this all started.

What he knew.

And what he didn't do.

He finished typing up his recommendations. The second Leonie, the perfect one, made the cut. Kennen had originally planned to stay up and see what the team came back with. But he felt abraded, worn away. He cut the lights and lay down, hoping to escape to sleep.

JULY 2017, 12:45 AM

Kennen was looking out the back window at the buzzards that were floating in lazy circles. They were right above where the road crossed the tracks. Where the woods on either side of the town leaned in to kiss, working with the tracks to cut Ashter in half, to keep apart the haves and the have-nots. But it had been quiet that day. Utterly silent in the morning. There weren't supposed to be voices. But Kennen could hear them, hushed but harsh. Too soft to stitch the syllables together.

Then there was knocking.

And Kennen wasn't looking out the window of his Ashter home anymore; now he was face down on a stale-smelling pillow. The knocking came again. Kennen rolled off the bed, flipped on the lights, and stumbled to the door.

Gemma stood there, and Kennen caught a glimpse of Greg and Cora heading around the corner at the end of the hall.

"You were sleeping?" Gemma sounded surprised.

"I guess I dozed off. What time is it?"

"About a quarter till one."

"You're back early."

"Can we talk?" Gemma asked, pointing to Kennen's room.

"Oh, yeah, sure." Kennen stepped hastily to the side and Gemma slid past him. "Did you guys see something?"

"Well, yes." Gemma dropped into one of the chairs at the table. Kennen hurried over and sat across from her. He wanted her to go on, to distract him from the annoying little voice in his head that was scolding him for sleeping while his team was out in the field. She seemed to need a minute though, like she was arranging her thoughts.

"Gemma," he said finally, "what did you see?"

"Don't get too excited. What we saw was flesh and blood. And really, quite cantankerous."

Silence.

"No… it wasn't—"

"Yup. That retired police chief. Of course, we didn't know that at first," Gemma said.

"Yeah?" Kennen asked, swaying slightly in his seat.

"Greeted us with a shotgun. Real charmer."

Kennen's elbows dropped to his thighs and his face landed in his palms. Gemma let out a short tired laugh.

"Don't worry, I handled him."

Kennen tilted his head to look at her sideways and dropped his hands.

"He came out of the woods, telling us not to move, he was armed. He claimed we were trespassing. I asked him according to whom, considering the house lots ended at the tree line and the woods were public land. He claimed we were trespassing on the rails. I pointed out that would only be true if we were crossing them at a non-designated crossing, which we weren't. We were simply walking along the edge, being careful to stay off the clearly maintained land on either side of the rails. He argued that the railway could claim land as far out as 200 feet from either side of the center of the tracks, and therefore we were on private property. I asked him if he was a railroad man. He hesitated, then answered no. So I said he sounded like a cop; walks like one, talks like one, must be one. He didn't have anything to say to that. So I took a guess; asked if he was retired Police Chief Jim Rasmussen."

"What did he say to that?"

"He lowered his gun and said, 'Oh, it's *you* people.'"

"Listen, I—" He should have told them. Why hadn't he just told them?

"Let me finish. I'm sure you'll have plenty to say."

Gemma wasn't exactly admonishing him; she said it gently enough, but Kennen couldn't help but drop his head again.

"He asked what we were doing out there, and we explained about the sightings. He said we must have been misled; he keeps a good eye out and he hasn't seen anything. And, to be fair, he did catch us. Then he asked where you were. That set off Greg. Started interrogating him, asking him why he wanted to know, why he was so interested in you. And so... he told us."

Gemma had been uncharacteristically wrong in her evaluation of Kennen. He didn't have plenty to say. In fact, he couldn't find one word to say. Gemma leaned over, clasped her hands, and spoke softly. "I know there must have been a reason you didn't want us to know he was your stepfather."

"The reasons don't matter," Kennen said, low. "I should have told you the moment he landed on your interview list. I just wasn't even sure he was still here. If he was even still alive."

Gemma didn't bother to cover her reaction to that comment. Her face told him everything she was thinking.

"Are Greg and Cora pissed?"

"More confused than pissed, I think." Gemma sighed and leaned back. "We all know what a dumpster fire this whole thing is for you. Or, actually, we don't. We can't even start to imagine. It's just—" Gemma cut herself off, but the silence that followed said enough to Kennen.

"You're right. We've got to be able to trust each other. And I have fucked that up."

"That's not where I was going."

Kennen eyed her. He knew his team was tight, and he had

just dealt them a slap in the face. But Gemma didn't really seem mad. Or betrayed. Instead, she was extending him even more grace. And this made Kennen feel that much worse. Because she should have felt those things.

In her place, he would have.

"I'm not going to say I don't feel upset. But we have to make this work. And Kennen..." She paused, her mouth partially open like she was practicing the next words in her mind. "He made us a deal."

"What?"

"He said he'd pull some strings and get us the entire police file on Leonie Tilden. No redactions."

This was huge. Even in the friendliest of cases, the cops hadn't granted that level of clearance. Legally, they usually weren't supposed to.

"If?"

"If you visit him."

"Well, that's settled then. I'll see him in the morning." Kennen said this directly to the floor.

"Do you... I'll come if you want me to."

"No. Remember, he already said he'd only talk with me."

Gemma's wide warm eyes stayed on him.

"I'll be fine."

Her eyes lingered a moment longer, then she nodded and moved to leave. Before she made it to the door, she stopped.

"Kennen, is there anything else we should know?"

Kennen was quiet for a long while.

"There is something."

Gemma turned, waited. He could see her, stiff as a mannequin. She was steeling herself. She had never behaved like that around him. And he had done this to her.

"Medina's motive. It was supposed to be a broken heart; he killed her after a lover's spat."

"Right. I read about that in the research. He had no witnesses to confirm his alibi and he seemed to be the only person with a real motive."

"There are two big issues with that. The first is that the 'break-up' fight happened four months before the murder."

"Okay," Gemma said, tilting her head to the ceiling. "That is significant. Plenty of time for emotions to cool off considering the brutality of the murder, but still, not impossible."

"Then there is the fact that they were never dating in the first place."

"What?! Did the police know that?"

"We'll find out when we get the file."

Gemma nodded slowly, closing her mouth. She stepped back over, put a hand on Kennen's shoulder for a moment, then turned and let herself out.

NOVEMBER 1997

Leonie answered the door with a smile. Kennen followed her to the living room, which was where they usually had their study sessions. As Kennen rounded the doorway into the living room, he found it empty except for Leonie. For a moment his heart leapt, hopeful. Then he scolded himself; if he was going to be so jealous over a guy, and genuinely nice guy who might be able to legitimately help him in math, maybe Leonie was right to be interested in Alex instead of him.

Kennen flopped into his regular spot in the red recliner and Leonie sat opposite on the floor in between the couch and the coffee table. She pulled the coffee table closer and leaned against the couch, her long legs sticking out the far side of the table. She started pulling out her textbook and binder.

"Hello, Kennen!" Mr. Tilden said, leaning his head around the doorway. Even at home, he wore a long-sleeved button-down and slacks. Sometimes he would still have on a tie, but not today. He had a bit of a receding hairline, but his hair was always perfectly groomed. Kennen thought Mr. Tilden probably fit the definition of a silver fox.

"Hey, Mr. Tilden," Kennen said.

"Just wanted to say hello. I'll let you get to it." Mr. Tilden gave a nod, a small wave, and disappeared behind the door jamb.

When Kennen first started coming over to Leonie's house years ago, he found it odd that they would always take over the living room. At other friends' houses, they would usually end up in the friend's room or maybe a basement den. Leonie had explained they were actually out of the way in the living room; her father did most of his living in the study. Whenever Leonie had friends over, Mr. Tilden would make sure to stop by and say hi, then give a small nod as if satisfied and retreat to his home office. He would leave the door partially open.

"Is Alex still coming?" Kennen asked, aiming for polite curiosity, but when Leonie paused, he tensed.

"Yeah," she said finally, eyes wide. "Why?"

"Oh, I just ... curious, that's all." Kennen forced a smile.

"Oh," Leonie said, visibly relieved.

"Is everything okay?"

"Yeah! Of course. I just thought maybe he had said something to you about not being able to make it or something."

"Oh, no, nothing like that." On the plus side, she wasn't seeing through his forced act; on the negative side, it was because her thoughts were squarely on Alex.

"I've been thinking about the Winter Snowball," Leonie said, putting her pencil down.

Kennen perked up. The Snowball was a semi-formal dance held in mid-January. Unlike Prom, it was held in the school gym and open to all grade levels. Since it was semi-formal, the girls would still dress to the nines while the guys could get away with slacks and a polo. Kennen always wore at least a dress shirt and tie. Previously, neither Leonie nor Kennen had gone to the dances with dates. Instead, they went with a group of friends, and it was always a great time. Last May, though, suddenly everyone in the group got dates for their Junior Prom. Kennen had wanted to ask Leonie, but she was gone that weekend, visiting her mom. At the time, the fact that she had been honest with him about her visit, something she rarely mentioned to anyone, had made up for the disappointment he felt about Prom. But, if she would be available for the Snowball—

"I'm thinking about asking him."

"Huh?" Kennen snapped out of his daydream.

"Alex. I'm thinking about asking Alex to the dance."

"Oh." Kennen tried to keep his face blank. "Instead of going with the group?"

"Well, Alex and I could still hang out with the group. I just…" She threw her head back on the couch cushions, sighing. "I suck at this. I want to tell him that I'm into him, which, you know, isn't me. I'm not the type to nurture a crush. But since I am so into him, I think I should do something like asking him to the dance, but then again, we'll all be off to college in just a few months, so why bother? But again, maybe that's the exact reason why I should. We won't get this time back–and now I'm rambling again. This is what I'm talking about. I've never been like this before."

Kennen couldn't help but agree and he wasn't sure what to do with this unfamiliar Leonie.

"What if, I don't know, he's turned off by a girl asking him out? Like, he thinks it's too forward?" Kennen asked.

Leonie's sharp laugh startled him. "Well, then I guess that would fix things. I'm not interested in a guy that would be threatened by that." The doorbell interrupted them. She crawled out from under the table and headed for the door. Kennen stood as well.

"I'm going to grab a drink," Kennen said.

"You know where everything is," Leonie said with a nod. He broke off toward the kitchen while she went to the door. Kennen grabbed a glass and went over to the fridge, using the ice and water dispensers to fill his glass. He listened to the voices from the entryway. By the time Kennen joined them, Mr. Tilden was there as well, smiling.

"Hello, Alex. I'm so glad to meet you. Leonie has been telling me all about you. Sounds like you are quite the scholar."

"It's nice to meet you as well. Thanks for having me over to study," Alex said, shaking Mr. Tilden's hand. Mr. Tilden's face all but glowed.

Kennen, Leonie, and Alex retreated to the living room. The study session went smoothly. Kennen found himself relaxing a bit. Alex laughed at Kennen's jokes and was patient with Kennen's mathematical mishaps. He was finding it hard to dislike the guy. They were all surprised when Mr. Tilden popped his head in.

"Would you gents like to stay for supper?" he asked. "It won't be anything fancy, just some cold cuts for sandwiches, but you're both welcome."

Kennen looked at the clock. When had it gotten so late? "I better not," Kennen said, shifting forward. "Jim will be expecting me home for supper."

"Too bad. Alex?' Mr. Tilden turned his full attention toward him.

"Sure, I'd love that, Mr. Tilden."

"I'll grab everything and meet you two in the dining room. Have a good night, Kennen!"

Leonie called thanks to her dad and Kennen gave a half-hearted wave. Mr. Tilden had never offered supper during any of their other study sessions. If Kennen had known, he could have planned to be able to stay, but Jim had probably already started something for their supper. Kennen started to pack up and saw that both Alex and Leonie were standing, waiting for him, their books and notes still spread on the table.

"You don't have to wait on me. Go ahead and eat. I'll see you guys tomorrow."

Leonie turned her attention to Alex and offered her arm as if to escort him. He laughed, took her arm, and they left the living room. Kennen dropped his head and went back to packing up.

He shrugged on his coat and slung his bag over his shoulder. He was about to leave when a photo on the mantel caught his eye.

It was a picture he'd seen a thousand times, one he always loved, but now it cut at his stomach. It was of Leonie. She was only five or six. Her hair was short and she had bangs, but the bright green eyes and freckles were dead giveaways. She held a hula-hoop, which looked comically large around her small frame, most of the hoop not fitting within the photo. The picture was taken from above, and Leonie was throwing her head back to smile up at the photographer. Kennen picked it up and looked at it closer. A burst of laughter from the other room startled him and he dropped it. He tried to catch it but only managed to deflect it enough so it didn't smash on the brick hearth below. It landed on its corner on the carpet. Kennen turned to the door, but the voices continued, muffled but happy, in the other room.

He bent to pick it up and grimaced to see a crack running across the glass. Kennen sent a quick look over his shoulder and then dropped his bag on the recliner. He slid the broken picture into his bag. Maybe he could get the glass replaced and back up on the mantel before anyone noticed. He threw his bag over his shoulder again and started toward the front door. Once in the entryway, he glanced towards the dining room, but seeing all three of them laughing, happy in the company of each other, he turned and silently left.

AUGUST 2017

Kennen got up early, dressed in a black short-sleeved button-down, gray slacks, and black leather shoes. He threw his messenger bag over his shoulder and headed down to the hotel's breakfast area. He had thought about his apology to Greg and Cora while getting ready, but they were nowhere to be seen.

"They went out early," Gemma said, appearing at Kennen's elbow. "They wanted some sunrise shots of town, so they've gone out with the drone."

"I was hoping to talk with them, but I guess I will catch them later." Kennen turned to leave.

"Don't you want to grab something to eat?" Gemma asked.

"I'm good. See you later." Kennen was already heading for the door when he felt Gemma's hand firm on his arm.

"Are you sure about this?"

Kennen put his hand over hers, gave it a slight squeeze, nodded, and pushed through the door.

It was a pleasant morning and Kennen needed the time to get his thoughts in order, so he started down Main Street, the long way to his stepfather's house. He had checked Gemma's notes; Jim had never moved. With all those years on the force, Jim would have been able to afford something better. But he really didn't need anything bigger. It wasn't like his stepson ever visited.

As Kennen walked, he eyed the woods that acted as a back-drop on his right, past all of the businesses and houses. He wondered a bit about the fact that he thought nothing of walking through those as a teenager, but now …

And if he had a teenage kid? Would he be comfortable with that? He shuddered a bit.

When he got to the house, Kennen all but ran up to the door and knocked before he could talk himself out of it. There was the creaking sound of old wood and then lumbering steps. Kennen stepped back so that he'd be easily visible, hoping for a less armed greeting than his colleagues had enjoyed the night before.

Jim opened the door and peered out through the screen door. His hair had thinned and was gray. There was stubble on his face, something he never let happen when Kennen was younger. His eyes were the same though, blue and quick. He stood silent, probably appraising Kennen as much as Kennen had just done to him.

"Suppose I should put some coffee on," Jim finally said, leaving the door open. Kennen opened the screen door and stepped in.

The smell of his old home hit him, a strange mix of old books and fried bacon. It seemed strange that a place could smell the same even after so many years.

Kennen pushed the door shut and went into the kitchen. Jim finished filling the coffee pot with water and leaned over to pour it into the back of a yellowed Mr. Coffee that had brown stains in all of its edges.

"Have a seat," Jim said to the cabinets. "Table's around the corner if you forgot."

Kennen humored the jab and crossed in front of the fridge to reach the small breakfast nook tucked away on the far side of the kitchen. Jim reached up in a cabinet, getting down another mug to pair with the one already waiting on the counter next to the coffee pot.

"Er–do you still take it black?"

"Yes."

"Good. I don't think I've got any sugar, and the milk is probably bad–is every time I go to use it for something."

"Well, not to worry. Black will be great."

Kennen took his bag off and set it on the floor next to him. He wasn't sure what to do with himself. Had this been a normal interview, he'd be pulling out prepared notes, a pen, a digital recorder, and double-checking that all of his release forms were in order. But that was not what this was. Kennen wasn't even sure who would be asking most of the questions.

When the coffee finished, Jim poured two cups and walked over to the small table. He sat Kennen's down first before landing in the chair across from him. Kennen reached out a hand and touched the handle of the mug with the tips of his fingers, his eyes trying to drown themselves in the coffee's rich color.

"Give it a sec to cool; it'll still be very hot."

Kennen nodded and pulled his hand back.

"So, how are you?" Kennen ventured.

"Oh, can't complain. Got my health for the most part, though my right knee's been bothering me a bit. Doc says I should get it replaced, but I don't think it's that bad yet. You?"

"Good," Kennen said, nodding. "Yeah, real good. Like you said, can't complain." Which until he entered this kitchen, had mostly been the truth. Kennen's investigations sometimes took him to some really disturbing places, but none of that had been as painful and uncomfortable as this conversation was starting to feel. "Are you enjoying retirement?"

"Oh, it's fine. A bit boring. How's your work?"

"Well..." Kennen sat back, sighing and turning over his palms.

"Big ratings, huh?"

"Yeah, there's that."

Jim regarded Kennen with a tight look that pulled at his eyes and lips. It seemed familiar, but not a face Kennen remembered Jim making often with him; more like something he had witnessed Jim do to others. His brain tried to shift through long unopened memories; there was something important about that expression. The expression was like static, and it made the hairs on Kennen's arms stand up.

"Do you watch the show?"

"Yeah," Jim said, nodding slightly. Kennen waited for more. Jim took a sip of his coffee. "You like all that fame?"

Kennen let out a short sharp laugh. "No, not really."

"Then why stick with it?"

Kennen frowned. "The show has been a bit of a blessing in some ways. Investigative journalism is often dangerous, hard work for what is often little payout. Every once in a while, sure, you get lucky. The show acts as my luck, makes the odds better. People take you more seriously when you've got a show."

Jim let out a disgusted laugh. Kennen wasn't sure if it was at his expense or that of the people who thought a television show gave one "legitimacy." Maybe it was a bit of both.

"People also get excited about it. Then they tell us too much or make mistakes."

"Yeah, like that fella on the Krendel case."

"Yeah?" Kennen was a little surprised for Jim to list a specific case. Clearly, he did actually watch the show. The Krendel case was an investigation into a girl who had gone missing five years before in Iowa.

There was an old factory on the edge of town. When the company built a new factory, they gutted the old place but kept it for overflow storage. The holes for the razor wire fence posts were dug around it and the myths about it being haunted grew. Some of Krendel's friends were joking about checking out the haunted factory one night, and she had been especially keen, so the police investigated the grounds. They found no evidence she had been there, so they tracked down other leads. Eventually, the case grew cold and Marissa Krendel's disappearance became another ghost story. When Kennen's team investigated, they tracked down the old security guard for the factory. He had moved on to another security job in a nearby town.

"That security guard," Jim said. "He said in his interview that sometimes kids would try and sneak around the place at night, but that he never really had any issues with them. 'Kids scare easily,' that guard said. 'That girl wouldn't have given me any problems.'"

Kennen couldn't help but smile to himself. He had developed a lot of his investigative instincts from growing up around Jim. That line had struck a nerve with Kennen too, even though it really meant nothing at the time. "That girl" wouldn't have given him problems? Kennen's ears had perked up. Especially since there was no documented evidence she was ever at the factory. That was until Gemma got hold of one of Krendel's old friends, who admitted that about a month before her disappearance, they had snuck into the factory. She didn't admit it at the time because, for one, she didn't want to get into trouble, and for two, she didn't really think it had any bearing on Krendel's disappearance. As far as she knew, Krendel never went back.

About a month of sleuthing later, the team found the security guard had held jobs in other cities, some of which reported missing girls during the time he worked there. Apparently, the security guard found it necessary to occasionally teach a trespasser a lesson, and unfortunately, it was teenage girls with blonde hair he selected to 'educate.' Also, unfortunately for the police, he was smart enough not to abduct them while he was at or near his work. Krendel's body was found buried behind a shed far back on what used to be his property. Five other missing girl cases from around the state were closed as well.

"Guy thought he had got away with it, so why not enjoy being on the show," Kennen said.

"So why this one? Why now?"

"Producers. You control the money, you get what you want."

"So, it wasn't your idea?" That face was back, but this time it clicked for Kennen. This was Jim's interrogation face. A face Kennen had seen when Jim was on the job, but rarely at home.

"No, of course not. I don't really think there is a case for us here."

"You think Medina did it, then?" Jim sounded mildly surprised.

"I don't think there is any paranormal nonsense getting in the way of this case."

"Then why do it?"

Kennen sat back and sighed, frustrated. Did Jim really think that if a simple "no" would have gotten Kennen out of this, he'd be here?

"Do you think you'll solve it?" Jim asked.

Kennen had considered this and what doing so might do to Jim's reputation. The Tilden case had been early in Jim's detective career, but it was big enough, especially if the show *made* it big enough, that an exposed fuck up could cast a considerable pall over the rest of Jim's work.

"I think I'm paying up for my borrowed luck," Kennen said, leaving it at that.

"Hmm."

For a few moments, they drank their coffee in silence.

"I don't think I can help you with this one," Jim said finally.

"You made a deal with my team."

"Oh, yeah, that, I can do that, but that's it."

"To be honest, I wasn't planning on asking for anything else." Kennen took another sip.

"Well, then, I guess you're set."

"Why did you want to meet?"

"Just to catch up. Something wrong with that?"

Kennen needed absolutely zero investigative instincts to know that that was bullshit.

"Fine. We're caught up." Kennen downed the last of his coffee and stood, grabbing his bag. He carried the mug over to the sink. "Thanks for the coffee."

Jim sighed heavily behind him. "I was going to ask you to leave this one alone."

"Why?"

"Plenty of reasons. You telling me you can't think of one?"

Of course, Kennen had already come up with the damaged reputation rationalization. And there was another one, buzzing lightly at the back of his mind, but it wasn't one he was ready to look in the eye yet. Just entertaining that one could poison the ground; there would be no chance to rebuild if that one took hold.

"So, can I pick up the file from the station tomorrow?"

"Yeah. I'll call Chuck. Not that I'm really doing much. Chuck's not a bad chief. He's compassionate and hardworking and all, but he's always had a bad habit of being one of those folks that get dazzled by the showbiz lights. He probably would have rolled over and given it to you anyway for five minutes on the show."

"Well, thank you anyway." Kennen turned and headed out the front door. He was off the porch and halfway across the yard when he heard the screen door squeal behind him.

"What do you got against ghost stories anyway?"

Kennen stopped and turned back to Jim.

"I understand trying to solve a crime," Jim called from the porch. "But sometimes your show seems more interested in disproving a ghost story, solving crime just being a good side effect."

"What does it matter as long as the truth comes out?" Kennen called back, anger edging into his voice.

"But why focus on ghost stories?"

"That's just the framing. Just a filter to pick cases from," Kennen said, frustrated. He felt like he was explaining something to a deliberately contrary child.

"I just think … it's good to solve the crimes, but you should leave the ghosts alone."

Kennen turned and stomped back across the yard and jumped up on the porch so he was face to face with him.

"Why, Jim? Why? They aren't true."

"But they have a truth to them. They act as cautionary tales," Jim said gently. "They might even protect the innocent by keeping them away from dangerous places, like old secluded factories or," Jim paused, "or railroad tracks."

Kennen turned on his heel and left without glancing back.

Greg and Kennen stopped by the police station at 10:00 am the next day. Kennen attempted an apology, but Greg quickly waved it off as unnecessary. The station was short-staffed as far as office assistance was concerned, so Chief Chuck Nichols gave them all of the paper reports and access to the copier. Greg and Kennen carefully scanned all of the paper documents, being meticulous to keep them in order and label their scans as they went. It didn't matter if it was an eyewitness account or a receipt from the coffee bought for the witness while they were making the statement, everything got scanned and sorted. By early afternoon they were finished with the records and ready for the physical evidence.

Chief Nichols joined them after lunch and went to the evidence locker with them. Nichols' hair was skipping gray to go straight to white and his jowls hung from his face, but he carried a bright energy. Kennen could see where this would translate into good leadership, his looks said, "don't mess with me," but his behavior said, "we got this." Nichols stayed while they looked at and photographed the physical evidence, but he made it clear he was there just to do his job, not to bust their balls on anything. Nichols held the bags that contained Leonie's clothes flat so that Greg could get a shot with minimal glare. Nichols then pulled out a spiral bound agenda that Kennen recognized as the kind they used to hand out on the first day of school. Greg continued snapping away and Kennen took the moment to swallow down the bile climbing up his throat.

"If you need to see the planner, we can do that, but obviously, I can't send it with you," Nichols offered. Greg nodded and Nichols carefully removed the book from the bag with a pair of tongs, despite wearing gloves. It was like they were examining some ancient priceless book, not a school-issued agenda from the nineties. Kennen remembered using his religiously, but Leonie only ever put a few things down; she usually could hold it all in her head. Most of the pages were blank, but Greg captured the few notes throughout.

"Now, you'll probably want to do the same with this, but it'll have to wait until a later time. There is plenty you will want to see in here, I'm sure. Probably take an entire 'nother afternoon to get this one done," Nichols said, replacing the agenda and digging one more small object out of the box. It was an envelope. Nichols laid it on the table and unfolded the top, (no brads, those can cause tears) and he produced a small tattered red book.

"What is that?" Kennen asked.

"Her diary."

All the saliva in Kennen's mouth turned to acid and bathed his tongue in bitterness. He never knew she kept a diary. She had never struck him as a type sentimental enough to do so. If Kennen felt like he was barely holding the steering wheel straight on this ride before, now it had come completely off. Whatever Leonie had thought about everything, about *him*, could be in that book. And at best, his team, people he considered true friends, were going to read it. At worst, it would be fodder for the whole world.

Greg snapped a few shots of the outside and thanked Nichols

for his time, promising that they would be in touch. And then they were done, out of there. Greg looked tentatively over his shoulder as Kennen got in the passenger side of the rental. He wasn't even sure he had said goodbye to Nichols. Or thank you. Greg opened his mouth to say something, thought better of it, and drove them back in silence.

NOVEMBER 1997

Kennen's mom had loved Thanksgiving. This was probably why he now hated the holiday. Jim tried. He'd roast a couple of turkey legs that he would baste in spices, butter, and a little liquid smoke in an attempt to replicate the smoked turkey legs that Kennen used to love from the Renaissance Fair. Of course, they didn't turn out like the real thing. Just like Thanksgiving no longer felt like the real thing. Kennen wondered if it ever would again.

Jim was on call. It alternated every year; he'd be on call for Thanksgiving, then next year it was Christmas. New Year's was always a workday. Thanksgiving could be a surprisingly busy day as far as policing went. One year, Jim got called out on a kidnapping case. It turned out to be two separated parents having a dispute over which had custody for the holiday. Kennen imagined that Thanksgiving was never quite the same for that kid afterward either.

Whatever the call, Kennen's mom had never let it bother her. If Jim was called out, they'd spend the afternoon together, just the two of them.

So, when Jim was called out that afternoon, Kennen tried to be like his mom and not let it bother him. He was watching television when the phone rang. Kennen froze for a moment. No one ever called on Thanksgiving. Had something happened to Jim?

He swallowed and answered. "Hello?"

"Kennen?" It was Leonie.

"Oh, hey, what's up?"

"I wasn't sure if it was you. You sounded funny. Everything okay?" Leonie asked.

"Yeah, everything's good."

"I'm interrupting, aren't I?"

"What?"

"It's Thanksgiving. You're busy. I'll just—"

"No!" Kennen cut her off. "You're not interrupting anything. But … aren't you and your dad celebrating?" He was careful to not ask about her mom. He wasn't sure if they were allowed to visit her on holidays or not.

"We had just finished eating and he got a call. Told me it was some emergency with one of his clients up in Chicago, so he took off. I'm just cleaning up the dishes and thought maybe you'd be free to chat for a few."

"Yeah, Jim got called out too, actually." Kennen felt a little guilty that it hadn't occurred to him to do anything with the dirty dishes.

"Yeah. It sucks, but what are you going to do," Leonie said.

Kennen thought about the Thanksgiving afternoons with his mother. They would put together a Charlie Brown puzzle where the gang was decorating their sad little Christmas tree. It was only 250 pieces, and with their yearly practice, they could get it put together in around an hour. Then they'd pop some corn and curl up to watch a movie.

"Hey, do you want to come over? We could watch a movie or do a puzzle or something," Kennen said.

"I'd like that. I'll be over in twenty. I'll bring some popcorn."

Kennen loaded the dishwasher and straightened up a bit so that the coffee table was clear for the puzzle. They defeated it in about an hour and a half then decided a movie would be next.

While Leonie popped two bags of microwave popcorn and emptied them into a big bowl, Kennen fetched a couple of throw blankets from the hall closet. He tossed one to Leonie and they nested on opposite ends of the couch, the bowl of popcorn between them. Kennen flipped channels until he landed on *Trading Places*.

"Hey," Leonie said during a commercial break. "Thanks for this."

Kennen smiled. "I feel better, too," he confessed.

"It's good to have someone who gets it." Leonie grabbed some popcorn and turned her attention back to the screen.

Fifteen minutes later, Kennen looked over to see Leonie's eyes were closed. He took a deep breath and just looked at her. Even slouched over on the couch, she was beautiful. He hoped the fact that she had called him and not Alex might mean something. That hope filled his chest, warm like mulled cider.

When Jim got home about an hour later, he found two teenagers napping away in front of the television.

AUGUST 2017

The next forty-eight hours were filled with the nose-in-a-book type research that often made the days meld together in Kennen's mind. Gemma, Greg, Cora, and Kennen poured over everything they had got from the file in preparation for Marty's arrival. Each person covered each document or photo in the hope that they might see something that someone else missed.

Marty's plane landed at 2:00 pm at Midway. Gemma went to pick him up and Kennen worked on fortifying himself. Usually when Marty first arrived, they started sketching the first episode's treatment, which was basically the documentary world's term for a script. The purpose of the first episode was always to establish the case as it was last left, as what the team was starting with. The first episode treatment would remain in flux throughout the investigation, but it grounded the team, focused them. That direction and attention kept their show from becoming completely chewed up and spat out by internet trolls, or as Cora lovingly called them, "Wikipedia-wankers."

Kennen spotted Gemma pulling up front with Marty as he looked through his hotel window. He started organizing his notes and files, closing up his laptop. Marty would wait to settle in later; he always got right to business the minute his bags were stashed in his room. This was why Kennen was surprised to find Marty at his door a few minutes later, hands empty.

"Hey, Marty," Kennen said slowly.

"Hey, Kennen, good to see ya. Can we talk?"

"Sure." Kennen felt off-balance as he stepped aside to let Marty in. The last time he needed to talk, it had been the start of this whole mess. They should be headed downstairs to meet up with Gemma, Greg, and Cora.

"Gemma and I were talking on the way in," Marty started. His hands were in his pockets, and he looked fiercely at the carpet like he was working out something confusing and complicated. "We think, maybe, instead of sitting down in our normal group and trying to nail down the treatment, maybe ... maybe we start here."

"Here?"

"With you. Just get your–get your memories down first and then work through the file." Marty had caught himself just in time, but Kennen still knew the word he had cut off: version. Kennen tried to not take it personally. It was something he had said a million times, and he knew it was an accurate description. Whatever he remembered, it was his version. Didn't make it right or wrong, it just meant it was what he knew. It would be up to the team to find out if it was correct or not.

"Oh ... yeah, yeah, that makes sense," Kennen said, distracted by another knock at the door.

He opened it to find Gemma, her bag packed much as he had been packing his for the conference room downstairs. Clearly, Gemma and Marty had already decided on this; Marty's quick visit was just a courtesy. Gemma came in and set up, pulling out her digital recorder, notes, and laptop. Marty leaned against the window, an arm up on the sill. Kennen sat in one of the wooden chairs, his hands empty and evidently displeased to find themselves in such a state. His hands rubbed over his pant legs and each other's knuckles without any prompting from Kennen's conscious self. On the contrary, they continued even though Kennen knew how anxious such actions made him look. He'd seen other interviewees behave the same way.

"Okay, are you ready?" Gemma asked.

Kennen sat back, sighed, and nodded.

Gemma pushed the record button and leaned back. "When was the last time you saw Leonie Tilden?"

"The day before at school, May 13th."

"You didn't see her the day she passed?"

"No, she didn't come to school that day."

"Was that normal?"

"Not really," Kennen said. "She didn't miss school very often, and this was especially strange because she missed a day when seniors were having finals."

"Did you talk to her by phone?" Gemma asked.

"No."

Gemma paused, then leaned back and looked Kennen over. "I thought from the way you talked you two were ..." she waved her pen in the air, "pretty close. Good friends."

Kennen thought this was an interesting comment. He had spoken as little on the subject as possible up to this point. Maybe that had told Gemma plenty about his relationship with Leonie. But on May 14th, 1998, he hadn't been sure what their relationship was anymore, not that that had any bearing on the case. Or at least, he thought it didn't. The time might come when he would have to give that up for the team to decide. But his hand wasn't forced yet. Right now, Gemma was just trying to establish the events of the twenty-four hours leading up to Leonie's death.

He knew her method.

They had developed it together.

"Yeah, that's right," Kennen answered.

"But you didn't call her? Not even just to check on her?"

The accusation rang clear, and Marty stepped forward. "Gemma," he said, his warning soft but firm.

"No, no," Kennen said, raising his hand. "She's just doing her job. I plead the excuse of being a teenage boy. I wasn't always the most thoughtful back then."

Gemma looked sideways at Kennen but went back to making notes on her legal pad.

"What did you do after school?" Gemma asked.

"I headed home for a bit. Jim was there when I got there. Then I went out with Jesse, a friend of mine from work."

"Work. That was the gas station on the edge of town, right? Milton's?"

"Yes."

"You and Jesse hang out a lot?"

"No. Jim wasn't a big fan of Jesse. But Jim had pissed me off, so to rub it in I called up Jesse. He was free."

"What did you two fight about?"

Kennen sighed. "It was stupid. He was pissed I wasn't studying for my Calc final. We–Leonie, Alex, and I–had planned to have a study session that night. When Leonie didn't come to school, I assumed it was off. Jim thought I should at least try studying on my own."

"Why not still meet up with Medina?"

"I didn't hang out with Alex one on one very often."

"Why's that?"

Kennen shrugged. "Not sure."

Gemma waited and watched him. He usually found comfort and kindness in her eyes, but this was a hard stare. Sharp.

"Was he still in competition for Leonie?" Gemma asked. Marty scowled at her. She took the hint. "Alright let's get back to what you did do. When did you go out with Jesse?"

"Around 5."

"And you were with him most of the night?"

"Jesse was 21, so I gave him some cash, we bought a six-pack and some weed and headed to the river up north. Hit up a popular fishing spot and just drank, smoked, hung out. A few other wasters showed up a little past 11 and gave us some hassle, so we headed out. Jesse dropped me back home just a bit before midnight. Jim was gone. I didn't know why he had been called at the time, but it wasn't unusual, so I just went to bed."

"From what I saw in the report, Jesse backed you up on this?"

"Yes," Kennen said, trying to keep the irritation out of his voice. "My alibi checked out."

"When did you find out about Leonie?"

"It was the following morning," Kennen said.

"Tell me about that."

Kennen thought about how to describe that morning, but something caught his eye off to his right. There was a flicker of black. He turned and looked, but there was nothing there. Had the lights blinked? Was there maybe a moth that had flitted in front of the light? There seemed to be nothing. He turned back and found both Marty and Gemma with concerned looks. Great. The black shadow wasn't content simply transmuting into lightning in his mind, now it was manifesting at the edges of his vision.

"I got up and I went out the backdoor to go to school. It saved me about ten minutes to cut through the woods, and since I wasn't feeling great from my activities the night before I was already running late. I noticed there was a commotion over by the crossing. I headed over and saw cop cars, an ambulance, and a large white van. I found out later it was a van from the coroner's office. I saw Jim. He came over and told me to get out of there. I asked what had happened and found out they were picking up the pieces of Leonie that were scattered along the track. She had been hit by the train as it was passing. The conductor of the Union Pacific #9456 never saw her, but about twenty cars down from the engine they found the impact site on the front corner. Her clothes had caught and she had been dragged. The coroner said the corner of the car hit her pretty squarely in the back, which shattered her skull like an egg, killing her instantly. She didn't feel herself being torn apart over the rocks. Jim didn't get home until about 5 that day. It took them that long to find ..." Kennen stopped and put his fist up to his mouth.

Gemma was still scribbling. "You even remember the number of the train correctly," she commented without looking up.

"Well, as you said, she was basically my best friend. So, yes, I can remember the number of the train that killed her."

"Can you tell us about her funeral?"

"I didn't go."

Gemma said nothing, just tilted her head and let the air fill with a grating silence.

"And they immediately started investigating it as a suspicious death?" Marty asked. Kennen caught a quick flash of annoyance across Gemma's face. Marty was trying to keep the interview neutral. It must be driving Gemma nuts to not be able to push the hard questions. All the same, Kennen couldn't help but feel appreciative that Marty was there to intercede.

"The train hit her from behind, which suggested she had been pushed from the front. Train suicides usually face forward and aim for the engine. She was about to graduate at the top of her class and pursue her college dreams. Her family history wasn't perfect, but her dad was wealthy and influential. No one they interviewed said anything about depression or any other signs. Then there was the note to Alex, which definitely didn't sound like a suicide note."

"Right, they found a note on him from Leonie asking him to meet at the tracks. How did the police get on Medina's scent?" Gemma asked.

"First, a neighbor testified that they had seen him at her house that night."

"But her dad didn't see him, because he was out of town," Gemma said, flipping back to check some notes.

"Yes, he was supposed to come back Monday. And Alex knew that."

"How do you know that?"

"I was there when she told us her father would be gone for a long weekend. He was leaving on Thursday morning. But, in Alex's defense, he might have just been at her house for the study session."

"The neighbor testified that Medina was frantic, beating on the door, and that when no one came to the door he called out and even went and peeked in a window. Was he usually that amped up about study sessions?" Gemma asked.

"I don't know why he behaved like that," Kennen admitted.

"Then he left. But he told police in initial interviews that he spent the rest of the night home alone. His mom was working the night shift, so there was no one to corroborate his alibi. No Jesse for Medina."

Kennen let out a short harsh laugh. Marty and Gemma both looked at him, brows furrowed with confusion over his outburst, but he just shook his head. "Right. No Jesse for Medina."

"Tell us more about this note," Gemma said.

"Well, that was actually found after Alex died, but most people thought it was final proof that Alex was the murderer, even though it was just circumstantial. It was a note from Leonie, asking him to meet her at the tracks that night. It was found in his jacket."

"Do you think he went to the tracks?"

"I really have no idea."

Marty walked over and looked at some notes on the table over Gemma's shoulder. "He ran when they came to arrest him?" he said. Kennen shrugged.

"From what I read, Mr. Tilden immediately suspected Alex even before any of this came out. Can you tell me why?" Gemma asked.

"Well, he had recently discovered that Alex's brother had gang connections up in Chicago. He had told Leonie that Alex was no longer allowed in the house."

"So, he didn't know about the study session planned between you three at the house, I take it."

"No. The only reason we planned to have it there was because he was out of town."

"And it had nothing to do with the fight Leonie and Alex had had?"

"Like I said, that was old news by the time this all happened. From what I saw in the reports, the police didn't even focus on it much, though it did seem to lay in line with everything else. I think the papers just ran with it because Kelsie Lockland, one of our classmates, had witnessed it and was using it to get her fifteen minutes of fame with the story."

Marty was back at the window rubbing his jaw. "But they didn't pick Medina up right away. He still had the note on him a week later?"

Neither Kennen nor Gemma had a good answer for that.

"Well, thank you, Kennen," Marty said, signifying that that was enough for now, the interview was over. "Who else do you have lined up, Gemma?"

Gemma listed the teacher, counselor, and Medina's uncle, Hector.

"Ok, what about people who saw her in the 24 hours prior?"

"That is an issue," Gemma said. "Most of the sightings are what you would expect. At school. Grocery store. Bank. We've got the one neighbor who saw Medina, but she didn't say anything about seeing Leonie that day. Her sighting was about ten minutes before 9. The train went through the Ashter crossing at 9:07 that night. There were no other confirmed sightings of Medina or Leonie that night."

"Well, let's see if we can track down the neighbor. Probably won't remember anything different after all this time, but we should at least follow up. How about her parents?"

"I followed up on Mr. Tilden. He suffered a massive stroke about five years back. Lost language and most motor functions. He's in a care facility. I talked to his nurse. She said we'd have about as much luck interviewing a bowl of pudding."

This was news to Kennen. He looked at Gemma, but she kept her eyes on her notes.

"But I am working on tracking down the mother," Gemma offered.

"She won't be a credible witness," Kennen said.

"Why's that?" Marty stood up straight, moving away from the window.

"She's in a mental health center. Has been since before I met Leonie."

"Not anymore. She got out not long after Tom Tilden had his stroke," Gemma said.

"What?!" Kennen was shocked. "She wasn't ever supposed to get out!"

"What's that supposed to mean?" Gemma asked.

"Well … as I understood it from Leonie, her mom was never coming home. She actually escaped once, which I never figured out how she did it, but they took her right back."

"Well, she's out now. I'm working with the mental health center to get current contact information for her."

Kennen stood and walked over to the sink and got a drink. Tom Tilden was in and Emmaline Tilden was out. It felt utterly wrong, like he had just found out the real lyrics to a song he had misheard for too long, except exponentially worse. More like he had written a dissertation on the misheard lyrics, and just found out he was wrong in front of his doctoral advisor.

"Anyway, we can talk to her, and if she's a mess, she's a mess, but I think we still need to try," Gemma said.

Marty nodded. "What was she in for?" he asked.

"The nurse I spoke to wouldn't go into specifics. Do you know, Kennen?"

"Not exactly. She originally went in because she attempted suicide. It was when Leonie was a baby, she didn't remember it. But I don't know the diagnosis. I saw her once. It seemed like she needed permanent care."

"But there were no signs of mental illness in Leonie that anyone knew of?" Marty asked.

Kennen sighed. "No."

"But how could they be sure it was foul play?" Marty asked.

Gemma had this answer: "Tilden claimed Leonie's backpack was missing. It wasn't found at their house, in her car, or at the tracks. He said she had withdrawn some money earlier that day. He had wanted her to pick out the decorations for her graduation party. He thought maybe Medina found out she had money on her."

"That seems weak. What if someone just found it? How many people would actually come forward and admit to having it afterward when they knew a murder investigation was going on," Marty said.

"I hear what you're saying, but no one was talking like that at the time. It made more sense to everyone that a girl with so much promise was killed by the Mexican with gang connections," Kennen said.

"We have to be careful with that, Kennen," Marty warned. "We can't sound like we are accusing an entire town of being racist."

"Most people in town were completely decent, but that doesn't mean ..." Kennen sighed. "When given the right situation, the right conditions, when it is more convenient, people can fall into their worst selves. And all it takes is a few with a loud narrative and silence from everyone else. And according to Mr. Tilden, Alex killed his girl."

"What do you believe?" Gemma asked.

Kennen dropped his eyes to the floor, silent.

Finally, he spoke. "I honestly don't know anymore. Things that made sense to me then don't anymore."

Gemma tilted her head, her pen hovering.

"Anyone else you suspected, Kennen? Someone you thought they should have looked into more?" Marty asked.

Kennen squinted out the window. The sky was infuriatingly

bright and blue. "I'm not sure, but there was one guy. Dylan Whitacre. It's nothing concrete. Just a feeling."

"His name was in the file, but he was checked off pretty early," Gemma said.

"Your feeling is reason enough for me. Let's track him down," Marty said, nodding to Gemma who added the name to her list. "Now, where does the wailing woman come into all of this?"

"Honestly, fuck if I know," Kennen said.

"Greg seems to have had the most luck on that front, but keep it in the line of questioning as you go forward," Marty said. Gemma made another note, turned off the recorder, and started packing up.

"Why don't you take it easy the rest of the afternoon, Kennen. I'll meet with Greg and Cora, get them up to speed and then we'll get some supper. We'll take your recommendation, townie," Marty said in a sad attempt at levity. He headed for the door.

"Be there in a minute," Gemma said, still packing up. Marty took the hint and left. Once the door shut behind him, she turned back to Kennen. "I have a clarifying question."

"Okay," Kennen said, standing.

Gemma hesitated. "I don't know how to ask this without it coming out accusatory."

"You don't need to explain yourself. I meant it when I said you're just doing your job. Ask what you need to ask."

"Well, from your house the school is in the opposite direction from the train crossing. And I was in the woods out back of your house the other night when I was with Greg and Cora. It's hard to see the crossing that far down unless you leave the woods to walk along the edge of the tracks, and even then, your back would be to the crossing if you were headed to the school."

"Yes, that's all correct." Kennen knew the question, but for some reason, he wanted to make her ask it. If she wanted the answer, she could work for it.

"Well …" She sighed. "What made you go toward the crossing? You said a commotion, but it's not like there would have been lights and sirens at that point."

Black flashed at the edges of his vision again. He looked down at his feet for a moment, blinking hard and sucking on his bottom lip. When it passed, he lifted his head, looking her in the eye.

"You're right. I couldn't see the crossing from my backyard, or even from the woods if I had set out directly for school. But I could see above the trees from my backyard. When I came out that morning there were … well, had to be nearly two dozen buzzards up there circling. Big black silhouettes cutting up the sunrise. I walked that way because …" Kennen paused, rubbing his forehead and glancing out the window again.

"Because I wondered what had died."

Gemma dropped her eyes. She turned and walked to the door. "I'm sorry," she said softly over her shoulder and left.

DECEMBER 1997

Kennen leaned on the counter over the scratch ticket display. Colorful and shiny pieces of cardstock yelled, *Four Chances to Win a Grand! Scratch and Match! Peel and Play!* Kennen always felt his stomach turn when he sold one to someone who seemed desperate; some customers all but drooled over the display. Some won a little here and there, but most people just threw any money they won right back in. Hope could be an ugly thing.

Jesse was out taking a smoke break before Kennen's shift ended. It had been a pretty slow night, even by Milton's standards. Milton's had once been one of those gas stations that had stale coffee and a single car lift for minor mechanical patches. Milton himself had been the mechanic, and when the new owners took over, they dropped the service but kept the name. Ashter had grown to where the station was no longer a solo light on a dark highway but was now the welcome sign for the southern border of town. This brought competition from the town stores like 7-Eleven and Casey's, so, as cheaply as possible, the garage was converted into refrigerated units and Milton's became a true convenience store.

Kennen was watching the seconds tick by when the light tinkle of the bell tied to the door alerted him to a new customer.

He stood up quickly, not wanting to be seen slumped over the counter. It surprised him to see it was Leonie. It surprised him even more to see that her eyes were red and puffy. In all the time he had known Leonie, she had never cried. Not even close.

"What's wrong?" he asked. She ducked her head a bit, pulling at her hair. She hadn't realized it was written on her face, and Kennen felt bad for calling her out that way.

"When do you get off work?" she asked, eyes still low.

"Like 30 minutes. What's up? Is everyone okay?" Kennen couldn't help but assume someone had died. He couldn't fathom anything else that would get to Leonie like this.

"Yeah, yeah," she said, waving him off. "I just … I think I messed up. Just call me when you get off work, okay?"

"Yeah, of course," Kennen said.

She turned quickly and headed for the door, almost running down three men that were coming in. The third stepped back and held the door for her, and all three of them watched as she rushed past them. The man at the door turned back to the other two and shrugged his shoulders before following them in. They were all Latino, and Kennen thought that their tired faces and matching scuffed steel-toed shoes suggested they might have just gotten off from one of the local factories. The first two headed to the beer selection, and the third, who looked younger, maybe just out of high school, went down the chip aisle.

Before the door could completely close, Dylan Whitacre slipped in. He was dressed head to toe in black, which set off his pale skin and thin blond hair. Why did it always get busy right at the end of his shift? Kennen called out a greeting to Dylan. They weren't really friends, but they were classmates. He got a quick head nod from Dylan for his troubles. Dylan started down the candy aisle, but his interest seemed to be with the other customers. After a few minutes, the three gentlemen came up. The oldest one put a pack of Coors up on the counter, and then signaled with a quick bob of his head for the young guy to put his Doritos and Cheetos up on the counter as well.

"Can I see an ID?" Kennen asked. Technically, Jesse was supposed to be present to sell alcohol since Kennen wasn't 18 yet, but as long as Kennen carded everyone, Jesse really didn't care.

"Sure, man," he said, digging in his jeans pocket and pulling out a worn black leather wallet. He passed over a faded driver's license. Kennen gave it a quick look over, handed it back, then continued checking them out. The guy paid in cash. When he reached over to get his change, Kennen saw he had a black tattoo on the underside of his right wrist of a five-pointed crown.

"Thanks, man," the gentleman said, grabbing the beer while the others grabbed the snacks.

As they headed for the door, Dylan sauntered toward the front counter with a jar of Tostitos cheese dip and off-brand tortilla chips, watching the trio as they left. He dropped his food on the counter and leaned over it, almost leering at Kennen.

"You know who those guys are?" Dylan whispered. Kennen glanced around, trying to figure out why Dylan was whispering when they were the only two people in the store. This guy was so weird. Kennen shook his head and started scanning the items.

"They're Latin Kings, from up in Chicago," Dylan said, looking over his shoulder at the door while absentmindedly picking at a scab on his wrist. "I think I'm going to join them." He was back to whispering.

"Four dollars, twenty-seven cents," Kennen said. Dylan had tried to join Jefferson's Gang and they rolled him pretty quickly. There was no way a gang like the Latin Kings would even consider a punk like Dylan.

"They're in the real shit, if you know what I mean. Not like Jeffie's small-time stuff. I mean, I tried to get with them, but I just had to drop 'em. They are small-time and I'm not, you know? I mean, they don't usually let white dudes in, but I can prove myself." Dylan dragged a crumpled five out of his jeans pocket.

Kennen gave a little snort and shook his head. Mistake.

"What?" Dylan sneered, leaning even farther across the counter, eyes bulging.

Kennen counted out the change, giving himself a second to think of how to calm this dude down.

"Well, I was just thinking, how are you going to find any big-time stuff around here to impress them with? Like you said, even Jefferson's gang only does petty stuff."

Dylan screwed his face up for a moment, then leaned back and opened his cheese dip and chips, taking a big scoop of cheese. Kennen assumed that the painful look on Dylan's face was evidence of his attempt at thinking.

"I mean, you're not wrong. But there are things. I was talking to a guy that was going to join the Kings a few weeks ago, and he said if I did something big ..."

Dylan's eyes slid from his cheese dip to the register, and for a moment, Kennen started to worry Dylan was thinking that holding up a gas station would be a good place to start. But he went right back to eating his chips and dip, and Kennen let out a sigh. Really, leaving crumbs on the counter was probably the most rebellious act Dylan had in him.

"I could kill a kid. Or a chick. That would do it," Dylan said, as if he was brainstorming what to do for the weekend. Kennen couldn't help himself; he gave Dylan a wtf stare. Dylan missed it as his few brain cells were currently busy trying to get a piece of broken chip out of the thick dip.

Right about then Jesse came through the back door. When he saw Dylan eating at the counter, he gave Kennen a quick raised eyebrow, and when Kennen shrugged his shoulders, Jesse turned a stern face towards Dylan.

"You good, man?" Jesse asked. It took Dylan a moment to notice, but when he did, cheese stuck in the corner of his lips, he quickly tightened the lid on his jar, grabbed his chips, and headed out the door without another word.

"Friend of yours?" Jesse asked, grabbing a caddy and heading over to restock the water bottles.

"Hell no. That guy gives me the creeps. I just know him from school."

Jesse paused and turned back to Kennen. "Well, watch yourself then. Don't get mixed up with guys like that." Jesse came from a family of five kids and he was the second oldest. He just naturally big-brothered Kennen, who was the only Milton's employee younger than him.

"He's harmless," Kennen said, brushing the tortilla chip crumbs into his hand and tossing them in the small trash can behind the counter. Jesse gave an unconvinced grunt but went back to stocking.

When Kennen got home, he tried Leonie twice. She didn't answer.

TRANSCRIPT FROM

AUGUST 27TH, 2017, RECORDING CONT.

Kennen: In December Leonie asked Medina to the Snowball Dance. He suggested they go as friends. Leonie pushed a bit, trying to get him to agree to a date. She told me later that she thought he was just being shy. Alex said he just wasn't into girls like Leonie. One of our classmates, Kelsie Lockland, overheard. Kelsie had a bad reputation of being jealous of Leonie, often coming up second best in class behind her. Never mind that Kelsie was plenty popular and was queen as far as athletics were concerned.

She piped up and told Leonie to drop it, clearly, Alex wasn't interested in her. Leonie had some words with both her and Alex before storming off. God, she was so embarrassed later. She came by to see me at work, but then couldn't bring herself to tell me what happened for a few days. By then I had already heard a number of versions floating around school, but a succinct retelling was that she had said if Alex wanted to be a player, he could. Nice knowing him.

She didn't even know why she said it. It had just come out after Kelsie started butting in.

This is the fight that is in the police file. And, yeah, it was good ol' Kelsie that gave that up. Alex and Leonie made up a few weeks later. Leonie and Kelsie didn't, and I guess Kelsie was just waiting for another chance to get at her. And Kelsie did get the last word.

[pause]

I would bet she feels bad for it now, but we all feel bad about some shit from high school, right? And most people are lucky enough that the stupid shit from the time doesn't stick. But not everyone. You can hope, but that's it. It's a lot like the lottery.

AUGUST 2017

The team was ready. The hotel's conference room was a simple beige affair with a long table, a dusty fern, and a projector that sat on a cart with all sorts of cords and dongles coming out of it like some sort of AI squid. Greg and Cora were in the back, setting up minimal equipment, nothing too scary looking. Marty sat in the middle, and Gemma and Kennen were at the end where they would have the interviewee sit. They had dimmed the lights and dressed clean but casually. Even Cora, who usually rocked a nineties grunge vibe, had switched from her normal band t-shirts to a bright and busy calico-patterned blouse that matched her pink hair perfectly. Anything to put their guests, both of older generations now, at ease.

There were usually three types according to Marty: the nail–biters, the eager-beavers, and the naturals. The nail-biters, the most plentiful group in the team's experience, couldn't hold it together. It didn't matter if their story was the most compelling for the case, the team just couldn't put them in front of the camera. Anxiety would stick to every word of the testimony, tainting it. Usually, if what they said couldn't be found from someone in the other two groups, Kennen would end up presenting it on screen. That plus some reenactment shots usually took care of the problem. The next group, and the second most populous group, the eager-beavers, desperately wanted to be on television. To be the center of attention. Unfortunately, more often than not, their contributions were nil. They'd advertise filet mignon and deliver beef broth. Sometimes they were coachable, other times not. Then there were the naturals, who did fine in front of the camera, and even if their input was slim, they could take some of the basic stuff off of Kennen's plate and add to the authenticity of the show.

The counselor turned out to be in the first group. Margaret Simons had no issues dealing with troves of angsty teens over the years, but a room with five other adults was another thing entirely. Despite giving a pretty good account of both Leonie and Medina's character in high school, she mumbled and told most of her answers to the edge of the table. She did say that she had grieved the loss of Leonie as she was such a nice and promising young woman, but that she also grieved the loss of Alex. She couldn't believe that Alex could have done such a thing, and claimed there were others like her. "Anyone who actually knew him knew that didn't make any sense," she said.

When she left, Greg gave Marty a disappointed head shake.

"Yeah, I know," Marty replied. A great testimony that would never succeed on camera.

Next was Sally Thompson. She could have been the mascot for the eager-beaver group.

"Hello! So pleased to meet you!" she said, shaking Marty's hand with bright eyes and a huge smile, all accentuated with professional-level makeup. Her thin hair had been teased and sprayed into quite a situation.

She laid her eyes on Kennen, and shoving his extended hand to the side, grappled him into a big hug. Kennen caught Marty's eye behind her head to try and telegraph that there was no reason for this type of greeting. Until Gemma showed him a yearbook picture she'd found online, he was having issues remembering this former teacher. When she finally did release his rib cage, she slid her hands to his elbows and held him, looking up at his face, then back at Marty.

"I always knew Ken would go on to do something amazing. Always such an inquisitive student," she said, a hint of the south resting on her vowels. She flashed her eyes back to Kennen's, her look softer now. "And so resilient."

Gemma caught his eye and twitched a quick smile at him. Thompson had given herself away: Kennen hated going by Ken. He humored the pet version "Kenny" from Greg out of love. But never Ken.

"Thank you. Please, Mrs. Thompson, have a seat," Kennen said, nodding to a chair.

Everyone settled back around the table. Thompson looked at Kennen expectantly. Gemma cleared her throat to catch her attention.

"Mrs. Thompson, maybe you could start by telling us a bit about yourself and your connections to Leonie Tilden and Alex Medina," Gemma asked.

Thompson flashed a quick look at Kennen, like she needed his permission. He gave a quick nod. "Well," she started, "I taught in Ashter from 1990 until I retired in 2015. I started teaching back in Oklahoma, until Steve, my husband, got transferred to Chicago. We weren't interested in big city living, so I looked around for a job in the smaller communities. When Ken's class came through, I was teaching English, but I was also the sponsor for the National Honors Society, so naturally, I had my eye on Leonie from her freshman year. She was such a bright and determined young woman. She had big dreams, much like our Ken here. Though I don't think you ever filled out your NHS application," she said with a wink and a wagging finger.

"So, you had Leonie in class?" Gemma asked, redirecting her.

"Yes, I had her the year she was murdered. I knew something was wrong when she missed her final, but I assumed she was just very sick that day, not in trouble. How wrong I was."

"Trouble with Medina?" Gemma asked. Thompson pursed her lips and nodded.

"Tell us what you remember about Medina," Kennen said.

"He and his mother were relatively new to the community, though I don't know exactly when they moved in. I only met him that year. He was in the Honors section of Senior English like Leonie and our Ken here. He did pretty well considering."

"Considering what?" Kennen asked.

"Well, I assume English wasn't his first language."

"Hmm. I didn't know that," Kennen commented lightly.

Thompson flushed slightly but said nothing. Kennen sent a quick glance over to Gemma, who was rolling her lips in; an attempt, he assumed, to cover a smirk. Gemma was half black, half Latina, but her features favored the latter, and nothing annoyed her more than when people assumed she could speak Spanish. After spending a semester abroad, though, her French was impeccable.

"What else do you recall about him?" Kennen asked.

"Well, did I think I had a cold-blooded killer in my classroom? Of course not. No one ever wants to think that of their students. But he did always seem a bit off to me."

"How so?" Gemma asked.

"Sometimes it felt like he wasn't quite in the here and now. I felt like he was always out of touch with reality."

Kennen frowned. This wasn't incorrect exactly. But Leonie and Kennen had been the same way. When she talked about them, she described them as big dreamers. For Medina, that meant he was out of touch with reality? Kennen knew how to read a witness, though. Thompson was convinced of Medina's guilt. Nothing could shut an interview down like contradicting a witness's truth, whether it was factual or not. Everybody liked feeling right.

"And he did have that unhealthy obsession with Leonie," Thompson went on. If she saw the quick flick of glances that fluttered between the interview team, she didn't react.

"How did you become aware of this obsession?" Gemma asked.

"His poetry tipped me off. The normal moony stuff teenagers write, all unrequited love. There was one in particular. I didn't really think about it until after he … well, he used a lion as a metaphor for this love, and of course, the root of Leonie's name is Leo, or lion."

Gemma frowned down at her notes. "Anything else?"

"Well, there was his gang affiliation, of course."

"Tell us what you know about that," Kennen prompted.

"Just the basic chit-chat around the teacher's lounge. That was the main reason Medina's mother moved him out to Ashter, to get him away from their influence. Seems she was just too late." Thompson looked skyward and shook her head.

"Did you ever hear him say anything about being a member? Or threaten anyone?" Gemma asked.

"Well, of course, he didn't talk about it. Being evil doesn't mean you're stupid," Thomson said, sounding a little flustered.

"What about doodling images or doing any strange motions?" Gemma asked.

"You mean like gang signs? Nothing that I witnessed, but then again, why would he? The other students wouldn't have understood. We didn't have that nonsense out here."

"At least according to lounge gossip, right?" Kennen had a hard time believing Jefferson's Gang had never been fodder for the teacher's lounge.

Thompson frowned. "Yes, I suppose."

"What about the wailing woman? Ever hear any rumors about her?" Gemma's question seemed to surprise Thompson, but the change of subject was a good tactic. After a moment Thompson's shoulders relaxed.

"Oh, yes. Apparently, the underclassmen wouldn't let that go. Too bad we didn't have a creative writing elective back then, we could have put all that imagination into good work. She was seen the evening of the Winter Snowball, so the kids were coming up with all of these stories about some girl who was supposed to go to the dance years before, but her beau never showed up because he was cheating on her or some such nonsense, so she threw herself in front of a train. Then she reappeared every ten years on the night of the Snowball, or something like that."

Kennen turned and looked at the wilting fern in the corner. Hearing these details did bring back some vague memory of a similar story, but from what little he could remember, the hapless girl had been hit by a car waiting by the side of the road. Nothing to do with a train. And he didn't remember the ghost being labeled as a "wailing woman." But then again, that moniker could have been attached later. And anyway, in the aftermath of the night of the dance, he had been pretty distracted.

He saw it again, the black fluttering at the edge of his vision. A loud clicking brought him back to the room. He looked across at Gemma who was staring at him. She had been clicking her pen loudly, trying to pull him back in. He opened his mouth, but only managed to gasp in a breath and close it again.

Marty cleared his throat. "Well, Mrs. Thompson, I want to thank you for coming in. You have provided us with some invaluable information. We'll be in touch again when we are ready to start shooting."

"Wait!" Kennen said, a little too loudly. "One more question. Do you remember Dylan Whitacre?"

Thompson looked a little perplexed for a moment, gazing up to the corner of the room.

"The name sounds familiar…"

"He was this skinny white kid, blond hair. Dressed in black. Thought of himself as kind of a badass?"

"Oh," Thompson said, looking back at Kennen. "I think I do. He was around your age, right?"

"Yes, he was in my class. Did you know him well back then? Or where we could find him now?"

"I'm afraid I'm not much help there. Quiet kid, always sat at the back. Probably scooted through with a C. I don't know what happened to him."

"Thank you anyway," Kennen said.

Thompson smiled broadly. When they stood, she went around and shook everyone's hand, then continued to call thanks and goodbyes over her shoulder as she headed out the door. When the door finally closed, Greg spoke up.

"I think with some coaching, she'd be fine."

Cora rolled her eyes. "Lion means Lion-ie, which is a contraction of lying and baloney," she said in her best Southern drawl.

Greg snorted a laugh. "Yeah, but Simons was no good."

"Agreed," Marty said. "We'll keep Thompson on the books unless something better comes along." He gave Gemma a look.

"I'll keep digging, but so many of the teachers have been hard no's. But Cora is right; she is a bit full of it."

"It's like she really didn't know either of them. She just came to her conclusions after the fact," Cora said.

"Well, she was more aware of what was going on than I was," Kennen said, still somewhat dazed.

"What do you mean? Do you think Medina actually was obsessed with Leonie?" Gemma asked.

"No, not that part, the wailing woman part."

The team went silent, all eyes on Kennen.

"I had worked and worked on getting Leonie convinced to go to the dance that night. Not with me, but just to go have fun. It was our senior year, last chance. She had agreed, but then she didn't show. At first, I thought she was just late, but after an hour passed, I left to go find her. She was in tears at her house, which was not normal for Leonie. Her mom had come by, she said."

"Wait, her mother? From the asylum?" Marty asked.

"Yeah. I didn't get it either at first. Leonie said she managed to get out and walked all the way to Ashter. Then I guess she got hold of some kid, gave him some candy she had taken from the hospital, and got him to give Leonie a note to meet her by the tracks. Leonie told her dad who called my stepfather, and together they all went and got her. I guess it was a bad scene. Leonie went to her and then our fathers ran in and dragged her to the patrol car. Leonie had gone home. I remember Jim coming home with a nasty scratch across his face. He said Leonie's dad was more worried someone might see his wife in that state than how she actually was. Jim sounded pissed. I assume he was thinking about my mom ..." Kennen trailed off.

"Does this have to do with the fact Leonie died at the tracks?" Marty asked.

"I don't know. You see, there was a not-so-secret secret place down by the crossing. The woods come right up to the road there at the railroad crossing, but if you walked about twenty yards along the tracks away from the road, there was a break in the trees and a few feet in is a little rocky shelf, maybe a foot high and ten feet wide. It's hidden from view from about every-thing but the tracks."

"I think we saw the remnants of that the other night," Cora chimed in. "It's overgrown, but it's still there."

"Teenagers and kids home from college had used it for gener-ations as a little hideout," Kennen continued. "It wasn't completely strange that Leonie's mom would pick that as a place for a meeting, especially if she somehow knew the dance was going on at that time so it would probably be empty. But that's not what I'm getting at. I guess I always assumed she walked in along the highway, but that doesn't make sense. Someone would have seen her, picked her up, or notified the police."

"So how did she get there?" Greg asked.

"The tracks run between Chicago, which is where she was institutionalized, and Ashter. What if she walked in along the tracks? What if Emmaline Tilden is the wailing woman?"

DECEMBER 1997

Leonie could sing. She was a mezzo soprano and a member of the Ashter Chamber Choir, an audition-only group. So, when Kennen heard that the choir would be performing at the Chicago Ridge Mall the second weekend in December, he started hatching a plan. On Monday, he approached Jim.

"Hey, what would you think of heading into town and doing some Christmas shopping this weekend? Maybe Saturday afternoon?"

Jim looked Kennen up and down once, like he was trying to decide if this was the teenager he usually lived with. "I suppose. Do you have a place in mind?"

"I was thinking about the Chicago Ridge Mall."

"Hmm." That was all Jim gave as a response.

The next day as they were finishing dinner, Jim spoke on the subject again. "I don't see any reason we can't go shopping this Saturday. During the afternoon, right?"

Kennen took this to mean that Jim had completed his investigation into why his stepson, who usually did most of his Christmas shopping on the short aisle labeled "Gifts" at The Drugstore, suddenly wanted to go to the mall. But Jim said nothing else on the matter, and Kennen appreciated that Jim wasn't giving him any grief over it.

When they reached the mall that Saturday, Jim and Kennen split up, planning to meet back at the food court at around 2:00. A number of local vocal and instrumental groups were playing that day, but Kennen knew the Ashter Chamber Choir had the spot from 1:30-2:00, so he needed to get his shopping done before then. Not that he had a lot to buy.

Jim had a favorite ballpoint pen, so Kennen found some refills for that in a stationery store. Next, he stopped in a bookstore to pick up the fourth installment of Stephen King's *Dark Tower* series, the only one Jim hadn't read yet. In past years, this would have meant Kennen was done with his shopping, but this year he wanted to get a little something for Leonie. Nothing that would come off creepy or weird. Something he could play off as being no big deal if she seemed unsure about him giving her a gift.

He spotted a gift store that had a window full of grandma-gift figurines on one side and stuffed toys on the other. He figured with that range he might be in luck. There were some cool embossed leather journals, but he wasn't sure Leonie was the type to keep a journal. What had ever happened in Ashter that was worth writing about anyway? There was an entire wall of stuffed toys, but that felt too girlfriend-boyfriend-ish. There was a set of friendship necklaces in the shape of interlocking keys, but Kennen figured that was probably the best way to permanently lock himself away in the friend zone. He spotted some decorative picture frames and felt a pang of guilt at never fixing the broken one from the mantel. It was stashed under his bed.

His eyes fell on a little wooden box with a treble clef carved on top. There was a small golden catch, and the inside was lined with felt in a rich shade of burgundy. Kennen paid for it and then headed for the food court.

He snagged a chair at a table near the back of the food court just as the choir was filing onto the risers. The guys wore matching tux-like outfits with bright red cummerbunds, which matched the school's colors of black and red. The girls wore long black gowns with scalloped necks and red ribbons around the empire waistlines. They performed a number of traditional carols accompanied by an amped keyboard and the constant clatter of mall shoppers. Leonie even had a short solo at the beginning of one, which she nailed. After the last carol, the singers stepped off the risers and headed to a few tables where parents had been watching the group's bags and coats. Kennen rose and grabbed his bags, heading over to say hi. Leonie seemed to spot him and headed his way.

"I didn't know you both were coming," she said as she reached Kennen. Kennen looked around surprised; who did 'both' consist of? Then he spotted Jim, just a few steps behind.

"You all were great. I enjoyed every minute of it," Jim said with a big friendly smile.

"Yeah, great!" Kennen echoed pathetically. He hadn't realized Jim had been in the crowd.

"Got some shopping done?" Leonie asked, pointing at Kennen's bags. He quickly hid the bags behind his back, like she could somehow see the box through the thick plastic. Realizing how foolish and suspicious this had looked, Kennen tried to mend things by causing even more of a trainwreck.

"Yeah," he said, "we were just up doing some Christmas shopping and then we saw your choir headed up to sing. What a coincidence, right?"

"Yeah, what a coincidence," Jim said. Luckily, Leonie didn't seem to note the sarcasm in his voice.

"Well, I'm glad you took time to hear us sing," Leonie said.

"We won't keep you. I'm sure your dad is waiting to congratulate you on your performance," Jim said.

"He couldn't make this one," Leonie said with a slight shake of her head.

"He might surprise you," Jim said with a sly grin. Leonie and

Kennen both started looking around, but Mr. Tilden was nowhere to be seen.

"Huh. I would have sworn–sorry, Leonie," Jim said after a moment of looking.

"No worries, Mr. Rasmussen. He was busy with a client today."

"A client? Is that what he told you?" Jim asked.

"Uh, yeah," Leonie said, clearly caught off guard by the question.

"Well, it was very good to see you and listen to you. Kennen, I'll meet you by the doors." Jim turned abruptly and left.

"What was that about?" Leonie asked.

"I really don't know. He made an arrest last week. Maybe he is afraid your dad is repping them and will get them off. Cop logic." Kennen said it with a laugh, hoping it would come off as a joke.

Leonie grinned. "Fair."

"Leonie!" another girl from the choir called, waving frantically to get her attention.

"They're buying us all Subway. I'd better go get in line. Thanks for stopping to listen. I'll see you at school." Leonie took a step away.

"Yeah, see you later." Kennen turned and headed to find Jim over at the doors.

Jim seemed very interested in a receipt as Kennen approached.

"All ready?" Jim asked.

"What was that about?" Kennen asked.

"Hmm?"

"The stuff about Mr. Tilden."

"I thought I saw him earlier while I was shopping. But I must have been mistaken. Did you find everything you were looking for? Hanging out in the food court made me hungry, but I want some real food. How do you feel about hitting Olive Garden on the way out of town?"

It was clear Jim didn't want to talk about it, and when Jim didn't want to tell Kennen something, he didn't.

It was odd that Jim would have made that kind of mistake though. He hadn't become a detective without having a good eye for faces.

AUGUST 2017

The team's next move was pretty clear: find out more about Emmaline Tilden's escape. Kennen could clearly remember Jim and Leonie's reactions to the event, carved into his memory like cuneiform into ancient tablets. In the days that followed though, it was apparent Leonie wasn't interested in talking about it any further. Or wasn't ready too.

What should have been the easy solution, talking to Jim, was currently out of reach considering his previous comments on the matter. Marty had suggested maybe he could approach the retired chief but as a last resort. So it was decided that the next day Gemma and Kennen would head to the mental hospital and Greg and Cora would go work with the diary. Marty would hold down the fort while working on arranging plane tickets for the actors and extra crew hands they would need when filming started in earnest.

Both pairs left early despite Kennen and Gemma's appointment at St. Catherine's Institute of Mental Health only being scheduled to take roughly an hour of their time. The hospital sat on the far side of Chicago, and it was almost a ninety-minute drive with the morning rush hour traffic.

When Kennen and Gemma arrived, they found a tall brick

and stone building. Round columns supported an archway over the entrance with broad wings stretching out from either side, partially obscured by a number of large elms and oaks. A tall wrought-iron fence sat between the slim parking lot and the grounds, interrupted by two stone pillars on either side of the main walkway. Two dark metal gates met between the pillars, and on the right was a small keypad. Kennen pushed the silver button at the bottom of the keypad and waited.

A fuzzy voice came over a speaker. "Can I help you?"

"This is Kennen Clarke and Gemma James. We are here to meet with Dr. Cho."

There was a buzzing sound and Gemma pushed on the gate. It opened easily and, once they were through, fell back with a satisfying thunk. A slight whir sound let them know they were locked in.

Once inside they were greeted by cool blue walls and warm woodwork. Gemma introduced them both to the receptionist who quickly guided them to the director's office. They passed down a hall with windows into a common area on the left. There were a number of patients in the room. Some were playing board games, others watched television, and a few chatted. Orderlies floated around the room, wiping tables and checking in on the patients. One young man sat alone, rocking back and forth, uninterested in his compatriots. His eyes were focused firmly on the massive birdcage that dominated the middle of the room. The cage reached from floor to ceiling, with plexiglass panels at the bottom that stretched up to about two feet below the ceiling, where they gave way to a metal mesh. Birds of varying sizes and colors flitted around inside, landing on branches that leaned at odd angles in the cage, or tucking themselves through the small holes of the birdhouses that were attached on the sides. As the boy rocked, his head pivoted so that he could keep his eye squarely on a little bird whose feathers shined oily blue-black and pecked away at a feeder.

They took a right and entered through a door labeled

"Director's Office." It was filled with dark wooden bookshelves built into the walls. Brass plaques engraved with the names of doctors spotted the shelves. The books on the far side of the room were considerably older than those behind the desk.

"Must be the collections from previous directors," Gemma said, running a finger over a faded spine.

"Mr. Clarke, Ms. James. It's nice to meet you in person. I am Margaret Cho, director of St. Catherine's." The slight woman had entered all but silently through a door behind the desk. She had long black hair pulled into a low ponytail and wore a navy-blue suit with a silky V-neck blouse. She shook their hands, then motioned to the high-backed leather chairs across from her desk. "I'm aware of your show. I have to assume since you are asking about Emmaline Tilden, you are looking into her daughter's case."

"That is correct, Dr. Cho," Gemma said.

"Did you know Mrs. Tilden?" Kennen asked.

"She was released a year before I took over as director for Dr. Nielsen. He was director here for many years, including the entirety of Emmaline's stay."

Kennen scribbled down the words *first name*. Despite being very formal in addressing Gemma and himself, as well as referencing the previous director, she referred to Emmaline Tilden by her first name. It might be nothing, but Kennen had to trust his intuition, and it was telling him that there might be some sort of relationship there.

"Did you know Dr. Nielsen well?" Gemma asked.

"Before transferring here, I worked many years at the VA hospital. We sometimes would contract with St. Catherine's, which always seemed to be well-funded and had abundant resources."

"Did you have occasion to meet many of the patients here prior to being the director?" Kennen asked.

"Sometimes Dr. Nielsen would ask me for a second opinion.

It was the least I could do considering how willing he was to work with the VA. He impressed me with his generosity."

"Do you have contact information for him?" Kennen asked.

"I'm afraid I've lost contact with him since he retired."

Kennen noted a sudden coldness in her voice.

"That seems a bit strange after he worked here for so many years. Do you think he is okay?" Gemma asked.

"I don't know," Dr. Cho said but offered nothing more.

"Did he ever ask you to give a second opinion on Emmaline Tilden?" Kennen asked.

"No."

Kennen and Gemma caught each other's eyes for a moment. Dr. Cho had agreed to give them an hour at the facility, but the way things were going, they were going to be out of there in fifteen minutes unless they could get her to open up.

"Dr. Cho, we recently discovered that Emmaline Tilden once escaped from St. Catherine's. Do you know anything about that?"

"Other than it happened, no. I reviewed her file before you came. It was noted but in very little detail." Dr. Cho opened a drawer in her desk and pulled out the file. It was an innocuous gesture, most likely only to prove that she had indeed dug into the file, but for Kennen it was almost like a taunt, having so much information so close at hand, yet completely unreachable. It didn't seem to be bothering Gemma, though. Out of the corner of his eye, Kennen could see she seemed preoccupied with her phone.

"I obviously cannot divulge much about Emmaline," Dr. Cho said, her hand on the file, "but it seems other than that, she had a very uneventful stay here at St. Catherine's. It was just ..." She paused, tilting her head and running her fingers over the unopened folder. She lifted her eyes and locked them on Kennen's, giving weight to her next words. "She was here for a very long time." At that moment, there was a knock at the door.

"Yes," Dr. Cho called.

A young man in a white dress shirt and dark tie peeked his head in. "I'm so sorry to interrupt, Dr. Cho, but we have a woman on the phone that is demanding to speak to you. She is very agitated."

Dr. Cho sighed. "Please excuse me for just a moment." She rose and followed the young man out.

The door had barely closed when Gemma was out of her chair, grabbing the file. She flipped it open and started skimming and snapping pictures. Kennen sat frozen for a second, stuck between appalled and impressed.

"Don't just sit there. Go watch the door," Gemma hissed without interrupting her photoshoot.

Kennen hesitated just a moment, then stood and went to the door. He cracked it just a bit so that he could see out into the hall. He hoped Dr. Cho would return the way she left, but if she used the other door she had originally come in, they were screwed. He watched the empty hall, the sound of Gemma furiously flipping pages behind him, and wondered how he was going to explain all this to Marty. It wasn't like he and Marty hadn't done a few underhanded things in their day, but to get a medical file without permission was something else entirely. And for Gemma to be doing it; rule-following, do the work, and do it the right way Gemma? When Kennen did spot Dr. Cho coming back, it took his shocked brain a moment to process and turn to warn Gemma. They both landed back in their seats, the file left, seemingly untouched, on the desk.

"I apologize." Dr. Cho sat back down in her chair behind the desk.

"I hope it was nothing too serious," Gemma said.

"No, not at all. Turns out the woman wasn't even calling the correct institution. You know, people think these walls are meant to keep the craziness inside, but really, it's just to protect some of our most sensitive from the craziness out there."

Kennen gave a commiserating smile. "Is there anything else you can tell us about Mrs. Tilden?"

"I'm afraid not, but after you contacted me, I called her. She asked that I pass on your contact information, and if she decides she is up to it, she will contact you. It is no guarantee she will call, but it is the best I can offer you."

"That would be extremely helpful, thank you," Kennen said.

"I will send her your information tonight then."

There was another soft knock at the door.

"Dr. Roland. Please come in."

The same young man opened the door as before, but this time he wore a long white lab coat.

"This is my assistant, Dr. Roland. He is going to give you a tour of our facilities. I thought a chance to see where Emmaline spent so many years of her life might be useful to you."

"Thank you," Gemma said. They both stood and followed Dr. Roland out.

Dr. Roland gave what turned out to be a very prosaic tour. They passed back by the common room where orderlies in scrubs were now handing out little paper cups with small, colorful pills. Next Dr. Roland took them by the cafeteria, which looked much like a high school lunchroom, and then to a few of the patient rooms, which resembled single-person dorm rooms. Kennen wasn't sure if the likeness to public education was comforting or disconcerting. They looked through a window at a group therapy session before exiting to a courtyard at the back of the building. After a quick visit to the gardens, where some patients trimmed rose bushes or carefully selected tomatoes that were ready to harvest under the watchful eye of people in long white coats and scrubs, Dr. Roland asked if they had any questions.

"Is this how you remember it?" Gemma instead asked Kennen.

"Close. Some things have changed of course, but nothing of note."

"You've visited before?" Dr. Roland asked.

"Just once. When I was a teenager back in the nineties."

"Well, I've heard it was quite something then. We are operating with about half of the staff they had at that time, or so I've been told. Funding is tight nowadays. But Dr. Cho does the best with what we've got."

Kennen and Gemma thanked him for his time, and he led them back to the main hallway. As they reached it there was a horrible drumming sound.

They all looked to see the young man who had been rocking back and forth slamming his arms against the plexiglass of the birdcage. The birds exploded into flitters and cried each time he hit the window. "Let them out! Let them out!" he shrieked.

"Please excuse me," Dr. Roland said hastily, running down the hall and reaching the door to the common room just as a few orderlies reached the young man. They carefully pulled him away from the birds, but he continued to scream and without the cage to hit, redirected his flailing arms to strike himself in the head. Dr. Roland arrived just then, trying to catch the young man's hands.

"Let's go," Kennen said. He turned and walked out the front door. Gemma soon caught up.

"I don't know what it was like back in the 90s, but really, it doesn't seem bad," Gemma said once they had landed back in the car. "Most of the patients seemed content, and they were very gentle with that boy who was upset. But it sounded like your stepfather didn't think Tilden cared for her."

"I don't know."

"Maybe this will tell us." Gemma held up her phone.

"What was that about anyway?" Kennen wasn't much of a scold, but it did come out condescending. Gemma glared at him and he turned his attention back to starting the car.

"I was getting what we needed," she said flatly.

"Lucky that call came in, I guess."

"Luck had nothing to do with it."

"What?"

"I have a friend who owed me. I called her last night and

prepped her. I hoped an opportunity would present itself, and I wasn't going to miss it. All I had to do was text her."

It now clicked for Kennen why she was on her phone instead of fixating on the file as soon as it was on the table. He shook his head.

"You know that isn't how we do things."

"None of this makes the show, it just puts us on the right track. And I've seen you do shady shit before."

"Such as?"

"Lying to interviewees to get them to talk."

"That's not the same thing. Lying isn't illegal."

"It's immoral."

"Yes, but—"

"Isn't immoral just as bad as illegal? Worse even?"

"What you did was both." But the fire was out of Kennen's voice. He didn't want to fight with Gemma. Or whoever this woman was because she sure didn't feel like Gemma. He pulled out onto the street. They rode along in silence for a very long time, Gemma examining the pictures.

"Shit, I think I might have something," Gemma muttered.

Kennen sighed and threw a look out his side window, but it didn't matter. He knew he was going to bite. "What did you find?"

"It's in the billing details. The invoices are very detailed. Line items for room, board, medications down to the milligram dosages. Counseling services with therapists listed. They are all pretty similar, but the weird thing is, there is one very vague line item: special services."

"That could be for anything. It could be just a miscellaneous category for all of the little things, laundry, phone access, I don't know."

"Seven hundred dollars for laundry and phone access?" Gemma asked.

Kennen paused. "How regular is this charge?"

"Every month. There is some evidence of insurance help, but

not for that. Tilden was sinking some serious money into keeping her here."

"Well, Dr. Cho did say the place always seemed well-funded back then."

"But that isn't all. One bill doesn't have this line item; the last one before she is released."

Kennen frowned. His skin crawled when he thought about how they got the info, but he knew she was on the right track. "Did you notice how she behaved when we asked her about getting in touch with Dr. Nielsen now?"

"Blizzard cold," Gemma answered. "Whatever their working relationship was before, they are not on good terms now. And Dr. Roland told us that money is an issue now, which it apparently never was with Dr. Nielsen as a director. I wonder how many patients had a similar line item."

"But we still don't know what it means. Mr. Tilden was a lawyer; he wouldn't have just been taken for a ride. It had to be for something that he thought was worth it."

"I don't know what it means. But I sure hope Emmaline Tilden decides to call us so we can find out."

DECEMBER 1997

Leonie was digging in her bag in front of her open locker after school when Kennen came up to her. She kept unzipping pockets, running her hand between notebooks and coming up empty. Kennen waited a full ten seconds, smiling at her, before he realized she was completely oblivious to his presence. He cleared his throat and his smile faded. Leonie jumped and dropped her bag. She scowled at Kennen for a moment before catching herself.

"What are you looking for?" Kennen asked as Leonie bent to grab her bag.

"My agenda. I know I'm forgetting something, but I don't know what. And I apparently forgot my planner, so I can't even look up whatever the hell it was."

"I was wondering if you had changed your mind about the Snowball. I think you should just come and hang out. You'll have a good time when you get there."

"Okay, yeah, I'll go," Leonie said, continuing her search.

Kennen was pretty sure from her tone that she was just saying it so he would drop it. He had noticed Leonie seeming more tired, more distracted the last few days.

"You okay?" he asked.

Leonie sighed and slumped her shoulders. "Just stressed.

Choir has all these extra performances, we've got finals next week, and Dad has been working so much that I've been needing to take care of a few more things around the house. Shit, that's it! I need to get home. There is a guy coming over to look at the water heater and Dad is in Chicago again. I'm sorry, Kennen, I gotta run."

"Here, before you go." Kennen pulled out a small package wrapped in green paper.

Leonie stopped mid-turn and looked at the box.

"What's this?"

"I just saw it in the mall the day you sang and I thought you might like it."

Leonie took it and unwrapped it. She ran her fingers over the treble clef.

"It's lovely, Kennen. You didn't have to do that."

"Merry Christmas," he said.

"Thank you." She had a sweet smile on her face that made Kennen's chest warm.

"Well, I've got to go. But do you want to come over and study for finals this weekend? Alex and I were talking about it earlier today."

"Alex? So, everything is like, fine now?' Kennen immediately regretted how catty he sounded.

"Yeah," Leonie said, fiddling with the catch of the box. Was she blushing? "We talked it out. It was just a misunderstanding. We're good."

This was an aspect of small-town living that Kennen had never gotten used to. In Chicago, if people fought, they would just avoid each other afterward. There were plenty of other circles to roll with. In Ashter, a fight could break out in the locker room on Monday and by Tuesday lunch, they'd be eating at the same table, chums again. Kennen wasn't sure if he should be impressed by the willingness of people to forgive, a clear dedication to community, or if he should be disgusted by how easily strong emotions could be washed away. Did those feelings mean nothing?

"Okay, I guess. I mean—"

"Do you have something against Alex?" Leonie asked.

Could she really not tell? Fair, Kennen was against Alex to start with because he seemed like competition for Leonie. That didn't seem to be the case anymore, but Alex had hurt her. If she was even a little bit aware of Kennen's feelings for her, his behavior would make sense to her. But it didn't seem to, so clearly, she wasn't aware of his feelings at all. And that stung.

"No. We're golden. You better get going."

"Okay," Leonie said, pausing. When Kennen didn't say anything else, she turned and jogged down the hall.

AUGUST 2017

Gemma and Kennen got back before Cora and Greg, so they decided to grab a late lunch at the Red Dragon across the street. When they entered, Kennen spied Jim sitting at a table by himself, reading a newspaper.

"Do you want to go somewhere else?" Gemma whispered.

"No. Just give me a moment. Go ahead and get started without me."

Gemma nodded and headed for an open table.

Kennen walked up to Jim's table slowly.

"Hey, Jim."

"Oh, hey, Kennen." Jim may have sounded surprised, but the way he leaned back, all calm and collected, told Kennen that Jim had spotted him the moment they walked in.

"How are you doing?'

"Oh, fine, just reading about all the dust you're kicking up."

"Excuse me?"

Jim slid the paper over to Kennen. It was today's copy of the *Ashter Gazette*, and on the right side, above the fold, it read, "Eyewitness Says Medina Got Off Too Easy".

"May I?" Kennen asked, gesturing to the paper.

Jim grunted permission, pushing aside his empty plate

streaked with a sticky red sauce and pulling his coffee closer. Kennen sat across from him and unfolded the paper.

Ned Turner had recently served on his first jury back in 1998, but he would have liked to have been summoned again, this time for the Leonie Tilden Murder. But Turner wasn't drawn, nor were any other Ashter citizens. Medina was shot during the arrest, so there was no trial. Even though Alex Medina, an 18-year-old senior at Ashter High School, died as a result of the shooting, Turner says that Medina got off too easy.

"That poor girl was dragged to death by that train. Who knows how much she suffered? He should have had to go through a trial, been found guilty, and suffer on death row until finally meeting his maker," Turner says.

Ashter was rocked the morning of May 14th, 1998, when it was discovered that Leonie Tilden, also a senior at Ashter High, had been pushed into the side of a moving train. When Detective Mike Milner and Detective Jim Rasmussen (previous to his promotion to chief) went to bring Medina in for questioning, he ran. During the chase, Medina ran through Sam Travers' backyard. Travers was working in his back-yard and had a loaded handgun in a holster. Fearing for his own safety and desiring to help the officers, Travers shot at Medina. Travers has always asserted he only meant to stop Medina, but Medina succumbed to his injuries from the shooting in the hospital that day.

Ashter Gazette archives show that many citizens wrote opinion pieces after Medina died, most of which align with Turner's opinion.

"I was at a neighbor's house for a barbecue when we heard shouting. When we heard a gunshot, we told the ladies to go inside, and my neighbor and I went to investigate. The officers at the scene kept us back, but we saw [Medina] laying on the ground. I was relieved to know a murderer was dead, but it didn't feel like justice," Turner says.

"I didn't know Leonie Tilden personally," Turner says, "but there were many stories in the paper about her after her death. She was a great young woman. It was a terrible loss for this community."

The popular streaming series Truth From the Shadows is investigating Tilden's case for their next season. This is in conjunction with tales of a 'weeping woman,' a town myth about a woman, betrayed by love, whose life also ended on the tracks.

"Fucking fabulous," Kennen muttered.

Jim laughed. "You've worked in small towns before. I'm sure this isn't a first."

"Yeah, it's just ..."

"I know," Jim said, now serious. "It's different when it's personal."

"I don't know how you stand to stay here," Kennen said.

"Best sweet and sour chicken I've ever had."

Kennen gave a good-humored grunt.

"I'm too old to live in the big bad city. You can keep it. And that," Jim said, tapping the paper, "is not the only type of folks around here." Jim paused to take a sip of his coffee. "But maybe you've forgotten. You've been gone a long time."

There it was. But Kennen wasn't going to get pulled in. He could play the game just as well as Jim.

"I've come across some news you might be interested in," Kennen offered.

"Oh?"

"Emmaline Tilden is out of St. Catherine's. Released with a clean bill of health."

Jim was practiced at receiving startling news. His mild eyebrow raise was all the reaction he made, but it was enough for Kennen to know it had hit home.

"That happen recently?"

"A few years back. Not long after Tom Tilden had his stroke."

"You don't say." Jim's eyes narrowed.

Kennen nodded. Waited.

"You going to make her wait on you?"

Kennen looked over to see Gemma had already ordered a drink and was handing a menu back to the waiter.

"You're right. I should be going. Well, thanks for sharing your newspaper."

"Sure. Sure. You staying across at the Regal?"

"Yes. The whole team is put up there."

"Well, I come over here every Tuesday for lunch. Sweet and Sour Chicken is the Tuesday special. Maybe we can get lunch together if you can break away."

Kennen hesitated for only a moment. "I'll keep that in mind. I should be able to catch lunch sometime." Whatever his feelings were, Kennen knew he couldn't pass up an asset like Jim. Not on this case. If there was any chance to get more out of him, Kennen needed to play nice. They both stood, Kennen heading over to Gemma and Jim heading to pay at the counter. Jim turned and gave Gemma a small polite wave before heading for the door.

"That seemed to go okay." Gemma took a sip of her drink.

Kennen watched the glass door close behind Jim.

"We'll see."

JANUARY 1998

Kennen looked up at the gym clock. He had to wait for the lights from the DJ's booth to flash over it, and even then, with the shadows from the cage that surrounded it, it took him a few moments to make out the time. The Snowball had been underway for an hour and there was still no sign of Leonie. Kennen waved at some friends on the way out who shouted friendly insults about him abandoning them so early. Leonie's place was a 15-minute walk from the school. He made it in 10.

At first, he got no answer when he rang the doorbell, but the living room light was on. He walked around the small perfectly edged shrubs that ran along the front length of the house and peered in the living room window. He spotted Leonie, sitting on the floor facing the fireplace. On the brick base, she had placed one of the few pictures of her whole family. She sat still, rigid.

Kennen took a deep breath and then rapped on the window. Leonie jumped as if shot. She turned around and glared at Kennen with an anger that made him jerk back from the window. Her face softened and slowly she stood and headed for the front door. Kennen went to meet her. She opened the door, her eyes red, and without speaking a word she turned around and returned to her spot in front of the fireplace. Kennen stepped in, hesitantly shut the door, then followed her. He went to the red chair that he usually sat in during study sessions.

"Leonie," he murmured, "tell me what's wrong." When she didn't answer, Kennen felt a tightness enter his shoulders as they crept up near his ears. He didn't know what to do or what to say.

"It's my mom." Leonie visibly shivered.

When she offered no more, Kennen stood and went to the kitchen. He found some packets of hot chocolate in a cabinet and microwaved some milk. He stirred in the mix, started back to Leonie, then paused by the small cabinet that he knew held Mr. Tilden's tastefully small liquor selection. He pulled out a bottle of Vodka and poured in a healthy shot.

"Here," he said. For a moment he was worried she wouldn't take it. Finally, she reached out for it. He had never noticed how delicate, how frail, her hands were. She took a sip, sniffed in surprise at the alcohol, then took another sip.

"Thank you," she said.

Kennen lowered himself down in front of the chair this time, joining her on the floor.

"Did the hospital call?"

"She was here."

"What?!"

"You know little Wes, from up the street?"

Kennen knew the curly-haired boy; he regularly rode his bike up and down the street.

"What about him?"

"He came by the house right as I was getting ready for the dance. He gave me a small note. He said a lady in a white night-gown had given it to him as well as a handful of peppermints as payment for delivery. It was my mother. She wanted me to meet her at the tracks."

Kennen sat, waiting for her to go on, but her eyes had gone back to the picture on the hearth. "Well, did you meet her?"

"Yes." She sounded so far away. Even though he was only a

few feet from her, he felt that if he reached for her, the space between them would stretch, keeping her just beyond his fingertips.

"Leonie ..." Kennen needed her to keep talking, to explain. She started drinking her hot chocolate, fast. "Leonie!"

She lowered the cup and ran her wrist over her mouth. "I told my dad. I don't know why—" Her last word was cut off in a stifled sob.

"How did she get here?" Kennen asked.

Leonie shook her head, tears streaming down her face. "I ... I don't know." She looked back at Kennen. "I told Dad and he called your dad and I went along and—"

Whatever else she had to say was lost to her sobs. She dropped the mug, the last of the hot chocolate spilling on the floor. Kennen grabbed for it, setting it on the brick hearth next to the picture. He then took her by the arms, lifting her and guiding her to the couch. He expected to feel her full weight, but she felt like nothing. Like she was a ghost. He sat down next to her, and she wilted, her head landing on his thigh. He let her cry, and when her sobs were replaced with regular breathing, he knew she had fallen asleep. She had exhausted herself. He rested a hand on her arm and looked up at the mantel where the picture of her should have been.

Kennen awoke at the click of the door, realizing he had nodded off as well. He moved his hand from Leonie's arm to the back of the couch. Mr. Tilden came in followed by Jim.

"Honey, let's get you to bed," Mr. Tilden said. She lifted her head slightly, looking confused from man to man. Mr. Tilden helped her sit up. He didn't even look at Kennen.

"Kennen, c'mon," Jim said softly. Kennen stood and followed him out the door.

Once in the cruiser, Kennen broke the silence. "Is her mom okay?"

"She'll be okay."

"How'd she get out?"

"They're going to conduct an internal investigation at the hospital. Luckily, it looks like she didn't harm herself or anyone else."

"Leonie seemed pretty hurt," Kennen said.

Jim grunted and nodded. He started the car and backed out of the Tilden driveway. "What did she tell you?" Jim asked.

"Not much. She got a note. Called her dad. He called you."

Jim sighed. "Yeah, I guess that's pretty much it."

"No. No way," Kennen said. "You've got to tell me what happened. That doesn't explain why Leonie was like … well, like that."

Jim shook his head a bit.

"This wasn't just any call. This is my friend!" Kennen knew that was a weak argument. If anything, it was all the more reason for Jim to not talk to him. But as Jim slowed at a red light, he looked over at Kennen.

"We used her as bait."

Kennen just gaped at him. "What?"

"Tilden thought that would be the safest way to get Mrs. Tilden. But she said something to Leonie. Something before we got to her. Whatever it was, it shocked Leonie. She was yelling at us to stop, to wait, but Tilden had his wife by one arm and I had the other, and he was literally dragging her back to the cruiser. And then he just screamed at Leonie to go home."

"How could you just stand by?" Kennen was angry. Hell, wasn't Jim the cop? Why wasn't he calling the shots?

"Kennen," Jim's voice was firm, but not upset, "just keep an eye on Leonie the next few days. She's been through something rough and she is going to need a friend. Lord knows—" He trailed off.

"She'll be fine, I'm sure. She's strong." Kennen kept his final thought, *no thanks to you, Jim,* to himself.

They rode in silence for the last few minutes it took to get home. Kennen followed Jim up on the porch. As soon as Kennen was inside, he started for his room.

"Hey," Jim called after him.

"What?"

"Mr. Tilden is a piece of work," Jim said. "Watch out for him."

"Um ... okay."

"His priorities aren't straight. You can't trust a man like that."

Jim turned and walked into the kitchen, leaving Kennen standing alone in the hallway. He shook his head and went to bed.

AUGUST 2017

Greg and Cora texted they were on their way back a little after 6:00, so the team reconvened in the conference room at 7:00 that night. Kennen and Gemma went first, briefing everyone on the trip to St. Catherine's and the implications of the financial records. Marty didn't ask, so Kennen didn't mention how they had obtained their information. Then it was the diary team's turn.

"We started from the beginning," Greg said. "We still have about thirty pages to go. The first entry is from August 1994. We're guessing she got the journal to write about high school. There are quite a few entries right at the beginning of her freshman year, mainly about her classes, her friends. Then it drops off, and she makes short entries maybe every three or four months. Sometimes there are mentions of teenage dramas, but they are not things that she seems to be directly involved in. She doesn't talk about her family much other than occasionally saying something like, 'We visited Mom last weekend.' She doesn't seem to describe the visits. We just got to the beginning of her senior year, and here it seems like her number of entries pick up.

"She starts talking about looking forward to college, and then after she meets Alex, she writes a decent amount about him. Starts off pretty innocent, but you can see how her interest in him develops. She also starts mentioning how busy her dad seems to be. He's gone a lot more, telling her he has client meetings."

"How did she describe Medina?" Marty asked.

"Well, obviously she is biased toward him, but there were no red flags," Cora said. "For the most part, she wrote about things he said that she found funny, or things he did that she thought might be indications that he was into her too. The only somewhat off thing was that she said he would often 'help' underclassmen with their papers, but that this meant he usually ended up writing most of it for them."

"He charge for that?" Gemma asked.

"It doesn't sound like Leonie was aware of anything like that going on."

"She could have found out later. I guess the next section of the diary might tell us," Gemma said, but there was no conviction in her voice. It didn't seem like she really believed cheating on some high school papers was a motivation for murder in this case. "How did she feel about Mr. Tilden being so busy?"

"She seemed proud that he was doing so well, but I also get the vibe that it was causing stress in her life," Cora said.

Kennen found himself nodding. It made sense with what he remembered.

"Did you get as far as the fight?" Marty asked.

"There is a gap in the entries around the time the fight happened. Seems like she didn't even want to write about it." Greg swiped through some images on his tablet. "We took shots of every page that mentioned Medina. When she does talk about Alex again, all signs of romantic interest are gone. She mentions that you, Kennen, talked her into going to the Snowball and she hopes Alex will go as well and that there will be no hard feelings. She said…" Greg paused to pinch-zoom into a shot. "*We finally talked and I get it now. I still feel embarrassed, but I'm glad he didn't just go along with it. The fact that he didn't, that he was honest with me, tells me all I need to know about our friendship.* Her next entry is about her mother's escape."

"Any guesses as to what they talked about, Kennen?" Marty asked.

"Maybe, but I want to talk with Hector Lopez first. If we can't get someone to corroborate what I think this is about, it could be a major tripping point for our investigation. It's something that can't just come from me."

Marty rubbed his chin but nodded. "Tell us about the escape."

Cora took this one, reading from the photographed page. The writing of the events leading up to the meeting sounded like Leonie was rushed, trying to put it down before she lost any of it, but much as Kennen remembered hearing about it.

"Then this part was interesting," Cora said, pausing to grab a drink. "She writes, *She didn't even say hello or 'I've missed you' or anything about how she escaped. It's like she already knew Dad must be around, that she was about to get caught. But that wasn't what really mattered. She ran up to me, grabbed me in a hug, and said, "Don't trust your father. I wasn't safe with him and I know you aren't either." Then Dad and Mr. Rasmussen were there, grabbing her. She sounded so lucid. I needed Dad to explain, but he just screamed at me to go home.* She goes on to say you came over after." Cora stopped reading and Kennen ran a hand over the back of his neck, looking at the floor. But Cora didn't look at him; she seemed to be skimming the rest of the entry. He felt acid crawl up his throat. He knew Cora wasn't going to leave something out to keep from embarrassing him. Greg might, but that wasn't Cora's style. It wasn't that she was a deliberately mean person; she was just brutally honest and to the point.

But she stayed quiet, as did the rest of the team, letting the words settle in. Finally, Marty spoke up. "Kennen, anything ever make you suspect Tom Tilden?"

"No, but …" Kennen trailed off. He blinked, the blackness flickering at the edge of his vision away. He had to focus.

"Go on," Marty urged.

"Jim said that night, after he came back from St. Catherine's, to watch out for Mr. Tilden. And maybe he was right. Mr. Tilden cared a lot about image. I mean, his wife was suicidal and he basically made her disappear. If his daughter found out something …"

"He was out of town the night she died," Gemma said.

"So he gets someone else to do it. Even if he is a sociopath, it'd be hard to off your own daughter yourself," Greg said.

"And he did champion Medina's guilt, which could have been a tactic to cover up his own," Cora said.

"It's possible, but with what we have so far, it's a stretch. We need a better picture of Tilden. Kennen, how can we do that?"

"I'm not sure."

"So, all we have is some financial records that we are making guesses about, and a cryptic message from someone who just escaped a psychiatric hospital," Gemma said. "And who could Tilden have hired to carry out his dirty work?"

"That Whitacre character? Seems like it would have lined up with his goals," Greg said. Gemma sighed and sat back, giving a slight nod as she considered this.

"Your instincts have always been pretty good, Gemma. You don't seem to think Medina or Daddy Tilden is good for it. Who are you thinking?" Marty asked.

"I don't know, but you're right, Marty, neither of those feels right to me."

"We still have a ways to go. Maybe the answer is still in the diary," Cora said.

"Well, Greg, Cora, keep on it. Kennen, Gemma, we've got to find a way to get more information on Tom Tilden."

FEBRUARY 1998

The day before Valentine's Day the school scheduled a "Fall in Love with College" program. There were going to be booths from community and state colleges, a booth of college English professors that would give feedback on application essays, and at the end of the night a presentation about filling out the FAFSA. The irony of this college love fair falling on Friday the 13th was not lost on most parents.

There was no NYU booth, but Kennen and Jim walked around the gym getting a handful of free notepads and pens, then headed for the main event. They reached the auditorium at the same time as Leonie and her father. The four of them found a spot at the end of a row halfway down the ramp to the stage. A counselor in a beige dress suit stepped out onto the stage with a microphone to announce they would be starting in about five minutes.

"Isn't that your friend, Alex?" Mr. Tilden said, leaning over to Leonie. Leonie and Kennen both followed Mr. Tilden's gaze to the aisle on the far side. Leonie stood and waved, catching Alex's eye. There were no more seats left in their row, but Alex was able to grab one just in front of Leonie and Mr. Tilden, waving hellos to everyone.

"You here alone, kiddo?" Mr. Tilden asked.

"Yeah, my mom had to work tonight," Alex said. Mr. Tilden gave Alex's shoulder a pat and a squeeze just as the lights turned down.

Leonie flipped open a notebook and pulled a pen from her small purse. Kennen followed suit with the freebies he had just snagged. Soon Kennen was completely lost in all the talk of tax returns and income brackets, Pell grants and Stafford loans. He leaned back to stretch, trying to will his mind into working. He noticed that while Leonie was taking down basically a transcript of the presentation, Mr. Tilden had barely written a word down. Maybe being a lawyer meant he was already well-versed in all of this legalese.

As the meeting ended and they started to file out of the auditorium, Jim checked his pager. "Shoot. Kennen, I hate to do this to you, but do you think you can walk home? I've got to get to the station ASAP."

"Oh, we can take him," Mr. Tilden offered. "We were going to hit KFC on the way home for dinner. That sound okay with you?"

"Thanks, yeah!" Kennen said.

"How about you, Alex? You want to come along?" Leonie asked.

"That would be really nice. Thank you," he said.

In the parking lot, Jim thanked Mr. Tilden again and broke off, walking quickly to his car. The rest headed to Mr. Tilden's car, Kennen and Alex crawling in the back.

"So, where are you thinking of going next year, Kennen?" Mr. Tilden asked as he pulled out onto the road.

"NYU, just like Leonie. I want to study journalism."

Mr. Tilden was silent for a moment, apparently considering this.

"And you, Alex?" Mr. Tilden glanced at him in the rearview mirror.

"I'm pretty solid in math and science, so my mom and my

teachers have been pushing me towards engineering. But I also really love poetry. I know there isn't much money in that, but I've started looking at places where I could do engineering but still maybe minor in Lit or writing or something like that."

They pulled into KFC's parking lot. As they headed for the door, Alex broke off. "My mom gets off her shift at 7:00. I'm going to call her and just have her pick me up from here," Alex said.

"I can take you home. It's really no hassle," Mr. Tilden offered.

"I appreciate it, but she works at the hospital, so this is already on her way home."

"What's your mom do?" Kennen knew that Alex lived with just his mom, but he had never asked what she did.

"She's an RN," Alex said, digging change out of his pocket. He headed to the pay phone in the parking lot.

By the time Kennen, Leonie, and Mr. Tilden got up to the counter to order, Alex had returned. They got down on some original recipe and mashed potatoes. As they were picking up their trash to clear the table, Alex's mother arrived.

"Hi," she said. She was short and plump, but her eyes were packed with energy, even after what must have been a long shift. She wore blue scrubs, tennis shoes, and a black coat.

"Hey, Mom," Alex said. "These are my friends, Kennen and Leonie, and this is Leonie's father, Mr. Tilden. He was nice enough to drive me over. This is my mom, Lily."

Lily looked puzzled. "I think I've seen you before. But you're the lawyer, right?"

"Guilty as charged," Mr. Tilden said with a little laugh.

"Could I–I know this is strange, but–could I talk to you outside for just a moment?"

"Of course," Mr. Tilden said, following her out the door.

Kennen threw a confused look at Leonie, and she returned it. Alex seemed to be wilting, dissolving away on his little plastic chair.

"Is everything okay?" Leonie asked.

Alex sighed. "My brother has got himself into some trouble. I asked her to not bother your dad with it." He looked at a small stain on the table in front of him and wiped at it with a napkin. It did no good.

"I didn't even know you had a brother," Leonie said. Alex shrugged.

Leonie seemed lost in thought for a moment, her brow wrinkled. Kennen hadn't known Alex had a brother either, but then again, Alex just didn't talk about himself much. Leonie sighed. "Well, if he is in trouble, she's right to talk to my dad. He can help. That's what he does." Leonie reached across and squeezed Alex's wrist. Her eyes searched for his, but he failed to meet them.

Kennen had no idea what to say or do. He fidgeted in his seat. "Um, do you guys want refills?" he asked.

Alex shook his head. "No, but thanks, man."

"Sure," Leonie said, taking the lid and straw from her cup. "Thank you."

Kennen went over to the drink dispenser. As he was filling, he spied Lily and Mr. Tilden speaking outside. She seemed upset like she was holding back tears. Her hands cut through the air in sharp motions as she spoke. Mr. Tilden put up his hands in front of him and she stopped. He dropped his hands.

Kennen switched cups and looked back.

The two seemed frozen for a moment, and then Lily said something, looking out at the parking lot and shaking her head. Mr. Tilden put his hands out to his side in a what-do-you-expect-me-to-do motion and dipped his head to look at her sideways, his face now tight and stern.

The pop overflowed and started running down Kennen's hand. "Shit," he said under his breath, shaking off his hand. He grabbed some napkins and tried to clean up his hand and the cup, then returned to the table. Leonie had finished cleaning up the trash and was just sitting with Alex, who had his hands in his pockets, looking at the table. Leonie sent Kennen a sideways glance. Kennen sat her drink back down and sat next to Alex. Kennen felt the skin on his arms crawl. It was like sitting next to someone who had just been turned to stone.

"Kennen, Leonie, let's go." They both turned to see Mr. Tilden leaning in the door.

Kennen and Leonie stood and slowly started towards the door, looking at Alex, who still didn't move. Finally, he sighed and stood. As they walked out Alex broke off towards Lily's car, where she was waiting with the driver's side door open. Kennen was reaching for the door of the Tilden car when he heard a car door slam followed by quick footsteps. He looked up and Lily was coming straight for Mr. Tilden.

"You know, I remember where I've seen you. I saw you in Chicago. At Ricardo's." Her chest was heaving with each breath she took. She jammed her finger toward the ground. "And I've heard about your wife."

"Mom! Come on, that's enough!" Alex called from their car.

Mr. Tilden folded his hands in front of himself and stared down Lily. She met his gaze for a moment, then finally turned and headed back to her car. Mr. Tilden watched until their car left the parking lot, then got in. Leonie and Kennen had stood frozen the entire time. Kennen shot a look at Leonie. She looked utterly shaken. Kennen reached out and squeezed her elbow. She nodded slightly and they got in the car, Leonie in the front and Kennen in the back.

They rode in silence. Lily's last statement kept running through Kennen's mind. Why was she attacking a woman who was sick and institutionalized? Lily was a nurse; wasn't she supposed to be caring? Kennen looked at the back of Leonie's shoulder and wondered if she was asking herself the same questions. As they neared Kennen's place, Mr. Tilden slowed the car.

"You both listen to me," he said, "I don't want either of you hanging out with Alex anymore."

"But—" Leonie started.

"Listen!!" Mr. Tilden yelled. "He has family members connected with gangs in Chicago. Major gangs. He is not a safe person to be around. He is not allowed in the house anymore and don't hang out with him at school. Do you understand me?" He looked at Leonie, who turned to look out the car window. Then he turned his gaze to the rearview mirror to match eyes with Kennen. "Do you understand me?" Kennen gave a small quick nod. He had never seen Mr. Tilden act aggressively. He felt his fried chicken trying to climb back up his throat.

The car finally slowed to a stop in front of Kennen's house. He got out of the car quickly, muttering his thanks under his breath. Mr. Tilden quickly backed out and drove away before Kennen had even gotten to his front door. When he reached for the doorknob, he realized his hand was shaking.

AUGUST 2017

Their research into Tom Tilden led them to the local library, which meant Gemma was all smiles. When she had joined the team, it quickly became apparent she was some sort of research master. Whereas Kennen would always be more comfortable interviewing people to get his answers, Gemma seemed as content poring over dusty old records as interviewing crusty old folks. Kennen felt relieved to see Gemma being the Gemma he was used to. Hopefully whatever had come over her at St. Catherine's was done with.

For a small town, Ashter sported an impressive library. It was a white stone building with columns and wide, shallow steps, giving it the look of a state house. Once inside, large skylights filled the lobby with natural light, catching the swirls in the green marble floor. Gemma's contact met them, a short older woman with tight gray curls, finely lined skin, and a wide smile that dominated her face.

"I'm Martha," she said, shaking their hands and leading them to a stairway. "We keep our physical archives down here."

Kennen gave a light groan that he tried to cover with a cough. Martha didn't miss it. She laughed.

"Don't worry, you won't have to do any digging through old articles. It's point and click. I thought you might like the privacy of the archives."

Gemma smirked at Kennen.

"I've been looking into our newspaper databases and I had plenty of hits." Martha flipped on some lights, but the basement was far from bright. There were rows of shelves with pale archival folders and boxes, and along the close wall were five computers spaced out at regular intervals.

"Do you know Tom Tilden?" Kennen asked.

"Only by reputation. Luckily, I never had need of his services." Martha shook a mouse and the corresponding screen blinked to life. She leaned over and after a few taps and clicks a newspaper database page was pulled up with a folder to the side that read, "T. Tilden."

"Would you prefer to split the work or work from one machine?" Martha asked.

"I supposed that depends. How many articles are we talking about?" Kennen asked.

"One hundred twenty-seven."

Gemma raised her eyebrows.

"He was a bit of a local celebrity in his day. I pulled every article I could find that mentions him."

"I guess we'll split it up then," Kennen said.

Martha nodded and stepped over to the next computer, and through the same ritual as before, summoned an identical page. "I have you both logged into the research folder I made for you. If you accidentally close it or back out, or have any questions at all, I'll be right up the stairs at circulation."

Gemma and Kennen thanked Martha and set to work, Gemma starting at the top of the list and Kennen working up from the bottom. Martha was thorough. No ribbon cutting or charity event had been left untagged. Articles from both local and Chicago-based news organizations had been included. And Tom Tilden had been at them all. He never seemed to be the head of anything, but he had his fingers spread out in plenty of business. There were, of course, articles about trials that he worked on, and more often than not the next article would confirm his client's innocence. He was good at representation.

They worked quietly, article after article, taking small notes here and there. Finally, Gemma leaned back and sighed.

"It feels like he isn't even a real guy. Everything about him is too perfect. Tailored. Like some small-town Americana archetype."

Kennen nodded. He had been somewhat aware of Tilden's notoriety but had no idea of the scale. It almost felt like Tilden was the town mascot.

"I have to agree. There is something else that I'm seeing now that I didn't then. With his success rate, you would have thought Tilden could have joined one of the large firms in Chicago, but he never made the leap. He seemed pretty happy being the big fish in a little pond." Kennen leaned back as well and tossed his pen on the table.

"Even the articles about Leonie's death feel off," Gemma said. "Unlike with his public appearances, he's never quoted directly, only through law enforcement. Though it was clear from the file that he was plenty loud about it being Medina when he did talk with investigators. You'd think a reporter with something to prove would have tried to do a close-up on him, but everything comes across as a landscape. And for a guy who was so big in the community?"

"He ran in so many circles. The Rotary Club, the Library Board, the Historical Society, the PTO. We could spend months interviewing members from those groups with no guarantee of hitting pay dirt."

"Kennen, the fact is, we may just have to—"

"How are you two holding up down here?" Martha called from the stairs. She descended carrying two steaming mugs of coffee, depositing one by each of them.

"Cream or sugar?" she asked, pulling some packets from the pocket of her knit vest.

"None for me, thank you," Kennen said.

"This was thoughtful, thank you," Gemma said, declining the cream and sugar with a pass of her hand.

"Any luck?" Martha asked. Gemma and Kennen sighed, looking at each other.

"It's impressive how much you were able to find," Gemma said, "but we still feel like we don't really know the man. You wouldn't know of anyone who was close to him, would you?"

"I'm afraid I don't. Sorry. Let me know if you need copies of anything." Martha turned to go.

Kennen glanced at his watch and almost spit his sip of coffee back into the cup. They'd already been at it for three hours. The coffee saw them through. Two hours later they had finished combing the articles, but no secrets were revealed. They thanked Martha and headed out into the afternoon heat.

When they were back in the rental, Kennen started to turn the ignition, but Gemma put out a hand to stop him. "Kennen, I don't know how to convince him, but I think we're going to have to talk to Rasmussen about Tom Tilden. We need someone who has first-hand knowledge of him."

Kennen started to speak up, but Gemma shook her head, "I know you were there, but we need an adult perspective. And preferably someone who saw past all of this." Gemma gestured at her notes. "From what you told us, it sounds like Rasmussen did."

Kennen was about to give up, to agree, when Gemma's cell rang. She grabbed it.

"Hello? Yes, this is Gemma James." Gemma's eyes went wide and she frantically pulled out a clean piece of paper to scribble on. "Yes ... that would be wonderful... yes, we'd really appreciate it. Name the time and place and we will be there ... thank you. I am so thankful you decided to call ... yes, you too. Bye." Gemma clicked off and stared at Kennen for a moment.

"Who was it?" Kennen said with a slight shake of his head.

"Our luck has changed. Maybe we should stop and buy a lottery ticket on the way home."

Kennen grimaced.

"That was Emmaline Tilden. She'd like to chat."

FEBRUARY 1998

The Art Institute of Chicago was boasting about their Egyptomania Exhibit and Kennen had to work hard not to talk about it like a giddy little kid. He had always loved anything that had to do with ancient Egypt. There was something magical about it. Kennen wanted to pull back the curtain, know its secrets.

He thought about mentioning it to Leonie, but she seemed indifferent about most things recently. She had been that way since the night of the Snowball. The college night had been a small bright spot until the KFC incident. They still hadn't really talked about that, but both Kennen and Leonie had continued to talk with Alex. It was clear the issue was between his mother and Leonie's dad, and it seemed wrong to drop Alex for that.

But to Kennen's surprise, Leonie brought up the exhibit to him.

"I'm going up to visit my mom next weekend. We could go together and see the exhibit while we're there. If I remember right, you're a bit of an Egypt-ophile," Leonie said. They were standing around after class, waiting for the parking lot to empty out a bit. Kennen stood there stunned. She might as well have invited him for a stroll on Saturn.

"Uh ... are you sure?" he finally managed to get out.

"Yeah," Leonie said, like it was no big deal. Like inviting Kennen to see her mother, a situation she basically didn't even talk about, was now about as normal as inviting him over to watch a movie. Kennen stayed silent, completely gobsmacked. Apparently, the silence dug at Leonie. "Unless, I mean, I don't want to make you do something you'd be uncomfortable with." Her voice had waned to a filmy substance.

"No, no, no! It's nothing like that. But what will your dad say?"

"It was actually his idea."

Add hula-hooping the rings to that stroll on Saturn.

"His idea?"

"Yeah. I was pretty surprised as well. But I think it's because of what happened the night of the dance. You and Jim are the only ones who know what happened, and you haven't said a thing about it. Well, little Wes down the street knows, but clearly, he is bought off pretty easily with candy. Anyway, I think maybe he knows he can trust you now. Like I do."

Kennen swayed a bit, tugging at his backpack strap. "I appreciate that. But just a reminder for the future, I can also be bought off with candy."

Leonie laughed, and it was just a short laugh, but Kennen felt a pang in his chest. Until he heard it, he hadn't realized how long it had been since she had laughed. Or how much he missed it.

That Saturday when Mr. Tilden rolled up in his car, Kennen felt his stomach clench, remembering the last ride in the car. He crawled in the back. The first hour of the ride was dappled with conversations that would start, but dwindle quickly, dying in the air before they were viable. Leonie eventually brought up the need to make a decision about the senior gift. It was something the graduating class did for the school with whatever funds were left over from prom the previous year and the profit from the magazine sales, the traditional senior class fundraiser. In short, something that could be done on a budget. A brain-storming session commenced that ranged from landscaping by the front entrance to repainting the tennis courts.

When they pulled up in front of St. Catherine's, they fell quiet again. That tightness returned to Kennen's stomach. Mr. Tilden put the car in park and turned to face Kennen.

"If at any point she makes you uncomfortable, just let me know and I'll give you the keys. You can come back out to the car."

Kennen nodded. Leonie and Kennen followed Mr. Tilden through the gate. Kennen looked sideways at Leonie. She looked pale. Even her freckles were faded.

The lady at the reception desk took their names and then nodded toward a small waiting area. About fifteen minutes later, a woman in a white nurse outfit came and led them down a hall to a small room which she unlocked with a key. There were few pictures of Leonie's mother left at the Tilden house, and the creature inside the room didn't look like any of them. She was propped up on pillows. Her face was drained of color except for a sickly red burning on her eyelids. Her cool blue eyes seemed muted, like there was a film of tissue paper over them. Her hair had been brushed, but it still stuck out at odd angles from the back where she had been laying on it. She did not give any sign she was aware of their presence.

Leonie took a deep breath through her nose and Kennen saw her unclench her fist, shoulders sagging.

"Hey, sweetheart," Mr. Tilden said soothingly. He took her limp hand in his.

"Hey, Mom," Leonie said, pulling a vinyl chair from the corner.

"Hi," Kennen squeaked out, taking the cue from the others and immediately feeling embarrassed. He melted away into the corner.

"On the way up, we were discussing Leonie's class and their senior gift." Mr. Tilden and Leonie took turns retelling the car discussion to Mrs. Tilden, whose total contribution to the conversation was the occasional slow blink and some spittle gathering in the corner of her mouth. How could a woman like this make it down the hallway, never mind break out and make it to Ashter? But Leonie and Mr. Tilden went on like this was normal. Kennen thought about Leonie's reaction when she came in and wondered if she had been hoping to find someone a little more lively than a lump of clay. They talked for a good twenty minutes, Kennen silently observing from his corner.

Leonie was mid-description of the terrible shape of the tennis courts and how that had resulted in the team losing every tournament that year when Mr. Tilden looked at his watch and announced they had better leave before they made her too tired. Leonie leaned in and gave her mom a kiss on the cheek. Mrs. Tilden flickered her eyes to Leonie, her first and only true reaction to the visit. A moment later her eyes slid back to stare into nothingness.

"Take care, dear." Mr. Tilden patted her hand and then gestured toward the door.

At the end of the hall, Leonie said that she needed to use the restroom and broke off. Mr. Tilden and Kennen stopped and stood across the hall from each other, leaning on the walls.

"I know what you heard about the night of the dance was probably frightening, and then there were the vile things Ms. Medina said, which to this day I can't figure out. But I hope you see that my wife is harmless," Mr. Tilden said. "She needs a level of care that Leonie and I can't provide for her at home. Anyway, I'd appreciate it if you wouldn't talk about what you saw today—"

"Oh, of course not, Mr. Tilden," Kennen interrupted. "It's no one else's business."

Mr. Tilden smiled. "I'm sure your father has taught you well about gossiping. That's important in his line of work."

Kennen let pass the drop of 'step' from Jim's title.

"And I understand if you have questions about what you just saw. I hope you will ask me if you do."

"Have they figured out how she escaped?"

"There was some mix-up with the drugs. As you can see, she is dissociative most of the time. This is because she tries to hurt herself if she isn't sedated. Because of that, she wasn't heavily guarded, and with the drug issue, she was able to take advantage of that. All of the people responsible have been dealt with."

"Oh," Kennen said, unsure what 'dealt with' meant exactly in this case. He didn't really think drugging her into oblivion sounded like good treatment, but he also knew he didn't know anything about this world. "I was surprised when Leonie invited me along, but it means a lot that you did. Thank you."

"I just wanted you, well, you and your father, to have peace of mind. While this isn't the happiest of solutions, it is the best for her. She truly does get great care here."

Kennen nodded and Leonie rejoined them. They returned to the car and headed to the art institute.

Kennen tried to enjoy the exhibit, but in every photo of a painted sarcophagus, the wide eyes looked blank.

Just like Emmaline Tilden's.

AUGUST 2017

That evening the entire group met in the conference room at 7:00. When Kennen came in, he caught a buzz of energy coming off Cora and Greg. Maybe the diary had revealed something.

"Okay, Greg, Cora, how'd things go today?" Marty started.

"Well, not as planned. We weren't able to get back to the diary today. Apparently, sometimes they are pretty busy with that whole 'protect and serve' thing there at the station," Greg said with a congenial smile. "But no worries, they will call when they can accommodate us again. Instead, we scouted out some neighborhoods that give off that pre-2000s feel. We've got some great locations to shoot and can start getting paperwork in order on that. Oh, and Cora hit pay dirt," Greg said, smiling at her.

"There were some folks, you know, checking us out because we were strangers in the neighborhood. I went up, introduced us so we wouldn't be the scary people casing the joint, and some were pretty chatty," Cora said. "Long story short, we finally got a lead on someone to talk to about the wailing woman."

This was a big break. Everyone was leaning in, ready to hear what Cora had discovered. True, Kennen's realization that possible sightings of Emmaline Tilden could be the source of the tale would be a great reveal, but the team still needed to get some information on the ghost story. There can't be a reveal without establishing a mystery in the first place.

"Great work, Cora!" Kennen said. Cora was nearly glowing. She was always a helpful member of the team, but rarely did she land in the limelight. Not surprising when a core part of her job as head sound tech was to be absolutely silent and catch what everyone else had to say.

"So, who's the source?" Marty asked.

"A lady named Velma Warren," Cora said. "We've got an interview set up for 1:00 tomorrow, and she's okayed us to film. From the stories I heard today, it sounds like she's kind of a keeper of tales here in Ashter. Is that enough time for you guys to be ready?" Cora's face dropped a bit, just now realizing that, in her excitement, she might have moved ahead too quickly.

"Oh yeah, we can get everything nailed down before we head out," Gemma said, and Cora's smile came back.

"Good work, you two. Really good work," Marty said before turning to Gemma and Kennen. "How about the Tom Tilden front?"

"We have a really good sketch of his public persona," Gemma said. "It's going to take a little more digging to get the real Tom, but we'll get there."

Kennen waited for her to go on, tell them about their big break with Emmaline Tilden's phone call, but she went back to looking at her notebook. He started to open his mouth, but Gemma caught him. She flipped her hair, but held his eyes in a piercing stare, sending the message loud and clear: shut it. Kennen slammed his jaw closed and gave Marty a slight nod to say that was all.

After a few more minutes of chatting the group packed up for the night. They'd all rise before sunrise to make sure questions were written and equipment was tested and packed, so an early night was in order. Kennen's room was just a few steps from the elevator. The crew said their goodnights to him as he stopped at his door.

He waited until they were halfway down the hall before shouting, "Hey, Gemma, one more thing."

Gemma waved to the rest of the crew and walked quickly back to Kennen, who was leaning on his door, hand still on the handle.

"Yeah?" she asked.

Kennen glanced over her shoulder to make sure the rest were out of earshot, then leaned in and whispered, "What is going on? Why are we keeping the Emmaline Tilden call a secret?"

Kennen braced himself, fearing a reappearance of the Gemma from yesterday, but she just furrowed her brow at him. She looked disappointed. Kennen crossed his arms. "What?"

"Kennen, you know it is okay to let someone else get some praise from time to time."

"What are you talking about?"

"Cora was really excited to share her news. And she should have been; she did good work. Emmaline Tilden doesn't want to talk until early next week, and with this interview landing in our lap, we won't be able to work that angle until after tomorrow anyway, so why not just let her be the star today?"

Kennen backed away. He was being scolded for just doing the job. Where was this coming from?

"Gemma, is something wrong?"

"Can you really not understand it?" Her eyes were hard.

Kennen decided to back down. This didn't seem worth fighting over, and anyway, it was done with. "You're right. Sorry."

Gemma hesitated. "Alright," she finally said before she turned and walked down the hall. Kennen stood and waited until she turned the corner to unlock his room. Maybe he just needed some sleep.

FEBRUARY 1998

Kennen had a shift Monday night after the weekend trip to see Mrs. Tilden. He was trying to just have a normal day, but images of the hospital kept sneaking into his mind when he got bored, which happened a lot at work. At ten minutes until 10:00, Alex and his mother, Lily, came in the door. She was dressed up; a gauzy black skirt with white polka dots hung below her black coat. She wore long black boots and her hair was down. It was much longer than Kennen had realized. She hurried to the bathroom. Alex went to the coffee station, poured himself a large black cup, and headed over to Kennen.

"She wasn't going to make it the fifteen minutes we had left before we got home," Alex said offhandedly as he came up to the counter.

"Coffee this late?" Kennen asked.

"Yeah, I got a bunch of homework to catch up on."

"That's right, I didn't see you at school today." Until he brought it up, Kennen hadn't noticed it. Maybe his brain had spent more time in the institution today than he had realized. "Is everything okay?"

"We had something to see to up in town," Alex said as he

pulled out his wallet. He offered nothing more about what had taken them to Chicago for the day.

Kennen rang him up and made him change as Jesse came out from the back. Jesse went to the self-serve doughnut section, condensing the meager pastry selection down to one tray and removing the empty ones to be washed in the back. Kennen tried to hand Alex his change, but Alex was looking over at Jesse. He seemed to be looking him over, head to toe.

"Alex?"

Alex jumped and looked back at Kennen wide-eyed. Kennen just nodded at his handful of change. Alex sighed and took it.

"Sorry. Guess I'm more tired than I thought."

His mother came out of the bathroom. "Ready, Bubby?" she asked softly. She nodded and smiled at Kennen. Now that she was closer, he could see there were bags under her reddish eyes.

"Yeah, Mom."

Alex held the door for his mother, then called goodnight back over his shoulder.

After they left, Kennen wished Leonie had been there. Clearly something major was going on. Leonie would have known what to ask. Leonie would have known how to show she cared.

Kennen always realized what he should have done too late.

AUGUST 2017

Velma Warren's place was secluded in the woods out east of town. The team took two vehicles, a car and a cargo van, and drove until the pavement gave way to gravel, then took a left into the woods. Her cabin was only about a half mile in, but the rough road made it feel like the longest part of the journey. To their right appeared a small cabin with a porch that ran the length of the structure. A stone chimney peaked above the roof on the far end of the cabin. There was a garage and shed set a little ways back. Out front, a large round tank pool had been filled with dirt and a number of colorful cone flowers grew from it, swaying in the breeze.

A woman opened the screen door and stood on the porch, and though the name Velma Warren had not rung a bell with Kennen, he recognized her immediately. She had aged considerably since he last saw her. Her hair, which used to only have a few wisps of grey, now only had a few streaks of brown left. But her sense of style had not changed. She wore a black top and skirt. Two necklaces, one with a pentacle and one with a lavender-colored crystal stood out against her black top. She had worn, dusty sandals on her feet.

Kennen remembered seeing her around town when he was a

teenager. At that time he avoided her because she creeped him out; to be fair though, he didn't know the difference between a pentagram and a pentacle at that age. He had never bothered to learn her name.

"Ms. Warren?" Marty asked, climbing out of the car.

"Yes, welcome!" she said, stepping off the porch and into the broken light that fought through the trees.

Marty introduced the members of the team.

"It's nice to meet you all, and it's lovely to see you again, Kennen. Please come in."

"Is it alright if my team brings in some equipment for recording purposes?" Marty asked.

"Of course! May I help?"

"It would be a great help if you would show us where you would like us to work," Marty said. She nodded and Marty followed her inside while the rest of the team grabbed the camera and sound equipment.

The main living area of the cabin was dominated by a long oak table surrounded by chairs. A small recliner and end table sat tucked into the corner of the room and a bookshelf sat along one wall. There was a doorway on each side of the room, one leading to the kitchen, the other to a bathroom and bedroom. After indicating where she planned to sit at the table, Ms. Warren disappeared into the kitchen.

Greg looked around at the cottage then smiled and nodded at Marty. "Great spooky story vibes," Greg whispered.

Ms. Warren returned with a tray of iced tea. She seemed utterly unphased by the team taking over her home and making it into a recording studio. Kennen glanced at the titles on the bookshelf. There were a number of the classics as well as a fair collection of Agatha Christie. A leather-bound book at the end caught his eye. He glanced over his shoulder; Ms. Warren was carefully listening as Greg explained what each piece of equipment was for. Kennen pulled the volume off the shelf and flipped it open. It seemed to be a hand-copied version of Gardner's *The Book of Shadows*. He slid it back on the shelf.

Everyone settled into spots with a glass of tea, the condensation shining in the lights Greg had set up. "Well, Ms. Warren, we have a number of questions for you. When we ask them, please look at the interviewer, not directly at the camera, when you answer," Marty instructed.

"I assume you also want me to use the question in my answer, like my elementary teachers told me to do when they wanted me to start answering questions with full sentences."

Marty flushed. Ms. Warren leaned over and gave Marty a grandmotherly pat on his arm. "I'm a fan of the show. It's exciting to be a part of it."

Marty smiled. "Well, take your time, and don't feel rushed to answer. And if you need to restart an answer, that is fine." Marty moved around the table and out of the way of the team.

They did a sound check, Cora sliding over to counterbalance the boom mic lower. Greg peered into his camera and gave a thumbs up.

"Please start by telling us about yourself, your name, how long you've lived in Ashter, that sort of thing," Kennen said.

"I'm Velma Warren. I was born and raised in Ashter. I worked at a local florist shop until it closed about five years back and then I retired."

"How long have you lived out here in the woods?" Kennen asked.

"I've lived in this cabin most of my adult life. It has been in my family for a few generations. I like the quiet, but it isn't too far from town either."

Gemma eyed the very long table. Ms. Warren didn't miss a beat. She laughed. "Yes, I actually do host get-togethers pretty often, so I don't lead a solitary life by any means. But it is nice that this cabin is out of the way. Occasionally, some of my visitors are a bit shy about anyone knowing they were out here."

"Because their visits are connected to Wicca?" Kennen asked, thinking of the leather book.

"The Coven I am a part of often meets here for our ceremonies. I have some nice space out back as well. But most of them aren't sensitive about others knowing their religious standing. There are plenty, though, that visit for other reasons."

"We hear people like to tell you ghost stories." Gemma's smile was warm. Genuine.

"People often come thinking that, because of my religion, I must know about ghosts. But there are no tenets concerning ghosts in Wicca. Actually, many Wiccans believe in reincarnation, which leaves little room for ghosts."

"So, you don't believe in ghosts?" Gemma asked.

"I didn't quite say that, dear. What I am saying is that my belief in ghosts has nothing to do with my being Wiccan. Many people confuse the two. But I've found with some patience and kindness, most people are willing to learn about both."

"What do you know about the tales concerning the wailing woman?" Kennen asked.

"Plenty of people have come to me with tales about the wailing woman. Some have seen her once, others multiple times. Some saw her crying, some didn't. Generally, she is described as pale and wearing white, but the description of the type of clothing varies. It's quite the amalgamation. Somewhere in all of it, there is some true source, but there is no way of telling what that is. There is one constant with all the stories, though."

"And what is that?" Gemma asked.

"The sightings always happen at the train tracks."

"Do you remember when you first heard this story? When someone first came to you with it?" Kennen asked.

"The first time I started hearing specific rumors about a wailing woman was not long after that young woman's death."

"Leonie Tilden?" Gemma asked.

"Yes. But people said their sightings actually predated that event. After Ms. Tilden died, people started thinking that what they had seen was a warning of the tragedy to come. A harbinger, if you will."

"Did you get a sense that these people believed there was a direct supernatural connection to Leonie's death?" Gemma asked.

"I don't know that anyone was suggesting that the ghost had any influence over the events at the time. You see, back then everyone in this town seemed convinced it was that Alex Medina boy. But that situation didn't come to a satisfactory end either. No trial. No judge or jury to say yes without a doubt. It didn't truly give closure. So, over time and with speculation, stories along those lines, stories about ghosts, started to grow."

"Do you believe that paranormal entities have that type of power?" Kennen asked.

"That's hard to say. We don't really know the limitations of the soul. Can they interact with our physical plane? Can they communicate? Influence us? Could it possibly be that they aren't locked by time the same way we are? I heard an interesting theory once that the woman seen months before *was* Leonie Tilden, her soul trying to prevent its own fate. Who knows?"

Kennen rolled his pen in his hand. This would all be great cut into the final product. The paranormal junkies would eat it up. But trying to make this distant spiritualism jive with the gut-wrenching event from his past was not working. He took a sip of his tea and tried to get the black shadow, joining him again as if it was another member of the team, to back down, to stop threatening his calm.

"We've heard there is an earlier tradition around the wailing woman. Another woman who lost her life on the tracks?" Gemma said.

"That's possible," Ms. Warren said. "But I must tell you I never heard about that until after the Tilden incident."

Kennen made a note, then slid an eye over to Gemma and saw she was circling a note as well. He'd bet she'd just come to the same conclusion he had: the prom date story was a late addition to the tale, developing after Leonie had passed. It was just a new iteration, something that filled in the backstory.

"What role do you think, if any, the wailing woman had in what happened to Leonie Tilden?" Gemma asked.

"I believe in reincarnation, but I don't know about the time-line. I think, just like when we are alive, that some people have such a sense of purpose, such a drive, that nothing can stop them, not even death. I think there was a reason that she was sighted when she was, but unfortunately, we may never know what it was. But it is hard to believe that it is just a coincidence. Especially considering that after all these years, just when your team comes to investigate, the sightings have started again."

Kennen gave a quick glance back to Marty and then to Greg. Greg gave a small head shake. Cora did the same. No one had mentioned the fresh sightings to her. Apparently, people were still bringing their ghost stories to Ms. Warren's door.

"Are the current stories the same as the old ones?"

"The only thing these sightings seem to have in common with the old one is the location: the tracks. Now people are seeing a man. Some have claimed they think it is the ghost of Medina."

"How many people have told you about these sightings?" Gemma asked.

"Two people have told me about the sightings so far."

The team switched gears, trying to see if she had any knowledge about Emmaline or Tom Tilden. She seemed to be in the same place as the rest of the citizenry: never met Emmaline, and only knew public-relations Tom, nothing real.

As the interview came to a close and the team started packing up their equipment, Ms. Warren put a hand on Kennen's shoulder. "Would you be able to help me with something in the shed before you go?"

"Sure." Kennen left the rest of the team rolling cords and carefully matching equipment with the foam molds in the transport cases.

He followed Ms. Warren out the back door and over to the small shed. He found himself shying back as she undid the padlock. What strange things might she keep in there? Kennen found it was just another occasion to scold himself. Inside, a shelf held some gardening tools, and there was a lawnmower and a wheelbarrow. In the rafters were rolls of green mesh gardening screen. Ms. Warren slid along the wall past the larger equipment and reached for an ancient suitcase that sat on a shelf in the back of the shed. It was so old that it would have looked natural strapped to the top of a stagecoach. Ms. Warren pulled at the worn handle gently as if it might let go at any moment, coaxing the case off the shelf with her other hand. It finally slid free and she caught it, cradling it in her arms. She pivoted around and Kennen reached out to take it from her so that she could maneuver her way back out.

"Put it there." She gestured to a low stump scarred with axe marks.

He consulted the latches, bent down to carefully balance the trunk, and then stepped away. She bent over and flipped the latches. One opened, the other took some tugging, but finally released. She lifted the top slowly, making sure it stayed balanced on the stump. Kennen peered over her shoulder to see the case was full of envelopes and pictures. He waited patiently while she dug through the contents with her long boney fingers.

"Aha." She rose and turned back to Kennen. She held out a picture frame with a folded piece of paper over the top, obscuring the image. He searched her face then reluctantly reached out and took the items. He pulled back the letter to look at the picture, and almost dropped it. Again.

It was the picture from the mantel. The picture with Leonie and the hula-hoop and the big crack across the glass that he never fixed.

He flipped up the top flap of the paper to see his name written in Leonie's slanted scrawl. He quickly closed it and put it back over the photo. Darkness filled his vision and he wondered if he was going to pass out.

Ms. Warren reached out a steadying hand and held his shoulder. That pulled him back. He shrugged her grip off.

"How did you get these?" There was bile in his whisper.

"You know, the past is as real as the here and now. It never really leaves us. And neither do the people we lose. Some people find comfort in this, others..." She paused, shifting her eyes to the team carting things out her front door to the van. "Others are haunted by it."

She stepped forward and reached a hand up to his cheek. Kennen stood still, glaring at her, but it didn't scare her off. Her hand was cool despite the August heat. "You can heal or be haunted, but you have to choose."

Kennen stepped back from her.

Her hand floated back down to the grasp of her other hand. "I don't know the meaning of this new harbinger, but you need to choose while the choice is still yours to make." She turned and closed the case then sat it beside the stump. Kennen started to look down at the contents of his hands but had to look away, like he held some grisly trophy.

He went back in to retrieve his bag and jammed the picture and letter into the back of it.

"Everything okay?" Gemma asked. She held the last case and extension cord in her hand.

"Yeah. Let's go," Kennen said, throwing his bag over his shoulder and heading out the front door.

FEBRUARY 1998

Kennen found himself running late to work. When he came in he was ready for Jesse to give him some crap, but when he opened the door he was hit with a wave of laughter. He found Alex up at the counter. Jesse was holding himself up on the counter, trying to recover from his laughing fit. Alex's face had a reddish glow and he was holding his side. He turned and spotted Kennen.

"Hey, man! Jesse said you'd be in in a minute. I thought I'd wait and say hi!" Alex lifted his coffee, toasting Kennen's arrival.

"You know this fool?" Jesse said, smiling and pointing at Alex.

"Yeah," Kennen said.

"This guy's funny. Bring him around more often," Jesse said. He turned back to Alex. "Well, now that tardy-bro has shown up, I got to go make some calls and get some orders going. Good shooting the shit with ya, man." Jesse gave a quick fist bump to Alex and walked to the back while Kennen took his place behind the counter.

"He's a real nice guy," Alex said, eyes lingering on the door Jesse had just gone through.

"Yeah, I like working with him."

"How are you feeling about the Calc test next week?" Alex asked.

Kennen felt his jaw tighten. He knew eventually this would come up. After the infamous KFC event, there had been no study sessions. Leonie wasn't afraid to go against her father and hang out with Alex during school hours, but once that last bell rang, she usually went straight home. Neither of them had told Alex what Mr. Tilden had decreed, but he also hadn't asked them to hang out. He was a smart guy, he had to know something was up. But it seemed he was now testing the waters.

"I mean, I think I'm good, but I've always struggled with logarithmic functions."

Right then the bell above the door rang. Calvin Travers came in wearing his black and red letterman jacket. Kennen looked outside and saw Calvin's car parked by the gas pumps.

"Well, if you need any help, let me know. I got you," Alex said, lifting his coffee again, this time in a farewell wave. He turned and left. Kennen noticed Calvin scowl at Alex as he passed.

"I need to pay for gas on pump 4," Calvin said once he sauntered up to the counter.

"Sure," Kennen said, turning to the computer to ring up the total. He told Calvin the total, who started digging in his wallet. He handed over a twenty.

"You hang out with that fag?" Calvin said.

"What? Alex?" Kennen asked, grabbing Calvin's few cents of change.

"I'm just saying man, if you don't want people talking, I wouldn't be hanging out with him. Just trying to look out for you man."

Kennen couldn't figure out why Calvin, who had barely recognized his existence the last four years, would suddenly be worried about his reputation. This wasn't about Kennen. This was just to dig at Alex.

Kennen just shook his head, and Calvin misinterpreted it to mean that Kennen wouldn't hang out with Alex.

"Good choice," he said, pocketing his coins. "See you at school." Calvin left and Kennen started checking the stock of cigarettes behind the counter, but he couldn't focus.

Maybe he shouldn't hang with Alex as much. Mr. Tilden had said he was dangerous. Maybe it would be better if Kennen kept his distance.

AUGUST 2017

Kennen hadn't been able to look at the photo or read the letter. He put the items on his bed and paced around it until he decided that it would be best if they switched places with the flask from his bag. He reduced the flask's content to a few drops that tinkled around in the bottom and, discovering he still wasn't up to looking at them, stashed the flask on top of them.

The next thing he knew, there was knocking at his door. And for some reason the sun was up, peeking through his blinds. He stumbled over to the door to find Gemma, who looked him over with an expression of surprise. He looked down and realized it was probably because he was still in his clothes from the day before.

"Everything okay?" she asked.

"Yeah, yeah. Guess I was just tired."

"You remember we have the Hector Lopez interview this evening, right?"

Kennen blinked. He had been so thrown off by the Warren interview he forgot that Alex's uncle was lined up for today. "Yeah, of course," he said after too long of a pause.

Gemma let it go. "I just wanted to go over the game plan since this might be a touchy one."

She was right. Lopez had been clear he was not willing to appear on camera or audio recording. He was talking to them so that they would leave his sister, Lily, alone.

At 7:00 pm, Hector Lopez arrived at the hotel.

Kennen and Gemma greeted him in the lobby and took him back to the conference room. Lopez was tall, broad at the shoulders and thin at the hips. He wore a baseball cap, a white t-shirt, and jeans. Since they were not recording, they were going to conduct the interview without Marty, Greg, and Cora. The guy seemed skittish enough without the entire team ganging up on him.

Kennen gestured to the chair at the head of the table while he and Gemma sat on either side. Kennen pulled out a small digital recorder.

"What's that?" Lopez asked.

"It's a digital recorder."

"I told you on the phone I am not comfortable being recorded." Lopez wasn't being impudent; he sounded truly concerned.

"And I have that documented right here," Gemma said, pulling out a carbon-copy contract. "Kennen and I are going to sign it," she said, scrawling her name, then passing it on to Kennen, "and we will have you sign as well. The recorder is just to help us in case we need to review what was said. This states that no recording of your voice will be used on the show and that you will remain an anonymous contributor. When the show goes to production, we will permanently delete the recording. We will send a copy of this contract with you."

Lopez read the document thoroughly. He glanced back at Gemma, sighed, and signed. Gemma took the paper, peeling off the top sheet, and returned the yellow sheet to Lopez. Kennen hit the record button and waited for Gemma to grab her notepad and pen. When she nodded, he started.

"Would you please start by telling us about what your nephew, Alex, was like when he was younger?"

"Alex was a sweet kid. Always happy to help out around the

house. Had lots of friends. He was very kind. And smart. Smartest kid I ever knew. He would have been successful in college."

"Did you know why he and his mother moved from Chicago to Ashter?"

"It was not long after Matt, his older brother, first got into trouble. Carlos, their dad, had too good of a job to leave Chicago, but Lily could get a job anywhere as a nurse. So they decided she should move and get Alex out of there, away from all that. That was such a hard decision, but they'd do anything for their kids."

"We've heard that Matt was involved in a gang," Gemma said.

"Yes."

"The Latin Kings?" Kennen asked.

Lopez took a moment before nodding.

"Did you know Leonie Tilden?" Gemma asked.

"Not personally. Lily told me a bit about her and her father over the phone."

"What did she tell you about Leonie and Tom Tilden?" Gemma followed up.

"She thought Leonie was nice. She heard that Tilden was a lawyer, and when things were looking bad for Matt in court, she went to talk to him. She couldn't afford much, but she tried to see if he would let her set up a contract where she made payments or something. She had looked into him, and thought he was a pretty successful lawyer. She wanted him to defend Matt."

"He didn't take the case though?" Gemma asked.

"No. He asked her if it was true, that Matt was really involved in the gang. She said he was, but that he didn't do what he was accused of."

"And what was that exactly?" Kennen asked.

"Attempted car-jacking and attempted murder."

Kennen waited, hoping Lopez would fill the silence, say more. He didn't bite.

"What really happened?" Gemma asked.

'Well, you know, Matt wasn't as good in school as Alex. He wasn't good at any sports, and Alex was always great at baseball. And Alex, he was a writer, too. I think Matt just got tired of being shown up by his little brother. So, he rebelled, went to the other extreme. He was nineteen when he got involved with some gang members. He thought they were just going out that night to have a good time, maybe score some weed. They were walking down an alleyway and saw this guy going to his car. Matt said there were three of them. One of them nodded to the other. Matt thought maybe this guy by the car was the dealer. Then the first dude pulls a gun on the guy, telling him to hand over his keys or he's dead. Guy doesn't hand over the keys, he turns to fight. The guy with the gun pistol-whips him and then shoots him in the back. They all ran." Lopez stopped and took a deep breath. Gemma offered him a bottle of water. He took a long drink and thanked her.

"Did the other guys go down with Matt?" Gemma asked.

"No. They were too important. Good soldiers. Probably already had multiple strikes against them. So he took the whole wrap."

"What about the weapon? If he never touched it—" Kennen started.

"They never found the gun, because the one dude still had it. Or got rid of it, right? There had been a witness, someone who saw it go down through a window. He gave the description of all three. Matt didn't know enough to get rid of his coat afterward, and he was picked up just walking down the street. The victim lived and recognized Matt as being there, though he couldn't remember which of them attacked him. It was enough though. Matt got ten years in prison."

"Where is Matt now?" Kennen asked.

Lopez hung his head. "Wish I knew."

"His mom, your sister, isn't well, is that correct?" Gemma asked.

"Yes."

"We're very sorry to hear that. You're helping take care of her?" Gemma asked.

"I'm all she's got left. Carlos died in a freak work accident a few years back. And now she's got cancer and ..." Lopez trailed off, looking down at his hands in his lap. Gemma and Kennen shared glances and gave him a moment. Kennen looked down at his notes. Despite the conviction, if what Lopez said was true, there was no evidence of violent behavior from Matt. He had failed to stop a violent act, but he didn't instigate one. Kennen was surprised to find how comforted he was by this.

"Are you familiar with the evidence against Alex?" Gemma asked gently once Lopez looked like he was ready to go on.

"Yes. A neighbor saw him trying to break in or something, he had no alibi, and they found that note on him where the girl had asked him to meet near the tracks."

"Do you believe he was capable of killing someone?"

"Of course."

Both Gemma and Kennen stopped, pens poised over paper. When they were planning their questions, they had worked on the assumption Lopez would defend his nephew. Kennen looked at Gemma and she looked as bewildered as he did. He looked back at his notes. It felt like all the gears in his brain had stopped. He had to get them turning again.

"Do you believe he killed Leonie Tilden?" Kennen asked.

"Don't you? You knew him, didn't you?" Lopez countered.

Kennen met Lopez's eyes. They stared at each other.

"We're trying to keep an open mind on all accounts. Follow the evidence, not feelings or beliefs," Gemma said.

"Will you answer the question?" Kennen asked.

"If he had a reason, yes, I think he could have."

"Why?" Gemma asked.

"I think most people could, given the right situation."

"Did Alex have any direct connections himself with any gangs?" Kennen asked.

"Not that I knew of."

"Then what kind of situation are you thinking Alex was in?" Gemma asked.

"Your guess is as good as mine, but we saw what happened. We know the outcome."

The interview paused again. Gemma picked up the ball.

"Have you ever heard of Dylan Whitacre?" Gemma asked. The question caught Kennen off guard and he felt it show on his face. He looked down quickly, trying to recover.

"The name sounds familiar, but I can't remember why."

"We are trying to see if he also had connections to the Latin Kings. Has Matt ever mentioned him?"

"Matt never talked to me about any of his contacts with the gang."

Kennen sighed. That stream was still dry. Gemma looked out of ideas. Kennen started to reach for the recorder, to call it, but his hand hovered over the button. Finally, he pulled his hand back.

"You are right. I knew him. And I knew Leonie. And I knew what they were like together. What I don't know is why Alex would ever kill her. What motivation could he have? You talk about 'situations' but I can't come up with a single one that would make sense in this case."

Lopez leaned back in his chair. Kennen thought he was going to fully ignore the question when he finally answered. "I don't know. Maybe that would have come out in court, but there was no chance for that."

"Did it have to do with Mr. Tilden not taking the case?" Gemma asked. Kennen cringed. Why was she giving him an easy way out?

"That must have been it," Lopez said.

"Do you know why Mr. Tilden said no to Matt's case?"

"He asked Lily point blank if Matt was in the gang. When she said yes, he said there was no way he would touch the case. She said she tried everything to reason with him."

Kennen thought back to the interaction he had witnessed. She hadn't stopped with reasoning. She had tried threatening as well.

"Did your sister know anything about Tom Tilden that she might have held over him?"

"Well, if she did, it didn't work. He never defended Matt."

"But could that be why Mr. Tilden immediately suspected Alex?"

"I assume he suspected Alex because all the evidence pointed to him. He was the only one who made sense as the murderer."

Kennen wrote down a word in caps on his paper and underlined it: <u>REHEARSED</u>. No matter what direction they came from or how incongruent it sounded, Lopez stuck to the guilty line.

"Uh, let's see, do you think we should move on down to this one?" Kennen said, showing his notebook to Gemma so that Lopez couldn't see it and pointed to the word.

"Um…" Gemma said, scribbling something down. "How about this one?" She had written down *lying* and circled it.

Kennen nodded. They were both right. Lopez didn't believe that Alex was guilty, and it seemed like he had practiced his lies. Kennen and Gemma had seen this before, and he realized that when Gemma had asked about Whitacre, she was falling back on her experience, which was what he should have been doing, but he allowed himself to get in too deep. This was exactly why people close to a case should not be investigating it. That's how he had lost control of this interview. But he knew what he needed to do now and what Gemma had tried to do and hadn't quite succeeded with: he needed to shake Lopez up. It was time to play his ace.

"Mr. Tilden and Ms. Medina's argument is one angle, but what about the fact that Alex was gay and Leonie knew it? Could that have been an issue?"

It was Gemma's turn to try and cover her surprise. Lopez's eyes landed squarely upon Kennen. Kennen could sense Gemma trying to telegraph something on the order of *what the fuck?!* over to him, but he kept his eyes on Lopez.

"Well, look at that," Lopez said finally. "You came up with a situation."

"So, you think that could be Alex's motive for murder?"

Lopez looked at him like the question was so dumb, it had to be some kind of trick. In Chicago, at that time, maybe it wouldn't have been as big of a deal. But in Ashter? During his time in Ashter, even in the late nineties, Kennen had never known a gay person besides Alex. At least, no one who admitted it. And Alex certainly didn't openly admit it.

"Did Lily know?"

"Lily loves her boys. It doesn't matter what they've done or who they were."

Kennen nodded. This time Lopez was telling the truth. No rehearsal needed.

"We've got one more subject for you," Gemma said.

Lopez nodded.

"Do you know anything about the wailing woman?"

"It's some ghost story they tell around here."

"Have you heard there have been new sightings? Some people are saying it's Alex this time," Kennen said.

Lopez's eyes sliced at Kennen, but he quickly recovered, lowering his eyes and shifting in his seat. "Just stupid stories." He glanced toward the door. Kennen could feel him shutting down.

"Is there anything else you would like to tell us before we conclude this interview?" Gemma asked.

"This is enough, right? You won't be bothering us again?"

"Unless some new evidence would come to light that we would need your insights on, I think we have what we need," Kennen said.

Lopez didn't seem completely satisfied with that answer, but he was ready to go, so he didn't argue. "Good. I need to get back to Lily. Good luck with your investigation."

They stood, shook hands, and he was gone.

"You're going to have to catch me up," Gemma said, shaking her head and falling back into her chair. "What the hell just happened?"

"I'm sorry about not letting you know that Alex was gay. I needed someone else who knew him to corroborate that. It couldn't simply be my word."

"I get that. But I'm not sure why you made it into a big secret from us, especially if it is possible that it has some bearing on the case. Why didn't you just say?"

"I just … Alex never directly told me. I had to know I wasn't wrong."

Gemma leaned in and put her arms on the table. She tilted her head to the side. "Were you embarrassed about it?"

"No! I just–I didn't want to make this case any messier than it already was without knowing for sure."

Gemma sat silent. She finally did lean back, but she had a strange look on her face. Watchful.

"Well, it seems his family did know, and that you were right. But his mother is dying. We are here, the only chance that her son might be exonerated before her death, and Lopez says he thinks Alex was the murderer?"

"That doesn't make sense to me either," Kennen admitted.

"Well, let's look at it this way. If Medina was guilty, we have two motives. One is that Tilden wouldn't represent his brother. The second is that Leonie supposedly knew he was gay and was going to use it against him. You suspected he was gay. Do you know for sure Leonie knew?"

"I think he told her. Remember, she said in the diary after the fight that she realized he was just being a good friend. I think he saw that she was falling for him, and even though he felt he needed to keep his sexuality a secret, he told her so she would understand why he wasn't going to return her feelings."

"Medina was smart," Gemma said. "He knew he had to be

careful anyway being a racial minority, and if people found out about his sexuality, well …"

"Go on."

"I was going to say it could have been a death sentence, but that's how it turned out anyway. So how did you know? Did he tell you?"

"No. I didn't know for a long time. I started to wonder about it, but, honestly, I don't think I was fully convinced of it until after he died. Jesse and I were talking about it. Jesse thought Alex was a pretty cool guy. He'd stop by and chat at the gas station. I remember Jesse saying later that if he didn't know any better, he would have thought the guy had a crush on him. And I realized, yeah, he had."

"Why risk it by flirting with Jesse? Especially if he had been so careful otherwise."

Kennen sat back and thought for a moment. "I think Alex and I were a lot alike that way. I always had an interest in Leonie, even though romantically she didn't return any. I think in some ways that was safer. I knew in the back of my mind that probably nothing would ever come of it. I could just admire her and pine for her and not have to deal with the reality of an actual romantic relationship. I think Jesse was the same way for Alex. Jesse was straight, and Alex probably knew that. He knew it would never be anything more, anything real, so it was safe. A harmless crush. And the only place they really talked was at Milton's, so, other than me, no real witnesses. Alex could always 'need to run' if another customer came in."

They both sat in silence for a minute. Then something shifted in Kennen's mind. He stood and walked around while in his thoughts he looked at the idea from different angles. "What happens if we can't find anything to disprove it was Alex?"

"Well, we won't have much of a show if that's the case," Gemma said, sighing and leaning back in her chair. "I mean, that was always the possibility when we picked the case up, but it sure won't make for a very engaging series."

"Exactly," Kennen said.

Gemma stilled, then looked up at Kennen. "Lopez *wants* us to stop investigating."

Kennen nodded.

"But why? Alex is already dead, he can't pay any more for it even if we do conclude he is guilty. And it's not like Lily can be a suspect, she was working that night."

"That doesn't mean she doesn't know something important to the case."

Gemma sighed. "Something she'll probably take to the grave with her."

MARCH 1998

Kennen caught Leonie by her locker.

"Hey," he said.

"What's up?" she said.

"In my last class, I heard there is a party down by the river tonight. Wanna go?"

She hesitated.

"Before you come up with some excuse about being too busy," Kennen said, "I know you are busy, I get it, but you haven't gone out for a long time. It's a Friday night. What were you going to do that wouldn't keep until tomorrow?"

She turned back to pulling notebooks from her locker. Kennen felt his heart sink to his heels.

"Okay, yeah," she finally said, shaking her head. "I'll pick you up, okay?"

"Great!" Kennen said with a little too much gusto.

"Yeah." She gave him a weak smile, but a smile nonetheless.

That night, they parked in the lot by the top of the boat ramp. Jim never kept much alcohol around the house, but Leonie had pinched a small bottle of rum from her father's liquor cabinet.

There were plenty of teenagers and twenty-somethings gathered in groups, huddled against the chilly night air. Kennen spotted Jesse with a group standing around drinking Coors and laughing. Kennen gave him a wave and Jesse hoisted up his beer can in response.

"Hey!" It was Alex, waving them over. He was near an open tailgate, some people sitting in the back, some sitting on blankets on the ground. Leonie followed the summons. Kennen held back for a moment, but not knowing what else to do, he gave up and followed. Leonie sat right next to Alex, so Kennen sat on her other side. "They're telling ghost stories," Alex whispered.

Leonie unscrewed the top of the rum and took a number of gulps before passing it to Kennen. He took a sip and handed it back. Leonie offered it to Alex, who waved it off. Gus, who was normally a bit of a class clown, was having a great time telling stupid stories like the one about the couple that heard scratching noises outside of their car and got home with a hook on the door handle, and the lady who woke up to some sound in the house, but thought she was safe because her dog was licking her hand; then in the morning her dog was dead and there was a note saying humans have tongues too. Everyone had heard these stories back in junior high, but Gus tried to say he had heard them from a cousin up in town who knew the victims personally.

Leonie made it through half the bottle during the two stories. A number of others had gotten enough alcohol and weed in them to loosen up and start dancing to someone's mixed tape.

"Come on, this is stupid," Leonie said, standing up and heading toward the improvised dance floor on the boat ramp. Kennen followed and she handed him the bottle. He took another swig, then tucked it in his coat. He'd never seen her have so much and figured it wouldn't hurt if she slowed down a bit. All the same, she seemed to be having a great time. She was dancing and smiling. Kennen stood near her, but just kind of bobbed his head to the music.

"Hey, hit me up with that!" she called over to a nearby bundle of teens. Someone tossed her a beer. She popped it open, took a long slug, and went right back to dancing. So much for slowing down.

Soon there were about twenty other people dancing. Down by the lip of the frosty river two girls were dancing and making out. Kennen wasn't truly much of a dancer, but Leonie was too gone to be dancing well anyway, swaying around with her can of beer held up high. Kennen started dancing as well, figuring most people were too drunk to notice his lame moves.

A beat-up old truck rattled in and parked. There were two guys in the cab and two in the back. Jeffie stepped out from behind the wheel. Kennen didn't recognize the other guy who got out of the front, but it was Calvin Travers and Dylan Whitacre who crawled out of the back. Kennen looked around, but no one seemed bothered by their arrival. He went back to dancing but kept an eye on where Jeffie and his crew were headed. Jeffie and the first two dudes dissolved into a nearby group, but Dylan held back.

"Whoo!" Leonie shouted, pulling Kennen's attention back. She was waving both her beer and her empty hand in the air and attempting to hop, but the slant of the boat ramp plus her current drunkenness meant she didn't get much air and then stumbled each time she landed.

"What are you doing?" Kennen asked with a laugh.

"I'm starting a mosh pit," she shouted, now trying to just bounce on the balls of her feet, not quite matching the beat of the song. "Come on, mosh with me!" she cried, and Kennen imitated her bouncing move. He laughed some more and this time she joined him.

Kennen watched her smile and dance, eyes half closed. Everyone else faded into the background until Dylan came up behind her. First, he just put a hand on her hip and swayed a bit, giving her some space. She looked over her shoulder and Dylan smiled at her. She gave him a hesitant smile, starting to lower her arms. Dylan looked off to his left, and Kennen followed his gaze to see Calvin. Dylan motioned him over with a toss of his head. Calvin shrugged and came over. He threw Kennen a cool look and then stepped in between him and Leonie. Dylan and Calvin closed in on her, Dylan grinding on her from behind and Calvin basically humping her hip.

"Hey, man, back up," Leonie slurred, trying to push Calvin away but getting nowhere.

Kennen weaved around them, trying to find a way in there. His weak protests of "Hey!" were drowned out by Dylan cackling and Calvin shouting "Whoo, yeah, baby!"

"Stop it!" Leonie shouted, dropping her mostly empty beer can to try shoving with both hands, but they both just moved in tighter.

"Hey!" Alex showed up to Kennen's right. "HEY!" he yelled again, tapping Calvin on the shoulder. When he didn't react, Alex grabbed his shoulder and pulled hard.

"Yo, back off man!" Calvin turned around and squared up with Alex, inches from his face.

Leonie tried to run, but Dylan grabbed her around the waist and held tight. Kennen wanted, needed to do something, but his body was frozen in place.

"Let me go!" she shouted.

"She's not interested, man, just leave her alone." Alex's voice was calm but firm.

"What, she doesn't like this?" Dylan said, and wrapping his arms around her tighter so she couldn't squirm away, ran his tongue from her jaw back to her hairline.

"Let her go." Alex pushed Calvin aside, eyes now on Dylan. Calvin threw a wild haymaker that caught Alex in the right cheek. Alex stumbled backward into Kennen, the jolt waking Kennen's body up. He caught Alex, keeping him from falling.

Alex regained his feet, pulled back, and laid Calvin out. He went down straight backward, then rolled over, grasping at his nose. Apparently, Alex could do more than just pitch with his right arm. Calvin shouted and cussed as blood escaped his fingers and dripped into the traction grooves sawed into the cement boat ramp. Dylan threw Leonie to the side and stepped up to Alex. By now most people had stopped to watch. Jesse came running up and put a hand on both Alex and Dylan's chests, pushing them apart. Jesse stood about a head taller than both of them, so it wasn't going to be easy for either of them to get around him.

"Okay, that's enough. Everyone was having a good time. Let's just get back to that," Jesse said. Dylan and Alex kept their eyes locked, but neither tried to advance. Jesse leaned over to Dylan. "Your boy needs to get some ice on that nose. Why don't you get him outta here?"

"This ain't over," Dylan hissed. He bent down, grabbed Calvin who was still down on his knees, and took him back to the truck. Jeffie looked over, spotted Jesse, threw his glass beer bottle to the ground where it shattered, then headed back to his truck along with his fourth companion. Once Whitacre had helped Calvin into the back of the truck and crawled in after him, Jeffie revved the engine, then tore out in a wide arc back to the main road.

"I wanna go home," Leonie said weakly.

"I'll drive. I haven't been drinking," Alex offered. Kennen looked at Alex's cheek; it was already swelling and red where a bruise was brewing. His right hand was scuffed up.

"I can—" Kennen started, but Alex was already guiding her back to her car, taking her keys.

"Let her go. I can give you a lift home later," Jesse said.

Kennen watched as Alex drove Leonie away.

AUGUST 2017

The rest of the crew, along with the actors, were arriving today. The actors and actresses were flying in and the crew was coming in with the big equipment via vans. Greg had been a mess the night before. This always happened at this point in the process; it was like Greg's normal personality went on vacation for about two days. No matter how detailed the instructions, how competent the crew head that packed the vans, every time there seemed to be something missing. Greg always met this with as much calm as a broken nest of hornets. Cora talked him into going with the rest of the group to pick up the acting staff. That way the poor crew could get themselves organized before the onslaught of Greg's anxiety-driven interrogation. Kennen fully supported this idea, volunteering to stay back at the hotel, where the crew was scheduled to arrive at approximately the same time as the actors' plane. He wanted to sit down with the files again anyway.

According to the records, at first, the cops seemed to be looking into not only Leonie's friends but every young man with an arrest record. Every member of Jefferson's Gang was on the list, including Dylan Whitacre. Hell, they had even checked in on Jesse, not only because of Kennen's alibi but also because Jesse had been picked up a few times for underage drinking in that three-year window of being an adult but not being able to drink. Dylan's alibi had been that he was in Chicago that night. There was an arrest record to back him up; apparently, he got picked up with another guy trying to check door handles in a parking lot. They didn't actually steal anything, so it turned into a catch and release. They were picked up around 10:45, but the report showed they had been questioned and both said they arrived in Chicago around 9:30 pm and got to the lot at about 10:15. But was there any proof of that timeline?

Kennen pulled up Google Maps and did some calculations. It would have been tight, but Dylan, with or without the help of his friend, could have met Leonie, killed her and still have made it to the parking lot by 10:30, but he wouldn't have entered Chicago until 10:15. Was there any proof he made it to Chicago before then? And if he didn't actually get to the lot until 10:30, that only left a fifteen-minute gap between getting to the parking lot and getting caught. Was it bad robbery skills or bad luck that had led to Dylan getting caught at that time, or something more deliberate? Kennen sat back, mulling this over. Dylan struck Kennen as someone who would botch up basically anything he tried. Could he have deliberately gotten caught to establish an alibi after murdering someone? That would be both impressive and terrifying, two feelings Kennen had never experienced in regard to Dylan Whitacre. But his friend, a George Sillens, whom Kennen had never heard of, could have been acting as Dylan's brains. A panicked call from Dylan, a friend from Chicago helping a buddy out. That's all it would have taken.

Kennen scribbled down Sillens name as a person of interest and returned to the files. There was no in-depth follow up on Dylan. And why would there be? Between the eyewitness account from the neighbor and Tom Tilden's influence, Alex became the solid lead.

Kennen tapped his pen on the desk and flipped over his phone to glance at the time. There was still half an hour before the team would arrive. Plenty of time to purchase a refresher for his flask. He figured he might need it after meeting the new Leonie, Medina, and himself when they arrived.

He struck out on foot for a liquor store that wasn't particularly far away and, most importantly, had not existed when he lived there before. As he walked, he pondered the actors and actresses that would be arriving. They weren't A-listers by a long shot. Most of them weren't even going to need to speak on camera, just exhibit whatever emotion was needed for the content of the scene. And obviously, he had worked with actors before, but Kennen had never really stopped to think about the implications. It was one thing to play a completely fictional character, but these people were taking on tragedies that were often the worst part of a real human's life. Did they end up carrying a weight from that? Or were these people they imitated, people they often never knew, as fictional to them as any other character they portrayed? Kennen smirked, realizing what a shit actor he would make. Of course he had a persona in front of the camera, but he wasn't being someone else entirely. But for a good actor, it didn't matter if the character was real or not, they had to believe their character could be real to execute the art. Kennen was just wishing it all could be fiction. He wondered how many other people who had watched their filming for previous shows had known the real people. What was it like for them, to see other people play lost neighbors, guilty friends?

He reached the liquor store and was impressed by the choices he found in the whiskey aisle. He was reaching for a bottle of Pike Creek when the door opened with a harsh little jingle. Kennen glanced up unconsciously and was about to finish making his selection when something clicked in his mind. He looked back at the new customer, who was headed to the refrigerated beer. It wasn't the man's looks that tipped him off; he was a white middle-aged man, blonde hair cut short to halo a bald top, wearing a black and red checkered button down and khaki shorts. Fairly common. It was how he walked, hunched as if to counterbalance the fact that there was nothing between his hips and ribs but a hollow place. It was in his wrist that twisted nervously as he pulled at a string coming off of a corded bracelet.

Kennen wasn't sure what was happening. Had the black shadow come back with a vengeance, taking the form of his greatest wish, just to taunt him? Was he sending out signals so loud and strong that the universe was just trying to appease him so he would shut up for a bit? Could he actually be right, and somehow Leonie was pointing him in that direction from the grave?

Or could his brain have put together all the subtle clues from the file and somehow figured out that the place Dylan Whitacre would most likely be on a Monday morning would be a liquor store? He didn't care if it was divine intervention or dumb luck; all that mattered was that, right now, Dylan Whitacre was across the store, trying to select a six-pack.

Kennen waited until Dylan opened the fridge door before he started for the counter. He sauntered up as Dylan made his selection and was signing the credit card receipt when Dylan lined up behind him. He tucked his brown bag under his arm, then turned wide down an aisle, keeping the back of his head to Dylan, acting like he was fiddling with his wallet. Once outside he slid his sunglasses down from the top of his head, stepped around the corner of the store, and pulled out his phone, pretending to text. When Dylan came out, he paid no attention to Kennen. He took the six-pack and set it in the back of a beat-up old chevy before crawling inside. Kennen repositioned himself, straightening up as if to read a long text reply. Dylan started backing out, and Kennen snapped a photo of him in profile as he craned around in his truck, looking for traffic. Once he was out on the street, Kennen took a slow step forward, still trying to look like he was simply reading his phone, and caught a picture of Dylan's license plate as he drove away. Kennen put his phone in his back pocket and started back toward the hotel.

For the first time since he had been on this case, Kennen felt like smiling.

He made it back with just enough time to stash his whiskey upstairs before the two large vans arrived with the rest of the film crew. They were checked in and ready for Greg when he arrived with the actors about 45 minutes later. Kennen went out to meet them as they pulled up. His accidental success with Whitacre gave him a sense of strength, or at least of good luck, and he was now ready to meet these imposters head-on. The Leonie look-alike stepped out from the van, but the shoulder strap from her backpack caught on the armrest. As she stood there, Kennen felt his chest fill with something warm and lighter than air. The make-believe Medina popped his head out and slipped the strap loose.

"There you go," he said with a smile that she returned, but as soon as she turned away from him, she rolled her eyes. And that was all it took. That one small gesture destroyed any illusion Kennen had about her being like Leonie. His chest deflated, ribs dropping to grate on his lungs, his heart. Hopefully, she was a better actress than she was a person.

"Hey, Kennen, any trouble with the film crew?" Marty slid out from beside the van.

"No, all good as far as we know. Greg will tell us otherwise, I'm sure," Kennen said, smiling. But Greg took no notice; he was already charging for the door to find the crew. Cora shrugged her shoulders. Kennen looked around. "Where's Gemma?"

"She didn't come with us," Marty said.

"What are you talking about? I saw her leave with you this morning."

"She headed out at the same time, but she said she had a lead to follow up on and she went off on foot. I'm sure she'll be in touch in a bit."

"Well, I struck up my own lead," Kennen said. He leaned in closer to Marty and lowered his voice. "I found Whitacre. He's here, in town."

The look of surprise that crossed Marty's face quickly grew into a manic grin. "That's my boy!" he shouted, clapping Kennen on the back.

Kennen pulled out his phone and showed the pictures he had snapped to Marty.

"Why don't you send those off to Gemma? Whatever she's on, she's going to want to see that. Ask her to get digging on him," Marty said.

"Oh," Kennen said, taken aback. "I figured I'd follow it up."

"I've got other plans for you this afternoon." Marty glanced over at the three actors who stood waiting on the curb.

Half an hour later, Kennen, Marty, and the acting crew had gathered around the conference room's table, all fighting varying levels of fatigue from jet lag and hotel living.

"This is going to be good," Marty had assured Kennen before opening the conference room door. Kennen wasn't so sure about that. He was fairly sure he'd rather be taking a nip off of his new bottle.

"Everyone, I'd like to introduce you to Kennen Clarke," Marty said.

The Leonie look-alike flipped her hair. "We are all big fans of the show. We talked about it the whole way up. We know all about you. Maybe we should start by telling you about ourselves?"

Kennen and Marty exchanged looks. "Um, this is Julia Rivers," Marty said.

"Yes, I'm Julia and I'll be playing Leonie Tilden," she continued, fake-as-fuck smile plastered on her face. Did she think anyone in the room didn't know who she was supposed to play? "I'm so excited to meet you. I'm originally from D.C. I've done a number of advertisements. You may have seen me in the recent spots for Tanqueray." She tilted her head and gave a flirty little smile.

"How old are you?" Kennen asked.

She blinked for a moment before reapplying her smile. "Oh, don't worry. I'll have no problem pulling off a teenager."

"And how about you?" Kennen asked, unceremoniously turning his attention to the actor who was to play Medina.

"Oh, uh, I'm Kyle Mendoza. I'm from L.A. I do mostly stage work. I got my Equity Card two years back and have been in a number of off-Broadway shows. This will be my first role on a streaming series. I'm excited about this opportunity."

Kennen smiled and nodded at him. "Happy to have you on board." He turned to the final guy.

"Well, I'm Roger Smithfield, and I'm supposed to be playing you, so it's nice to meet you in person," he said. "I guess I'm the non-trad guy. I haven't done much acting, though I have been involved in the theater. I've worked in set design for a number of years. Anyway, a friend of mine who is an actor saw the casting call and thought I fit perfectly. Got me in touch with his agent and here I am. It's pretty surreal." Roger let out a little nervous laugh and everyone joined in except Julia, who seemed to find the partially dead fern in the corner more interesting than Roger.

"Well, what questions do you have?" Kennen asked, opening up the floor.

Julia jumped back in, ready to take charge again. "Maybe you could just tell us a bit about all of our characters."

"The *people* you are portraying, well, I can give you some traits now and feedback later, but I think it's better if you read up on them yourselves. What I don't want to see is just my version, my interpretation, up on the screen. I want to see the truth of things, and the investigation so far has shown me I did not see that before. I was just a teenager." He turned to Roger. "I was not to be trusted," he said with a little laugh. "I was naive, inexperienced, biased without a clue." Kennen paused. No one moved. "Well, there you go, Roger. Run with that."

More nervous half-laughs filled the room. Kennen turned on

Julia. "Leonie was so much smarter than any of us. She always knew what was going on."

A smug little smile crossed Julia's face, and Kennen could just imagine she was thinking, *I've got that, no problem.*

"But she was also the most kind, most accepting." Kennen bore his eyes into Julia, daring her to look away. "The most big-hearted person you'd ever meet. She was real. Genuine."

Everyone was silent. Julia shifted in her chair. Kennen turned to Kyle. Damn, he looked just like Alex, right down to the slight wave in his glossy black hair. Kennen felt his face soften. "The same could be said of Alex."

"I've already been reading about him. I don't know what you all have found, but I just can't buy that he did it," Kyle said.

"And I think you should play him as such."

Marty shot Kennen a warning look. All of the team members had to sign non-disclosure contracts that lasted until the premiere, but leaks still happened. To prevent this, Marty, Greg, Cora, Gemma, and Kennen were often the only people who got to see the full hand of cards, at least until post-production. Kennen met Marty's look, and after holding his eyes for a moment, Marty nodded. Kennen stood and left. He didn't know if the rest of them were done, but he was.

At least it wasn't all bad. Kennen thought that Kyle was perfect for the part. But then he grimaced at the irony of it. Medina had seemed to be the easiest choice twenty years ago as well.

TRANSCRIPT FROM

AUGUST 27TH, 2017, RECORDING CONT.

Kennen: There was another fight you won't find recorded in any of the police files. In this fight, Alex fought for Leonie. He was protecting her from some creeps at a party. I called her the next day, and she was so worried about him. Afraid he'd get in trouble with the law, or that Jefferson's gang would come after him. She had to refer to him as Allie over the phone so there was no trouble from her dad. I didn't follow how Alex helping her would get Alex in trouble. I thought if anything it might heal some things. Leonie didn't think so. I assured her she didn't need to worry about the law, because there was no way anyone could tell on Alex without snitching on the whole party, and no one was going to do that. As far as for Jefferson's gang, I thought Alex might actually be safer now. Most of us were easy pickings for the gang whenever they felt like it, but they knew Alex would fight. They also saw Jesse there with Alex. Jesse and Jeffie always seemed to have some sort of unspoken truce. They had grown up together, and I think there was some sort of respect there.

Leonie saw the sense in all that, but she was worried about the fact that the fight was literally written on Alex's face. I knew from Jim's work that people lied about this sort of thing all the time, unfortunately. He could just say he fell down the stairs. I reminded her that he was super smart and that he could talk his way out of it.

But, and this is the fucked up thing, no one did ask him about it. I mean probably most of the kids already heard about it.

I guess we were both right. I was right that no one would be talking about it.

She was right that we should have been worried for Alex.

AUGUST 2017

That night Kennen couldn't sleep. Gemma had come back mid-evening, saying she would get right on the Whitacre trail in the morning. Her lead had turned into a wild goose chase, and she was pissed that she had wasted a whole day. She seemed stoked about Kennen's lead though. She hadn't divulged what her hunch had been. Now Kennen was lying awake, debating whether he should be paranoid about that or angry at himself for feeling paranoid. He needed to be able to trust Gemma like he always had. Were this any other case, he wouldn't have thought twice about it. But it was so hard to trust anyone right now. Then of course there was the meeting with the actors. Kennen still wasn't sure about how he felt after that situation. And tomorrow was the Emmaline Tilden interview. With all that, the few shots from his freshly filled flask fell powerless.

Around 1:30 am he decided a walk was his best chance to settle his mind. He hadn't had any particular place in mind, but he found himself in the woods, lit by the full moon that sat high in the sky. Walking through these woods felt like being in a good memory, but he watched for the bad memories, like they might jump out from behind a tree, ready to slice him like Jeffie all those years ago. But nothing happened. Even his dark shadow seemed to have taken the evening off.

The hollow howl of a train horn filled the air like the call of a siren. Kennen veered to the edge of the woods, near the tracks. He looked to the side to see the bright round light moving toward him, so blinding he couldn't see the actual train behind it. It was only light and sound.

Then something on the far side of the tracks, just inside the treeline, caught his eye.

"Hey!" Kennen shouted above the growing roar.

The figure paused and turned. Just enough light from the train reached the person for Kennen to make out a man's face, dark with a scar running deep and wide from his cheek up to his hairline. Then the man turned and started to run.

"No! Wait!" Kennen looked back down the tracks as he scrambled forward. He could make it. There was time. He hit the rough rocks of the track ballasts. They did not give under his weight and their rugged angles rolled his ankle. He fell forward, the sharp edges of the rocks sending pain ricocheting up his arms. He needed to get his footing. There was no way he could cross now, the train was too close, wide and low on the tracks. He was too close, the rail a mere foot from his face, but he couldn't get his weight shifted. The rocks that had been so unforgiving to his feet seemed to wobble now under his grip.

There was a tugging at his waistband and he was dragged backwards just as the screaming train hurled by. Kennen felt a heavy arm steady him.

He turned to find a very angry Jim.

"What the hell were you doing?"

Despite the track noise and horn, Kennen had no issue hearing Jim's booming voice.

"There was a man!" Kennen yelled, pointing.

"What?!"

Kennen wasn't sure if Jim couldn't hear him or if he just thought Kennen had lost it. He sighed and threw up his hands, stumbling around on his sore ankle. The driver finally let off the horn and the roar of the train settled into a rhythmic ka-junk, ka-junk as the train kept rolling by.

"There was a man!" Kennen tried again. "People have been seeing a man around the tracks. A ghost."

"Well, which is it, a ghost or a man?" Jim was still shouting.

"I–I don't know. It was a man. It had to be a man."

Jim scowled. "You know vagrants and homeless people camp down by these tracks, in these woods. I warned you about them as a boy. You *know* this, and you almost get your damn head knocked off by a train because you saw a man?!" Jim's voice cracked and he stepped away, running both hands through his stubby hair. He shook his head and bent to the ground. That's when Kennen noticed the shotgun, moonlight shining off the barrel.

For a moment, Kennen wondered if Jim would turn it on him out of frustration, but instead he lifted it and just shook it a bit. He turned and headed back toward home.

Kennen looked back up at the train, steel gray, chalky yellow, and flashes of graffiti whipping by, all the colors muted in the moonlight. He shook his head and turned to limp after Jim. They walked back in silence through the dark woods until the faint pool of light from Jim's back porch light gave color back to their silhouettes.

"Thank you," Kennen said. His eyes searching the back of the house, landing on the window that was once his.

Jim grunted in response. He paused. Kennen stopped, still a few steps behind him.

"You want to stay here?" Jim asked flatly, without turning around.

Kennen looked down at his swelling ankle. "I don't have any pressing engagements right this minute, so I think I'll take you up on that."

Jim grunted in reply. He grunted when Kennen thanked him for the bed pillow and light blanket he brought to the couch, when he gave Kennen some tylenol and a bag of frozen peas to put on his ankle, and one more time when Kennen said good night.

Kennen had set an alarm on his phone so that he would have time to limp back to the hotel for a shower in the morning, but it proved unnecessary. When Kennen first opened his eyes, he felt a moment of panic, not from being confused as to where he was, but from wondering how he could possibly be there. His mind cleared as did his contacts, dry and itching from being slept in. It seemed the sun itself was still struggling to get up. He then realized what woke him: there were voices coming from the porch. He ran a hand through his hair and tested his ankle. The pea bag was tepid and soggy, but it had done the trick. The swelling was down and he only felt a mild twinge as he put weight on it. He stood and crossed to the front window. Jim was out on the front porch and Kennen could make out the figure of a man in the yard, the low light making him featureless.

"You don't need to be messing around here." Jim was muffled but decipherable.

"I just thought you might need some reminding." The other man was easier to understand despite being farther away. It seemed to be a combination of the fact that he was facing toward Kennen and that, whomever he was, he was nervous. His voice was high, forced.

"My memory is just fine, son."

Kennen was annoyed to find the challenge in Jim's voice was still enough to raise the hairs on his arm.

"I'll be keeping my eye out." The stranger then turned and left.

Jim stepped back in and was surprised to see Kennen standing there.

"Is everything alright?" Kennen asked.

"Just a neighbor blowing off steam. He doesn't like me

wandering around at night with a shotgun. Most of the rest of the neighborhood feels better that I do. You can't win 'em all." Jim headed to the kitchen and started for the coffee pot. Kennen didn't buy that story, but he didn't hear enough to have anything to work with.

"I'm not sure these would be good to eat now," Kennen commented as he entered the kitchen behind Jim holding the bag of peas.

"I never remember they're in there when I'm cooking anyway. Throw them back in the freezer for the next time you hurt yourself."

Kennen did as instructed.

"Did you sleep alright?" Jim asked as he sat down. His eyes were down, scanning yesterday's newspaper.

"Yeah, thanks." Kennen paused. "And thank you for last night. I'm—" Kennen cut off, confused where the wet lump he now found in his throat came from. He looked at the door, then the time, then Jim.

Fuck it, he thought.

"Can I be honest with you?"

Jim looked up and studied Kennen's face. He leaned back. "Please." Jim gestured to the space across from him. Kennen walked closer, but stayed standing, leaning against the wall.

"I fucked up. When I left, I fucked up. When Leonie died, I hurt so much and I just wanted to get away from it. So I left you, I left this entire town. I should have been grateful–I am grateful– that you took care of me when I wasn't really yours to worry about. But I just–I couldn't understand why you didn't let me go to Leonie's funeral. That was just … that was the breaking point for me."

For a moment Kennen thought Jim was going to shut back down, give him another grunt and let him go on his way. Then Jim sighed.

"Looking back, that was a mistake."

Kennen swallowed. "I'm going to ask you a question, and,

just ... can you just be honest with me? Whatever the answer, I need to know. Did you ever think, even for a second, that I did it?" Kennen couldn't believe it was out–that question he had tried to tuck away and ignore for most of his adult life.

"Is that why you thought I made you miss the funeral? Is that why you left?"

Kennen took a deep breath, but he couldn't summon his voice. It had left him, absolutely deserted him. Maybe it was out for its own walk in the woods.

"I never once thought that." Jim set his jaw, looking Kennen straight in the face. He furrowed his brow. "But I know what investigators do at the funeral of a murder victim. They look at everyone, trying to find a suspect. I wasn't going to have them look at my–at you that way."

Silence settled between them for a moment. "You didn't think my absence would raise some eyebrows?"

Jim smiled. "I did not give one fuck."

Kennen couldn't help himself; he laughed. Jim joined him.

"How is the investigation going?" Jim asked.

Kennen sighed. "I have a theory, but ..." He hesitated.

"You're not going to hurt my feelings, boy. I never thought Alex did it either."

Kennen froze, surprised at Jim's candor.

"It was decided that there wasn't a strong enough case for anyone else after Alex died, so the investigation just dried up."

"I thought you didn't want me to dig things up."

"I didn't want you digging into Alex. That was a waste then and it would be a waste now."

"If you knew that, why did you go along with it?"

"You won't find this in the file, but Milner had a CI."

Kennen recognized the common abbreviation for Confidential Informant. So, the other detective had a snitch?

"And the CI said it was Alex?"

"Said Alex would have a note on him. I didn't believe it. I knew Alex, and I knew the CI. But when the note was there ..."

"Could it have been planted?"

"I really don't think so."

"Why?"

Jim looked at Kennen like he was trying to solve a puzzle. Finally he just shrugged his shoulders.

"You said you knew the CI. I take it you didn't trust him. Why?" Kennen asked.

"Because he was originally one of my top suspects."

Kennen nodded, letting this soak into his synapses. He knew he would get nowhere asking who the CI had been. Still, it was more than Kennen would have hoped for 24 hours ago. He glanced at his watch again. "I need to get going. I've got an interview with Emmaline Tilden today in Chicago."

"Give her my best, would you?" Jim said.

Kennen nodded and started for the door, careful to not put too much weight on his tender ankle. He heard Jim sigh from behind him.

"Let me give you a ride."

They rode in silence for the ten minutes it took to get to the hotel. Kennen looked out the window. It was strange how just sitting in the passenger side of Jim's car made the town seem like its old self again. There was the ancient towering birch that always looked otherworldly with its white boughs standing by the Presbyterian Church. The big storm drain on the corner of Main that Kennen had avoided for a month after seeing Tim Curry dressed up as a clown in *It*.

Jim pulled into a parking spot in front of the Ashter Regal.

"Thank you again," Kennen said.

Jim grunted, looking forward. Kennen carefully got out of the car, mindful of his ankle. He watched as Jim backed away and started down the street, raising his hand to give a small wave. That's when Kennen spotted the man across the street, eyeing Jim's car with daggers. As soon as he realized Kennen had spotted him, he turned quickly and headed up the street and around the corner, but it was too late. Kennen had seen him clearly, and he recognized him, despite the age. He had grown to look just like his father. It was Calvin Travers, and he looked suspiciously like the silhouette that visited Jim earlier that morning.

When the elevator delivered Kennen to his floor, he discovered Gemma in the hallway, knocking on his door.

"Oh," she said, surprised. "And here I was worried I might be bothering you too early. I didn't know you'd already been out."

"That's what happens when you don't make it in," Kennen said, pulling his key card from his wallet. "Come in, I'll explain. Please make me some of that shit hotel coffee while I take a quick rinser."

Gemma did as instructed and Kennen washed off the train dust from the night before. He wrapped a towel around his waist and opened the bathroom door enough that they could hear each other while still allowing him some privacy.

"So, what brings you to my door so early?" Kennen called out.

"Why don't you tell me first what brought you to it so late? Or do I not want to know?"

Kennen could hear the grin in her voice.

"It was nothing untoward. Actually, I was out ghost hunting."

"Anything nibbling?"

"I saw someone. It was definitely a person, because they ran when they saw me."

"Did you get a good look at them?"

"Not real great. Looked like a man, brown complexion, but I couldn't tell you a specific race. Had a gnarly scar on one side of his face though, pronounced enough that I could see it in the light from the train. Unfortunately, that same train gave him a chance to get away. Then I ran into Jim who reminded me that they have transients that come through those woods from time to time."

"So, you were down at the tracks. Do you think that is what people are seeing there? Just some transients?"

"It's possible. They probably see people out there all the time, but by now they know the show is in town, word has spread, so now they're ghost sightings instead. The power of suggestion."

Gemma was quiet. Kennen slid on some fresh pants and threw on an undershirt, wondering if she'd ask it.

"So, you talked with Jim?"

There it was. "Yeah. That's where I stayed last night. I rolled my ankle like an idiot. It was a shorter walk back to his place than to the hotel."

"How bad is it? I think there is one of those emergency care places across town," Gemma offered.

"I'm fine, really. Don't worry about it."

"Well, since you've answered my question, I will answer yours."

Kennen felt relieved that she wasn't asking any more about Jim or how he hurt his ankle. She seemed to always know when to turn the investigator side of herself off. It wouldn't hurt Kennen to figure that out sometimes.

"I've been looking into Whitacre," Gemma continued. "He currently works at a mill out west of town. And you know what is strange? After that little incident up in Chicago the night of Leonie's death, there has been nothing else. Not so much as a parking ticket on his record."

Kennen finished running a comb through his hair and threw a short-sleeved button down over his shoulders.

"Really? Nothing?" Kennen stepped out of the bathroom, buttoning his shirt and heading for the coffee.

"I know, weird right? He didn't just keep his nose clean, he polished it and put it under glass."

Kennen walked over to the file that he had left on his night-stand. He was about to mention what he had learned about the

CI when his brain came to a grinding halt. Jim had said he had suspected the CI. Whitacre had been pretty thoroughly looked into–definitely, a suspect except for the alibi–and Kennen already had his doubts on that timeline. He was suddenly aware of the shadow's presence again. But this time it wasn't the same panicking experience. This time it felt like it was waiting in the corner, patient as Kennen put all the little pieces together.

"What if Whitacre was a CI?"

"Excuse me?"

Kennen sighed. "Jim. He told me there was a CI that said there would be a note on Alex."

"I think you need more than coffee."

"No, hear me out," Kennen said. He brought the file over to Gemma. "I've already looked into his timeline, and there could be some room there. He runs into Medina. We know the CI knew about the letter, so let's say he sees it. Now he knows where Leonie will be that night and exactly what evidence will make Medina look guilty. I'm pretty sure he had an axe to grind with Medina anyway."

"So, let's talk this through. If Whitacre did this, what was his motivation?"

"The Latin Kings," Kennen said.

"Right. So, he meets Medina. Is that part of the plan from the start or a happy coincidence?"

"Not sure yet."

"Okay. Next, he meets and kills Leonie. Then he hightails it to Chicago where he and a buddy get caught trying to break into cars. They aren't successful, the cops let them off with a warning, but the timetables are so close it makes him look improbable as a suspect. But the plan fails, he doesn't make it into the Latin Kings. This is his love letter to them, his grand gesture, and they still reject him?"

Kennen waved her on. "I have an idea, but let's keep going first."

"So, he realizes it failed and that he needs to cover his ass. He comes in as a CI. And the letter checked out as genuine against Leonie's handwriting in the journal. That plus the nosy neighbor and Tilden's accusations, and people think when Medina is killed justice has been served. The investigation stops. Whitacre lucks out."

"And he plays it safe from there out. Figures he can't ever get that lucky again." Kennen took a deep breath.

"A plan like this requires determination, foresight, and a whole lotta balls. Why would the Latin Kings not take him?"

"Because none of that sounds like Whitacre."

Gemma looked at Kennen for a moment before her eyes grew wide again. "It wasn't his plan. Someone else put it together. Somehow the Kings must have found out, and that's why they didn't take him. He wasn't the mastermind he claimed to be. He was just a footman, and they've got plenty of members for that work already."

Kennen smiled. "It fits."

"So did this person plan the frame on Medina before or after the fact?"

"That I still don't know," Kennen said. He slumped back in his chair.

"Do you think it was the guy he got caught with at the car park?"

"I doubt it. That would be too close, too easy to connect. I don't think the person who planned this out would make that obvious of a mistake."

"But this just creates more questions. Who wanted Leonie dead?"

Calvin Travers flashed through Kennen's mind, but he couldn't make any connections there. The night of the party was the only interaction he could ever remember between Calvin and Leonie, and that ended with Calvin mad at Alex, not Leonie. Killing Leonie and blaming it on Alex seemed too convoluted for what had gone down between them. No, it would have made more sense for Calvin to just jump Alex. Kennen hadn't bought the walking around with a shotgun story Jim had given him that morning, but there were plenty of things that could have happened to create some issue between Calvin and Jim. It had been twenty years. Most likely it had absolutely nothing to do with the case. Kennen shook his head. "I suppose it is possible that it was someone else who was looking for a spot in the Latin Kings. They used Whitacre as a pawn. He wasn't the quietest about his intentions to join the gang, so another potential gangster sees the opportunity. Maybe this person even sees the interaction with Medina, sees the note, and acts fast. And when Whitacre realized he'd been used, he tries to save himself by becoming a CI."

"It's possible. Too bad the Kings don't publish updated membership lists," Gemma said with a scoff. "So, if Whitacre is the murderer, we now have a phantom controller to find."

Kennen let out a dry laugh. "Just what we needed. Another ghost."

TRANSCRIPT FROM

AUGUST 27TH, 2017 RECORDING CONT.

Kennen: I guess I've kind of always been this way. When I was a kid, back in Chicago way before I had ever heard of Ashter, I had a friend named Miles. Miles was about two years younger than me, and the coolest thing about hanging out with Miles was that there was a tire swing in his backyard. We had to be, I don't know, five and seven? I loved that tire swing and I was always trying to trick Miles into giving me an extra turn.

So this one day, it was a surprisingly warm early Spring day, we go out to play on the swing. It's my turn and Miles is pushing me, then he stops and walks over to the trunk. I call out to him, trying to get him to come back and push, but he just puts his tiny little hands on the bark and leans his ear against the tree. At first, I ignore him, assuming this is a trick to get me out of the swing, but finally, my curiosity gets the better of me and I slide out of the tire and go over to him.

"What are you doing?" I ask him and he shushes me. So I try to put my ear up to the tree as well.

"Do you hear it?" he asks me.

All I hear are normal tree sounds, right? There is a breeze and I can hear the branches moving. That's it. So I tell him I don't hear anything, and he gets pissed and goes and gets his mother. Drags her out to the tree.

"Don't you hear it, Mommy? The tree is cracking," he says.

Of course, his mom doesn't hear anything either, so she scolds him for dragging her outside and goes back in to watch her TV show.

I tried to convince him it was fine, that those were normal sounds. Heck, I tried to give him an extra turn in the swing. But he wouldn't have it. He just sat down in the corner of the yard, knees under his chin, staring at the tree. I played on the swing a while longer, but his pouting was getting on my nerves, so I left.

Five days later, the top half of the main trunk split in two. The part that fell caved in the neighbor's garage like it was made out of play-dough. The branch that held the swing went with it.

[Drops head]

I have tried so many times to remember what I heard that day. I think, maybe, I could hear the wood cracking, just like Miles did.

[Looks back at camera]

I just didn't want to hear it.

AUGUST 2017

Emmaline Tilden's conditions for the interview included no video, so again this interview was to be just Kennen and Gemma. To be truthful, Kennen wondered if they would be able to use anything. Testimony can only be as credible as the witness. One strange behavior, one comment that they could not contextualize anywhere on the messy road map of this case, and Emmaline's testimony would be infected by her past.

As they headed into Chicago, Kennen tried to keep the threat of normalcy from his mind. But it did feel normal. During past cases, he would usually drive, the action helping him to calm and focus his mind, keeping it from running rampant. Gemma would spend the time obsessing over her notes, a ritual of reassurance that she was prepped and ready for anything. Kennen had to admit, it felt good. Until they pulled in front of the yellowed apartment complex.

The building was U-shaped, leaving a courtyard area in the middle where a few kids were playing jump rope in the dead grass. The windows that climbed the walls looked old and leaky. A short, round lady stepped out of the entrance to the north wing, eyeing Kennen and Gemma a bit too obviously.

"Which one is it?" Kennen asked as they stepped into the entryway, looking at the panel of buzzers.

"It should be 407."

Kennen reached for the buzzer and paused. "It says E. Martin."

Gemma checked her text again. "Yeah, 407. Did she take back her maiden name?"

Kennen shrugged his shoulders and hit the buzzer. A moment later a staticky voice came from the small round speaker.

"Yes?"

"Is this Emmaline Tilden?"

"Is this Gemma James and Kennen Clarke?"

"Yes."

There was a buzz and a click as the door next to them unlocked. Gemma grabbed the door and pulled it open. They climbed four floors of open metal stairs with metal handrails that needed painting. The stairwell was at least clean. There were no musty smells, no cigarette butts or spiderwebs in the corners.

Kennen knocked on the door of apartment 407, and there were the sounds of a door chain and deadbolt. She was shorter than he remembered, but he had only ever seen her in bed. Had Leonie been that height? She wasn't a tall girl, but he wondered if she had grown in his memories. Emmaline's hair was thinning and graying, but there were still streaks of the honey-colored hair that she shared with her daughter.

"Come in," she said, holding the door. Her apartment was small but tidy, with a living area off to the left with a couch and two small chairs tucked close around a small round coffee table. Long white curtains with brightly colored flowers hung over glass doors that led to a small balcony.

"Thank you for having us," Gemma said.

"Thank you for coming all this way. Can I get you something to drink?" Emmaline started towards the tiny kitchen that sat on the opposite side of the door.

"Thank you, we're fine," Gemma said. Emmaline gestured for them to take the couch and she sat opposite them in a small rocker. Despite the heat, she wrapped a large green shawl around her, her pale hands blooming from underneath it like white trout lilies.

"We noticed you changed your name to Martin," Kennen commented.

"Yes," she said, "I have gotten pretty good at hiding after all these years."

Gemma covered the standard privacy information and recording policies. "We know this is a painful subject," she said as she finished.

"I wasn't going to call you back," Emmaline admitted with a small laugh. "But I started thinking about that poor boy's mother. Medina? If I were in her place, I would want me to call."

Kennen wondered what she would have made of Hector Lopez's interview.

"So, you don't believe Medina was guilty?' Gemma asked.

"We don't know, do we? There was no trial, no justice. His death was as much a tragedy as my Leonie's."

"I don't know if you remember me, but I was a friend of Leonie's," Kennen said.

"I heard that you had a personal connection with her. I'm sure she mentioned you on one of her visits, but unfortunately, I don't remember most of those."

"I actually came with her once."

"Oh," she said, surprised. "Then I suppose you saw what they were doing to me."

"I'm sorry?" Kennen asked.

"Dr. Cho called me. She's a great lady, and, unlike her predecessor, she doesn't have the stomach for doing anything unethical."

"Unethical?" Gemma asked.

"What did you make of me when you visited?" Emmaline asked Kennen.

Kennen swallowed. "Well, I was young and had never–I didn't really have any knowledge or experience with such a situation as yours. But you seemed ... well, I was shocked to hear you had been released and you were living on your own. It sounded like a miracle." This was so embarrassing. Why did it seem in every one of these interviews he was caught off guard? It was like he was a newbie again.

Emmaline turned to Gemma. "What a polite way to say I was a drooling zombie."

Kennen let out a tight laugh and gave a shallow nod.

"I'm embarrassed to say it took me years to really understand what was going on," Emmaline said. "It didn't help that for years they changed my meds so regularly trying to get some combination that worked that I legitimately did have dissociative spells.

"But eventually I started noticing a pattern. I always seemed to have a fit right around when Leonie would visit. I didn't necessarily have them when it was just Tom, but once I'd been put away for a while, he didn't visit as much. He'd just come with Leonie to her monthly visit. Dr. Nielsen told me it was my mind's way of dealing with the guilt I felt over abandoning my daughter. And I guess that made sense to me for a long time. But then I realized that wasn't true. I had made that choice once, yes. But I'd never make that choice again. Leaving Leonie was my last regret before the attempt, and the one mistake I couldn't make again after I failed."

"The attempt to take your own life?" Gemma asked softly.

"Yes," Emmaline said. "I was in a terrible place and I needed help. But I felt like I couldn't get help, so it seemed the only way out. But afterward, despite all the other things that happened at St. Catherine's, I did get help for that. But there was no need for me to be locked away all those years."

Gemma waited for a moment. Then, just above a whisper, she said, "Tell us your story."

"Well, it's a very common story. I was suffering from mental illness, depression, but I couldn't talk about it. Tom made that very clear."

Kennen opened his mouth, but Emmaline anticipated his question.

"Tom was never physically abusive. Can you imagine what a bruised wife walking around town would have done to his reputation? No, no, no, couldn't have had that. He had to make sure the wounds he inflicted couldn't be seen by a casual glance." She paused to tug at the tassels of her shawl. "You know, looking back, I think Tom had his own struggle with mental illness. He was utterly obsessed with appearances. What other people thought of him. And I just couldn't live up to it. I felt trapped in this storm of inadequacy. I finally convinced myself that Leonie would be better off without such a fuck-up of an influence."

"And Tom did that to you. Drove you to that point," Gemma said.

"That's not quite fair. While I was stuck at St. Catherine's, not able to live my life, I did believe that. And he definitely didn't help, but I don't know that his intent was ever to simply hurt me. He wasn't cruel just to be cruel; he did it to soothe his own ticks. Tom was only ever worried about Tom, and I only mattered to him in terms of enhancing his image. But when I became ill, when I started threatening that image–but this is beside the point. The truth is, I would have gotten sick anyway."

"How can you be sure?" Gemma said.

"We were happy once. When Leonie was born, we were over the moon. But you can't always trace the source of depression. Sometimes you are just susceptible to it, just like you might be to any other illness. Its presence wasn't Tom's fault. He just didn't help the symptoms. If an asthmatic fell in love with a smoker that just couldn't kick that habit, they'd harm their partner, but they wouldn't be guilty of actually giving them asthma."

"But would Tom have handed you your inhaler?" Gemma asked.

As if on cue, Emmaline started coughing. Gemma stood and

fetched a glass of water from the kitchen.

"Thank you," Emmaline managed to choke out after a few swigs. She took a moment before continuing. "After the attempt, Tom had to do damage control. So he hid me as best he could. And he was thorough. He even found a way to hide me from our own daughter."

"The pattern you mentioned," Kennen said.

"Dr. Nielsen was drugging me out of my mind before Leonie visited. It had to be Tom's idea." She looked Kennen in the eye. "That zombie you meet was a trick, a way to keep me from connecting with the one person who would have fought for me."

"Leonie," Kennen said. Her bright, fierce face flashed through his mind.

"We believe you, but do you have any proof?" Gemma asked.

"Nothing concrete. I've become close with Dr. Cho. She has given me continued support, and I think that maybe she knows, but she has never said anything conclusive. She has to protect St. Catherine's. She is doing good work there now. Helping people like me. I can't ask her to jeopardize that."

"When did you figure it out?" Kennen asked.

"Just a few months before Leonie passed."

"When you broke out?"

"That's why I had to. I had to get to Leonie. I was just trying to protect her. If Tom could do that to me, what could he be doing to her? I needed to see for myself if she was okay. Once, after that, she came without Tom. Over her spring break."

Kennen's head jerked up, attracting the full attention of both Emmaline and Gemma. He cleared his throat but said nothing.

"Do you think Tom found out?" Gemma asked.

"I'm sure Dr. Nielsen passed the word on. I didn't tell her exactly what I thought was happening, I wanted to ..."

"To protect her," Kennen said.

"Yeah," she said. "But she knew something was wrong when she came to see me. She said her friend had gotten into NYU, but she hadn't heard anything back. So she called the admission office. She called all the admission offices she had applied to. None of them had heard of her. She had left her applications with Tom to mail; he always had plenty of out-going with his job. He was going to keep her out of college. I don't know why, but I'm sure it played into his schemes somehow."

Gemma gave Kennen a quick glance, tapping her pen. "Could it have been money? It must have been expensive keeping you at St. Catherine's."

Emmaline looked out the window a moment. "I suppose it is possible. But we started a college fund for Leonie when she was a newborn."

"If Tom was all about appearances, wouldn't it feed into his egomania to have his daughter at a prestigious college?"

"When Tom couldn't look good, he would settle for pity. That's what he did when I embarrassed him. I asked him once, early on during one of his solo trips, if people were asking about me back in Ashter. He said no, everyone was too nice to bring it up. And I saw it then, how much of a tragic hero he must have become. He would have put some spin on it so it looked good in the long run. He must have assumed he could control her like he did me."

Kennen tried to swallow, but something had formed in his throat again. Maybe the black shadow had found a new place to stay, clogging his airway. He bent forward and coughed, trying to dislodge it. He felt Gemma's hand on his back. He shook his head. "I'm fine," he finally croaked out.

"Thank you for telling us all of this. We finally have a real understanding of Tom," Gemma said, returning her attention to Emmaline.

"Use it as you will, but please, don't vilify Tom. There's no point now. I just hope this will help you find the truth for that other mother."

"We understand. We will find it and we will get it out."

"I hope you do. Now, I need to get to work. My shift starts soon."

Kennen and Gemma thanked her for her time. Emmaline stood and quietly escorted them to the door. After the door closed behind them, Kennen turned to stare at it. It was a door like any other. He couldn't help but wonder what stories lay just on the other side of the rest of the doors they passed.

"When we get back, I'll get back on tracking down Whitacre," Gemma said, looking out the window at the passing traffic.

"I've been thinking," Kennen said. "Maybe we should look up Sam Travers as well." Kennen had tried to brush off the whole Calvin Travers thing from the morning, but it kept echoing around in his head. He couldn't see any connections, yet.

"I actually already have his address."

"Really?"

"Yeah, I figured he was someone we'd need to find at some point. We've got time, let's swing by."

When they got back to Ashter, Gemma guided Kennen to a small gray house with peeling white trim. The front yard was mostly weeds, but that had been cut.

Gemma rang the doorbell three times, and they were about to leave when the door creaked open. For a moment, Kennen thought it was Sam who opened the door, but then he realized no, the age was wrong, that it was Calvin. Up close, the resemblance between Calvin and his father's former visage was even more uncanny.

"Hello," Gemma said. "Is Sam Travers here?"

"Who are you?" he asked, though it was clear in his glare at Kennen that he recognized him clearly.

"I'm Gemma Jones and this is Kennen Clarke. We are investigating the Leonie Tilden case. We had some questions for Sam Travers."

Calvin stepped out onto the porch and nodded Gemma's comment away. His hand stayed on the doorknob.

"How is your father?" Kennen asked.

"Broken."

Gemma hesitated for only a moment. "We're sorry to hear that."

"Listen, I'm sure you both have a whole interview planned out there in your little book." Calvin pointed at the small note-book in Gemma's hand. "But you just listen. My father shot a murderer. The murderer of a young girl. And what did he get for his trouble? A year on the inside and five years on parole for manslaughter. But it might as well have been fifty with what it did to him. There's no hidden story here. The kid ran from the police. He had that note on him. It's simple. Simple enough for even you big-town folks to figure out. Now some of us have to work the night shift and would really appreciate being left alone."

The clink of the doorknob as Calvin turned to go back in might as well have been the sound of Kennen's brain working. The connection finally came to him. Kennen jammed his foot in the door before Calvin could shut it.

"Whitacre is a relative of yours, correct?" So many of the families in town had had some shared kin.

A snarl threatened to break through Calvin's face. "Yes. His father and my father are cousins."

"Thank you," Kennen said, slipping his foot back out of the door.

"But you already knew that," Calvin said, leaning just his face out. "I know Leonie was your friend. I understand that. I understand that her murder was hard to accept. But don't you dare drag my father's name through the dirt because of your damn issues. I know you've got a show and can do what you damn well please. But if you do this, then you're trash just like that murderer. If I see either of you on our property again or trying to contact me or my father in any way, I'll call the police. You have all you're getting from us."

He slammed the door.

MARCH 1998

Leonie hadn't answered the phone all of spring break. On Monday when they returned to school, Kennen watched as she walked straight past him and didn't say a word. Didn't even look at him.

"Leonie!"

She stopped and turned slowly. She looked up at Kennen like he had just woken her from sleepwalking.

"Leonie, I called you like ten times over break."

"Sorry, I was grounded."

"You were what?" Kennen said, laughing. Leonie had never been grounded in her life. This had to be some kind of joke. But Leonie wasn't laughing. She just looked up at him with her big green eyes.

"Are you serious?"

Leonie just shrugged.

"What happened?"

Leonie looked over at the lockers. Kennen stepped closer.

"Hey," he said, just above a whisper, "whatever it is, you can tell me."

The two-minute bell rang.

"Listen, if I'm tardy to a class or not home ten minutes after school, my dad is going to lose it. He is calling the school to make sure I'm not late and everything. He's lost his fucking mind. Meet me tonight, midnight, out by the clearing near the tracks. I'll sneak out and then we'll have time to talk." She turned and left before Kennen could argue.

At 11:45, Kennen carefully pushed open his window and slid out to the ground. The spring night still held on to winter chills, so Kennen jogged to the clearing to warm up, using a small flashlight to guide his way through the woods. As he came to the clearing, he spotted the silhouette of a thin body against a tree.

"Hey," he called, wanting to announce his presence and not scare her.

She turned around. As he came up, she walked quickly to him, wrapped her arms around him, and buried her face in his chest. It happened so fast and he was so surprised his arms were still at his side when he heard a sob escape her.

He wrapped his arms around her and lowered his face to the top of her head. Her hair was a little greasy, but he didn't care.

"Leonie," he whispered, "what is it?"

Leonie held tight for a few more seconds before her arms loosened from his sides, falling away like wilting petals.

She turned away.

"Did you get a letter from NYU?" Kennen couldn't help it; his anxiety spewed the words out. He had received his acceptance letter just before break. He was sure hers must be in the mail too, maybe they were processed alphabetically or something. There was no way they would take him and not her. But when she said nothing about it today, when she was clearly upset, he couldn't help but think that she didn't make it in. Maybe she got a rejection letter and lost it so bad she did something to end up grounded. But how could she have not made it in?

"Leonie?"

She was walking away from him, holding her elbow.

"No. I didn't get a letter from NYU," she said flatly. Kennen relaxed a bit. No actual rejection then.

"It's probably just lost in the mail. I'm sure you'll hear soon. Maybe tomorrow we could call—"

"No. This isn't just about school. It's–I don't even know how to explain—"

Kennen walked over to her and turned her to face him. He placed a hand on her cheek and wiped a tear away with his thumb. He had an overwhelming urge to kiss her.

So he did.

Somehow seeing her sad, seeing her vulnerable, made him braver than he'd ever been before. Her lips were soft enough to make him want to cry himself. But then she pulled away.

Kennen felt his cheeks burning so hard he wondered if he was lighting the woods up red.

"I'm sorry, I—"

"No, no," she interrupted him. "I'm sorry. I just ... I can't right now." She turned to the tracks. "What if we just left? What if we just hopped on the train like hobos or something? Just road until we found somewhere beautiful."

Kennen let out a nervous laugh. All his bravado had left him. "Leonie, just ... what's up? What's bothering you?"

"It's my dad."

"What about him?"

"You know, everyone thinks he's so great. But nobody really knows the real him. He even fooled—" A sob cut her off. She pressed her hand over her mouth.

"Is this about him grounding you?"

Leonie turned, her brow pulled together and her hand dropping to show her mouth hanging open. "What?"

"Listen, I don't ever remember him grounding you. Whatever argument you two are having, I mean, he's clearly upset, too."

"What are you trying to say?"

"Well, I mean, I think you should talk it out."

"Oh. Right. Just have a talk. Why didn't I think of that." Her tone cut him.

"What happened anyway?"

Leonie looked at him, scouring his face raw with her eyes.

"What are we, Kennen? Friends? More? Can you just tell me the truth so I know if I can trust you?"

Kennen opened his mouth, but she had scared away all his words.

She sighed and turned away.

"Wait!" he shouted. "I just–you're talking crazy and I don't know what's going on. The truth is you're scaring me."

Leonie threw her hands up wide. "You know, you're right." She had a sick grin on her face. "I'm crazy just like my mom. I don't know why I asked you out here. I need to go home before my dad sees I'm gone and he locks me up for good."

"Wait!"

But Leonie was already running, already gone.

AUGUST 2017

Gemma offered to drive them back to the hotel and Kennen took her up on it. Emmaline and Calvin's words rattled around in his head, punching holes in his memories. He wasn't sure of his own mind anymore. It was almost like his memories were just chapters in some fiction novel. Scenes that never actually happened.

When they got back the rest of the team was still out shooting, so Gemma and Kennen broke off to type up their notes which would be added to a drive shared by the main crew and producers. Once Kennen got in his room, he threw his bag down and went right to his flask. When he pulled it out, the note Warren had given him fell to the floor. He still hadn't read it. He looked at his flask. Maybe he could if he had some reinforcement. He grabbed the picture of Leonie and walked over to the edge of his bed. Expertly he loosened the cap of the flask with one hand, took a swig, then looked at Leonie. How much would she have looked like her mom now? Like Tom?

A sharp knock at the door surprised Kennen and he fumbled the picture. *For fuck's sake* he thought and stormed over to the door. He threw it open to find a startled Gemma.

"Is everything okay?" she asked, eyeing the flask. He hadn't dropped that. He didn't want to think about what that said about him.

"Yeah," he said, but his tone gave away the lie. "I was just thinking."

"Me too. Can I come in?"

"Sure."

Kennen backed away and Gemma stepped in, heading for the table. She spotted the frame, the glass now shattered so much that there was no way she could possibly see who it was.

"What happened?"

"What were you thinking about?" Kennen asked, bending over to pick up the picture. He carried it carefully to the trash and tipped it over, the glass clinking like ice on the bottom of the can. Gemma stood still, frozen. "Tell me your idea. It'll give me a chance to get a few more sips in and then I'll be able to tell you about this."

Gemma hesitated, but then she nodded and sat down at the table. Kennen crossed the room, putting the picture on the bed and grabbing the rest of the bottle from the drawer where he had stashed it. He put it on the table and then went back to the edge of his bed. Gemma picked it up, checked out the label, gave him a slight smirk, and unscrewed the top. She took a long drink.

"When we last talked about Whitacre, we came up with the idea that he was a patsy for the real mastermind, but we had no idea who was behind it. We thought it might be someone else who wanted to be in the Latin Kings because we couldn't think of anyone who would want Leonie dead. But that's not necessarily true anymore."

Kennen capped his flask and leaned back, crossing his arms. "You think Calvin?"

"No ... do you?"

"No. I do wonder, though, if maybe he helped out in some way. I remember him and Whitacre hanging out some, and we did just confirm they are related. And if Calvin's father knew anything about it, that might explain why he was so quick on the trigger to take out Medina. Make sure he didn't have a chance to talk."

"I don't know that Sam Travers felt like he needed any excuse." Gemma took another drink.

"So, who do you think our puppet master is?" Kennen asked.

"Tom Tilden," Gemma said.

Kennen blew out a breath.

"Just hear me out. That line item on Emmaline Tilden's bills; it had to be a bribe or something to keep her there, locked up and drugged at just the right times. Leonie confirms that something is up with that when she visits her mom after she broke out. And there are her college applications that he didn't mail. He's trapping her too, just in a different way. We've got to get back to her diary. There have got to be clues in there."

"She was grounded after visiting her mom," Kennen said.

"See! He knew that she knew. Dr. Nielsen tipped him off."

"As fucked up as it is, it's still a big leap from fraudulently keeping your wife locked away in a mental institution to hiring a hit on your own daughter. Like Emmaline said, she didn't think his intent was to really hurt her, it was a byproduct."

"Maybe not. In a way, he took his wife's life from her. Then, when his sin was possibly going to be exposed, he escalated. He was out of town when it happened to cover his tracks. Then he threw it on Medina, a kid he felt had threatened his status before by befriending his daughter, coming to his house, all the while having gang connections via his brother. Or maybe it was that he was gay or that he rejected his daughter. Maybe all of it."

Kennen looked to the corner of the room. The shadow was there again, waiting like before. He looked back at Gemma. "We need to see Tom. It may be pointless, but we need to try."

"I'll set it up for tomorrow. What about Whitacre?"

"If we're right, we need to talk with Chief Nichols before we corner him."

Gemma nodded. "So, it's your turn. What is that?"

"This is a picture of Leonie," he said, picking it up. Now that the cracked glass was gone, he could see her better.

"Where did you get it?"

"Warren."

"How did she get it?"

"That's the question, isn't it?"

Gemma stood to cross over to him. She suddenly changed direction, and by the time he looked up, she was bent over, picking up the letter. He stood and tried to stop her, but it was too late. She had it open and was reading.

He swallowed. The shadow was just behind her. It was the most defined he had seen it. He could almost make out the wavy hair. "What does it say?"

Gemma's eyes finished sweeping over the page and then landed back on Kennen. For a moment, he would have sworn she looked scared.

"Don't you know?"

"Warren gave me that, too. I haven't been able to bring myself to read it. I don't know how she got these things. But I used to have this," Kennen said, lifting the frame. "Now, please, before I change my mind, what does it say?"

"It's almost identical to Medina's letter," Gemma said and handed it to him. She took the picture as he took the paper.

Gemma was right; other than the name at the top, it looked exactly like Medina's right down to the place and time.

"What the fuck," he muttered.

"Why didn't you mention this note?" Gemma was trying to cover it well, but there was an edge to her voice.

"Hey," Kennen said, waiting until she was looking him in the eye. "I promise you, I never saw this letter."

Gemma didn't answer.

"I wouldn't lie to you about this."

Gemma's shoulders slackened. "I know," she finally said.

And that was it. All she had to do was trust him again for him to lose it. He landed on the edge of the bed and his face landed in his hands. He crushed his eyes closed, trying to keep himself from crying, but it was too late. He felt Gemma sit down next to him.

He dropped his hands. "I didn't know." God, he sounded so pathetic. "I never saw it. I should have been there for her, I should have—"

"Stop it," Gemma said, putting an arm around him. "This," she said, taking the letter from him, "is not your fault. You never saw it."

"This wasn't the only fucking sign. She knew something was wrong. She knew. That's why she tried to meet with Medina and me. She needed our help. And we weren't there. And that," he pointed to the letter, "that could have saved Medina. If it had ever been seen, things could have been different for him too."

"You don't know that," Gemma said, but Kennen couldn't stop shaking his head. "Kennen, listen to me."

"I'm tired," he said, turning away from her.

She sat silent for a minute, then stood. He figured she would see herself out, but instead she picked up the flask and took it with the picture and letter to the table. Then she came back and pulled down the blankets on the bed. He turned to look at her, and she patted the bed. He stood and walked over, dropping heavily back onto the bed. She bent over, loosened his shoelaces, and slipped his shoes off.

"Lay down," she said softly. She walked across the room to close all the blinds. Then she came back and pulled the sheet over him. He felt stupid being mothered like that, but he felt too broken to do anything about it. She crawled up on the bed behind him, slid an arm under his neck, and placed her other hand on his shoulder. She wasn't quite spooning him, but she was there, and he felt better because of it. She breathed slowly, and soon his breath synced up with hers. He drifted off, with Gemma's soft breath on his neck and the shadow still sitting in the corner, watching.

APRIL 1998

Leonie had kept her distance for weeks, which was an impressive feat considering how many classes they had together. Maybe it was because it was a team effort; Kennen didn't know how to approach her either. All he knew was that it was killing him. He hadn't felt as shitty as this since his mother passed. He felt like his chest had caved in. Then there was the fact that a girl ignoring him somehow made him feel as bad as when his mother died, which made him feel even shittier. It was exponential shit.

He saw Leonie sitting with Alex during lunch. He started to pass on by when Leonie called out.

"Kennen, just sit with us."

Kennen hesitated, but then he went ahead and sat down.

"Carver's homework is nuts," Alex said, apparently picking up where his and Leonie's conversation had left off. "It's going to take all night."

"I didn't even do the last assignment."

Kennen looked at Leonie, thinking she was joking, but she went right back to her turkey sandwich. Alex sent Kennen a quick glance but didn't say anything.

"Leonie, maybe we could all get together–at the library or

somewhere like that–and start our study sessions back up. Those were fun," Alex said.

Leonie gave a non-committal head bobble, eyes down on the table. Alex made eye contact with Kennen, rolled a glance to Leonie, and then back to Kennen, silently asking for backup. But Kennen felt like he had completely forgotten how to talk to her.

"Um," Kennen said, looking around for something to inspire him. His eyes landed on a baggy Leonie had in front of her. "Are those Fritos?"

Highly inspired.

"Yeah, you can have 'em if you want." Leonie tossed him the bag.

"Oh, thanks," Kennen said. Leonie went back to picking apart her turkey sandwich, discarding most of it. Alex gave him a raised eyebrow, but Kennen just shrugged and started eating the chips.

Alex got out a notebook and mumbled something about forgetting to catch up on the notes from physics. He scribbled something down and acted like he was putting it back in his backpack that sat on the ground between Kennen and him, but instead, he slid the notebook into Kennen's lap. Leonie was taking minuscule pieces of provolone and eating them while staring into space, so even though it wasn't a particularly sneaky move, she missed it. Kennen glanced down. Alex had circled what he wrote on the page:

She's talking to you again! Don't mess it up!

Kennen sighed.

"Well, I gotta run. See you all later," Alex said, carefully grabbing back his notebook and standing up. Leonie didn't say anything, but she watched him head off.

"Hey, Leonie—"

When she turned her gaze back on him, he felt his jaw start to lock up again. He shook his head. "I just wanted to say I'm sorry. I should have just listened better."

"I'm sorry, too," Leonie said. "I've been a mess."

"I want to help. Just tell me how I can help."

"I shouldn't have bothered you—"

"No! Really, Leonie. Is there something I can do?"

Leonie looked back at her mangled sandwich remains.

"You really mean it?"

"Of course," Kennen said.

Leonie stared out into space and nodded her head slightly, thinking. "Okay. Next weekend is prom, right?'

Kennen laughed despite himself. Every day for the last two weeks the morning announcements had been dedicated to buying tickets, signing up out-of-town dates, helping with decorations. There were posters all over the school, including one on the column just to the left of Leonie. Kennen motioned to it. "Yeah, it's next weekend."

"We should go."

Kennen looked at her to see if she was going to follow that up with a laugh, something to show she was joking, but she was as serious as she had been about not finishing her assignment.

"We should?" he asked slowly.

"Yeah. You wanted to help, right? You'd go with me, right?"

"Um yeah! Of course! I'd love to go with you."

"Okay. It's settled then. Thank you," Leonie said, gathering up her trash and leaving Kennen to sit by himself, dumbstruck. He didn't move until the bell rang.

Kennen couldn't focus on anything the rest of the week. Well, that wasn't quite true. He took his one suit to the dry cleaners and arranged with Jim to borrow his car for the night of prom. He went to the flower shop and ordered a corsage that had carnations dyed a dark blue, little white roses, and silver ribbon. He bought tickets from the main office. He'd already spent an entire Milton's paycheck getting ready for the night, and he knew he'd probably spend another one on dinner and pictures, but he didn't care. It felt like all the years, starting with the moment he met Leonie on his first day of high school, had led to this.

Saturday came and Kennen couldn't relax. He tried to eat breakfast, but he couldn't finish. He left to pick up the corsage early in the afternoon. When he got home, he cleaned an entire shelf off in the fridge to keep it safe. He got out his shoes and tried to buff them with a soft cloth. He showered, shaved, and scolded himself for not getting a haircut, even though he usually let it get much longer before chopping it. He ironed his shirt. Practiced tying his tie.

Finally, it was time. He was picking Leonie up at a quarter till 7. They were going to Tino's, a little Italian place where he had reservations, and then they'd head over to the high school.

Jim got home right at about 6:30, leaving just enough time for them to switch out. Kennen grabbed the corsage and called, "Seeya!" on his way out, but he froze on the porch. Jim stepped out behind him. The car shined in the light.

Kennen walked up to the car slowly and Jim followed a few steps behind. Kennen peered in the window. "Did you get it detailed?"

"Inside and out," Jim said.

Kennen let out a little laugh and turned around. "Thank you," he said.

Jim patted him on the back and turned back toward the house. "Have fun," he called over his shoulder.

Kennen pulled up in front of the Tilden house. He got out and straightened his jacket. When he knocked on the door, it was Mr. Tilden who answered.

"Oh, looking good, Kennen," Mr. Tilden said. "Come on in. She's almost ready."

Kennen followed him in. He looked down at the corsage that was still in the plastic clamshell. Should he have taken it out? It looked kind of tacky in there, like the type of thing a diner sold pie in. Mr. Tilden went up to check on Leonie. Kennen opened the container and tossed it in the trash, holding the corsage tenderly. He heard footsteps and turned to see Mr. Tilden coming back down, a big grin on his face. He got to the foot of the stairs and looked up.

Leonie appeared at the top of the stairs. Kennen swallowed to actively keep his jaw from dropping. Her hair was pulled back into an elegant twist and there were little pearls dotted through-out. Her dress was a silky navy with spaghetti straps. When she stepped off the stairs and turned he could see it had a lace-up open back. For a moment he thought about how, if it was short, it would almost look like a piece of lingerie. He felt a twinge down south and panicked. Luckily, Mr. Tilden picked that moment to grab his camera and declare he was ready to take their 'glamour shots.' That was creepy enough to kill it.

Leonie stepped into the kitchen and came back with a boutonniere wrapped in plastic with a deadly-looking pin. Mr. Tilden insisted on getting shots of her pinning it to Kennen's lapel, a small red rose with greenery. Then he put the corsage on her wrist. Mr. Tilden ushered them into the living room for a few more pictures in front of the fireplace before they were able to escape.

"You look beautiful," Kennen said as soon as they were on the front steps.

"Oh, thanks." She seemed confused about the comment.

"Jim got it detailed," Kennen said as he opened the car door for her.

"It looks nice."

Kennen jogged around to the driver's side and got in. He started the car and pulled away. When they got around the corner, he noticed Leonie lean over and check out the dash.

"We're going to need gas."

"What are you talking about?" The car had just a little over half a tank, more than enough for their evening. Heck, with as small as Ashter was, it would probably last the rest of the week.

She reached up and started pulling pins from her hair.

"What are you doing?!"

"You said you wanted to help, right?" she asked.

Kennen just looked back and forth from her to the road, mouth hanging open.

"Listen, I'm sorry I couldn't tell you more before, but I need you to drive me to Chicago, to St. Catherine's. I've got to get in contact with my mom. This is the perfect night. Dr. Neilson goes home at 5 on Saturdays. I've got this note." She pulled a paper from her small clutch. "They'll know me, but I don't think they'll remember you. You can sign in as my cousin."

"You can't be serious."

"My father has been watching me like a hawk. I can't sneak off on my own. He's even been checking my odometer. It's got to be tonight. We can get there, give my mom the letter, she can write you a response, and we can get back before he ever knows."

"Are you telling me you never had any intention of going to the dance with me?"

"I'm sorry. I was afraid if you knew the whole plan, Jim might sense something was up and figure it out. It's literally his job to figure things out. And he would have felt it was his duty to stop us. But you said you wanted to help."

Kennen wrenched the car over onto the shoulder.

"What are you doing?" she cried.

"Get out." He couldn't even look at her.

"What?"

"Get out!" Kennen screamed at the steering wheel.

They sat in silence for a moment, and then he heard the click of her seatbelt. The slam of her door. He saw her figure out of the corner of his eye, starting down the road, off balance with the poor combination of heels and gravel. But he didn't give a fuck. He threw the car in drive and sped off.

AUGUST 2017

Gemma was gone when Kennen woke up the next morning. Kennen had a text from Marty that the team was out shooting again. He took a long shower. As he dried off, he decided he should take a look over the files again, but his room seemed too small. He loaded up his bag and headed to a nearby park. He found a secluded picnic bench underneath a large oak, where the heat of the sun couldn't distract him.

There were so many statements. So many people who knew Leonie or Alex in some way. Or didn't. Not really. Most of the statements were so vague, so predictable. Copy and paste. Kennen was about to shut the folder when a word caught his eye: bruises. It was a statement from a kid, Eric Bell, that was a year behind all of them in school. Kennen knew the guy was one of Jeffie's and figured that was why he'd been asked for a statement. When the police spoke with him, he said he didn't really know Leonie well. When asked if he had seen anyone acting strangely at school, he said, "There's a kid, Alex Mendoza. He has a lot of bruises on his chest. I saw them when we were changing for baseball practice. They were new."

Kennen couldn't remember an Alex Mendoza. He stood, packed his bag, and started off on foot. It wasn't a long walk to the high school, but even in the morning, the heat was growing. As he rounded the corner, Kennen wondered if the heat had gotten to him. The school was sitting there, completely unchanged. Impossibly unchanged. He went and stood by the fire hydrant out front. He looked across the street. There were houses and some new apartment buildings. He recognized some of the homes, but they all had some sort of update. He looked back at the school. It was almost like an old photo had been pasted into reality. He walked up to the door and was surprised to find not only was it locked, but there was no buzzer to get in. It was then that it clicked what was wrong. Even if school wasn't back in for the students yet, surely there would be some sort of staff on site. Secretaries, custodians, teachers getting their class-rooms ready. But the building was dead. Kennen spotted a lady across the street, watering her flowers.

"Excuse me, ma'am?"

The lady looked up from under a floppy sun hat. "Yes?"

"What, um." Kennen realized he didn't even know what to ask. "Is … is this Ashter High School?"

"Oh, it used to be, but about 15 years ago they built the new one on the north side. They used this building as a headstart and teacher training site for a while, and then it just closed up. Bit of an eyesore at this point really. I wish someone would buy it and do something with it."

"How far is the new school from here?"

"Oh, it's up on 21st Street and Oaklawn."

"Thank you," Kennen said. He backed away slowly. That was nearly 10 miles away. New plan. He turned and headed the other way.

When he arrived at the library, Martha was standing behind the circulation desk. She spotted him and gave him a big smile and a wave.

"How is your investigation going?"

"Well, I was hoping you could help me. You don't by chance have access to any old yearbooks here, do you."

"Follow me," she said, lifting the flip-up countertop and heading towards the stacks. She turned right, led him through a doorway, and past a desk where another librarian gave them a friendly greeting as they passed. "This is where we house local history and genealogy. We have Ashter High yearbooks on this shelf. We have almost all of the years, mostly through donations. These books are not in circulation, but Carly there at the desk can make copies if you need."

Kennen thanked her and she left him with the shelves of tall, worn yearbooks. His finger hovered over the spines as he read the years, stopping at the 97-98 edition. The red of the cover was faded. He took it to a nearby table and flipped open to the index.

Maggie Malcolm, pp. 25, 67, 107
Alex Medina, pp. 17, 21, 67, 95
Max Miller, p. 67

"No Mendoza," Kennen muttered as he snapped a picture of the index. He pulled out the file and checked the name again. Did this Eric idiot not know Alex's last name? Kennen lightly tapped his fingers on the table. Where to go next? If Alex had bruises, they would have been mentioned in the coroner's report. But Kennen didn't have it, only Leonie's. Alex's report must still be at the police station, most likely tied specifically to Sam Travers' case.

Kennen thanked Carly and Martha both on the way out and started for the station. He flew down the street now oblivious to the heat and distance. It wasn't until the station was in view that he realized he was short of breath. He slowed and composed himself just in time to see Chief Nichols pulling up. They meet at the front door.

"Sleepy start?" Chief Nichols asked with a little chuckle.

"Excuse me?"

"Come on, I'll show you where your partner is working."

Kennen followed the Chief, confused. They rounded a corner

and faced two desks. One had an officer working on paperwork. The other held Gemma.

With Leonie's diary.

Gemma looked up and her eyes flashed wide at the sight of Kennen. She quickly recovered.

"Hey," Gemma said.

"Hi," Kennen said.

Chief Nichols seemed to sense the tension. "I'll let you two get to it," he said, backing away. The other officer glanced up at Kennen and then went back to work.

Kennen grabbed a plastic chair and walked over next to Gemma. He sat down. They both looked at the journal.

"I called this morning and they said I could have a look. You seemed so tired—"

"It's okay," Kennen said, trying his best to fake a calm tone. He was impressed; it came off as believable.

Gemma slowly looked toward him.

"Really," Kennen continued. "What did you find?"

Gemma just kept looking at him, unblinking. Barely breathing.

"Okay," she finally said, giving a heavy sigh. "I picked up after her mother came to see her. She writes about that, but then there is a big gap. Then, around March, she picks up again. Look at the dates."

Kennen took and put on the gloves she handed him then skimmed over the dates. "They're very regular. Almost always twice a week."

"Exactly," Gemma said. "She never wrote regularly like that before. And there is nothing in them."

"What do you mean?"

"Read a few for yourself."

Kennen flipped back to the start of March and read a few entries. She wrote a little about school, mentioning assignments and projects. Mentioned her dad a few times, mostly noting how often he was out. Talked about the weather.

"It's ... dull," Kennen said.

"I've read grocery lists that were more dynamic," Gemma said, taking the book back. "She isn't writing for herself anymore."

Kennen sat back. "She thinks someone is reading it."

Gemma nodded. "And the only person that makes sense is her father. Now, I know plenty of parents have probably done the same thing, but—" She cut herself off, shaking her head. "I just wish she had left us a better clue."

"I found something," Kennen offered. He glanced over at the officer that was babysitting them from the next desk, but the man was paying them no mind. He leaned over to Gemma. He showed her the statement and the picture from the yearbook. "He had to be talking about Medina," he said, keeping his voice low. "We need the coroner's report on Medina,"

"Are you starting to believe it was actually Medina who kill—"

"No," Kennen said, cutting her off. "But I think we were on the right track earlier. You see, Whitacre had threatened Alex before. We know Alex was at the Tilden house. He had the note. He goes to find her, but Whitacre spots him and follows. Alex gets to Leonie but so does Whitacre. They fight, Leonie tries to stop it, and ..."

"It might have even been accidental," Gemma whispered back. Kennen nodded. She sat back and tapped her pen against her chin. "Medina doesn't come forward because he knows it would just be his word against Whitacre's."

"That or the guilt."

"He couldn't save her," Gemma said.

Kennen nodded.

"We need that report." Gemma stood. "Excuse me."

The officer looked up at her, mildly annoyed.

"We're all done with this, thank you. But we did have a question. We need to see the file on Medina's murder."

"Check with Heather up front."

Heather sat at a desk near the entrance. She looked up at them as they approached, dark eye makeup accentuating her crow's feet.

"Heather, we are looking for the coroner's report on Alex Medina from 1998. Do you think you can help us?" Gemma asked.

Heather nodded and started typing away. After a few more clicks and some more typing, Heather squinted at the screen. Chief Nichols walked by.

"Hey, Chief, I'm trying to help these folks out, but I can't find anything. They want the coroner's report on Medina."

Chief Nichols stepped around the desk, looking over her shoulder.

"It wasn't in the Tilden file. I assume it is on its own or attached to Sam Travers," Kennen offered.

Chief Nichols and Heather tried a few different things. "Well, it must be somewhere. We'll just have to dig."

"Are you serious?" Gemma asked shortly with a tilt of her head.

The Chief dropped his chin and put his hands on his hips at her tone. "I'm sure it was just some sort of filing issue when we digitized everything."

"You have everything imaginable on Leonie, but not the report on Medina's murder?" Gemma crossed her arms. Kennen looked at her, trying to catch her eye.

"We'll come back later," he said and grabbed Gemma by the arm, all but dragging her out.

Once they were outside, he let go of her. "What was that about?" he asked.

She sighed and shook her head. "I'm sorry, that was unprofessional. But really, they don't know? Didn't anybody care?"

"Like Chief Nichols said, it was probably just a mistake. I'm sure they will find it. It could have happened with any case."

"It didn't with Leonie's." Gemma sighed. "Nevermind. So, what do we do now?"

"Well, I think we need to bring in Marty and Chief Nichols when we go after Whitacre, and right now might not be the moment to ask a favor of the latter."

"Well, we can still go visit Tom Tilden. Especially after what we found with the diary. Maybe there is something of him left."

"No stone unturned," Kennen mumbled as they headed to the car.

APRIL 1998

Kennen was busy scrubbing away dried cheese on the counter in front of the nacho station at Milton's, pondering, first, how people could be such slobs, and second, how people could possibly digest a product that turned into yellow cement after being exposed to air for a short time. Maybe it was an evolutionary thing; sloppy people could digest crap because they were exposed to said crap often because of their sloppiness. But then what came first, slovenliness or edible sludge? The bell at the front door broke into Kennen's internal rant and reminded him of the terrible headache he'd been suffering from all day.

He turned to see Alex. And he wasn't looking around like he was shopping. He was coming straight over to Kennen. Shit.

"If you're dropping by to visit Jesse, he's not here. I'm covering his shift tonight."

"No, I was coming to see you. I stopped by your place, and Jim said you were here."

Kennen swallowed and continued with his scrubbing. He hoped Alex hadn't let anything slip about why he was looking for Kennen, which he suspected had to do with prom. At first, Kennen had decided to go to the dance by himself. When he pulled up and parked, a limo was rolling up. The chauffeur put it in park and went around to open the door. A guy in a much nicer suit than Kennen's stepped out, turned around, and held out his hand, helping his gorgeous date out of the car. They smiled and giggled and looked so fucking happy.

Kennen started the car back up and swung by Jesse's house. Jesse was startled to see him but was cool enough to not pry. It couldn't be hard to put the general story together from the fact that Kennen had shown up alone. Kennen offered to cover Jesse's Sunday night shift if he'd head over to the liquor store and buy a six-pack of hard lemonade. Jesse hated the Sunday night shift; it was the slowest time at Milton's. Jesse agreed and took the cash Kennen had meant for pictures that night. He soon came back with the six-pack plus a small bottle of vodka and offered Kennen a place to drink, but Kennen declined. Instead, he drove over behind the Dollar General which was a straight shot up the road from his house. He downed three of the lemonades and the entire small bottle of vodka, ralphed most of it back up behind the dumpster, threw the rest of the alcohol and the empty bottles in the same dumpster, then coasted home. Luckily, Jim was scheduled for the early shift the next day, so he was in bed by the time Kennen got home.

"Missed you at the dance," Alex said, to which Kennen grunted. "I talked to Leonie."

Of course, he had.

"So, you wanted to drop in and what? Tell me what a shallow jerk I am?"

"Nope."

Kennen stopped scrubbing. Not only had he expected Alex to take Leonie's side, he realized he'd kind of hoped for it. He was hoping for a scolding, for someone to tell him how lame he was. It would save him from having to admit it to himself.

"Listen, I don't know as much about Leonie and her mom as you do. When someone trusts you with something like that, it puts a responsibility on you as their friend. So yeah, I guess you fucked up a bit. But she also had a responsibility to you," Alex said.

"How's that?"

"Leonie may have enough skeletons in her closet to open up a small graveyard, but, dude, everyone could see how much this meant to you. And then she just used you? She fucked up, too, man."

"It was just a stupid dance."

"It doesn't matter what *it* was, what matters is that it was something important to you. And I know she's been upset lately, so maybe she wasn't in a place where she could see what she was doing at the time. I mean, when I talked to her, she sounded plain exasperated. But she also felt bad about what she'd done." Alex paused. "To you."

"So, who is to blame?"

"Well, from where I sit, you both suck," Alex said with a grin, "but since you two are the best friends I've got, I'm willing to forgive you both if you'll consider doing the same for each other."

Kennen snorted a laugh. Alex was right. Kennen wasn't quite sure when the transmutation had started, but somewhere during the last year, Alex had gone from enemy number one to a truly great friend. He was always patient with Kennen during the study sessions, even though he wasn't as bright as Alex by a long shot. He cared for Leonie, but he apparently also cared for Kennen's feelings about Leonie.

"I'll call her tomorrow," Kennen said.

"Cool. What time do you get off?"

"Ten."

"You want to come by after? Watch a movie? We can't be too loud, because my mom will be asleep, but to be honest, she could probably sleep through a freight train running through the living room, so it won't be too big of a deal."

"Sure, okay," Kennen said.

Later that night Kennen did drop in at Alex's place. They put on *Twister*, but they didn't really watch it. They talked. They talked about school, their dreams for when it ended. They barely noticed the destruction on the screen right in front of them.

AUGUST 2017

Gemma had taken one of the cars to the station, so they loaded up and plugged in the address for Tilden. Gemma and Kennen arrived at Morton Hill Rest Home at around 1:00 pm. The complex was large, caring for residents with a range of needs. It consisted of a number of squat brick buildings tucked into little pods, like some sort of fairy tale village.

The building that housed Tom Tilden was far to the back of the complex, and as Kennen navigated the twisting path to it, he couldn't help but wonder if the people who had no one got stashed back there. It sure wasn't visitor friendly to get to.

They entered a small room decorated with fake flowers and trite paintings. A lady in scrubs stood behind a desk, clipboard in her hand and phone receiver in her ear. She got off the phone and greeted them with a tired smile.

"Hello! Are you all from Caring Hearts?"

"No," Gemma said, "we are here to interview Tom Tilden."

"Oh, from the show, right? I saw a note that you had been in contact. I don't think you'll get anything much, but you're welcome to try. I'll show you back." She stepped out from the desk and started down the long corridor to the right.

"What is Caring Hearts?" Gemma asked.

"That's about the only visitors most of the people on my watch get. It's a local group of volunteers that visit our residents who have no family close by."

"Sounds like a very worthwhile program," Gemma said.

"Yes, actually, Mr. Tilden has—" She cut off, noticing one of the long rectangular lights that lined the hall turned on near the end of the corridor. "Oh, that's Ms. Morris again. Tilden is right here on your left, room 602." She pointed and then hurried away down the hall.

Kennen knocked on the door lightly out of politeness then reached for the door handle.

"Come in," a man's voice called back to them.

Kennen froze and looked at Gemma, whose eyes were wide. She shrugged and Kennen opened the door, holding it so Gemma could enter first.

The room had the basic hospital room set up. The entrance was dimly lit, with a bathroom to the left and a series of cabinets on the right. In the main room, a hospital bed sat in the center and along the far wall were two chairs and a small table. One chair had a tall back and a controller hung from a wire on the edge of the arm, probably a lift chair. It was blue vinyl and had small, locked wheels on the bottom. It held Tom Tilden, his lap covered in a blanket, his arms laid across his lap, his head tilted to the side, his face blank and staring. The other was a standard vinyl and wood chair, like the subtle torture devices found in most waiting rooms.

In the small chair sat Dylan Whitacre.

Whitacre saw Gemma first, and apparently, he liked what he saw because his gaze settled on her too long. Kennen was already in the room next to her, the two of them blocking the exit before Whitacre shifted his eyes to Kennen. When he did, he shot out of the chair, which hit the wall behind him with a dull thud. Tilden didn't react at all.

"What are you doing here?" Kennen asked.

"I volunteer here. What are you doing here?"

So, Whitacre was going to try and have a backbone. That was somewhat refreshing, Kennen thought.

"We're investigating the murder of his daughter," Gemma answered.

"Well, you're wasting your time. He can't talk."

"We're lucky we ran into you then," Kennen said. "We'd love to hear what you have to say."

Whitacre blushed. Kennen glanced at Gemma, who was already stony-faced. Ready to run with it.

"You should track down his wife. I've heard she's out, not that she ever visits him." Whitacre said, shifting his weight and nodding at Mr. Tilden.

"We already did that actually," Gemma said. "You seem to know a lot about the family. Did you know a lot about Leonie?"

"Everybody knew Leonie," Whitacre answered.

"But you were in her class, right?" Gemma asked.

"You already know all of this from him." Whitacre glared at Kennen.

"We'd like to hear what you have to say, though. Kennen can't speak for you."

Whitacre snorted. "Right. Like you would take my word over his. But it doesn't matter anyway. I've got nothing to do with any of it."

"Did you point the cops to Medina?" Kennen asked. Gemma shot him a warning glance.

"What? I–that bastard!" Whitacre sputtered. The redness reached his forehead and exploded down his neck.

"Who's the bastard?" Kennen asked.

Whitacre tilted his head as if to say, *You know damn well who I'm talking about.* And Kennen did, but he found a sick pleasure in toying with Whitacre.

"Jim didn't say anything about you. We figured it out on our own," Kennen said.

"I can verify that Jim didn't name you," Gemma said,

keeping an eye on Kennen and putting her hands up as if she was trying to calm the waters. "But we also know there was a CI."

Whitacre just shook his head.

"If you'd be willing to meet with us...maybe we could schedule a time?"

Was she really going to give him an out?! Whitacre could disappear and dry up for good. This wasn't what they had planned for, but this was their chance. He stepped in front of Gemma. Whitacre was exactly where he wanted him: cornered.

"It's an easy question, K? When the cops came to talk to you, did you mention Medina?" Kennen knew everything that was in Whitacre's statement, but Whitacre didn't know this. Maybe he would slip up and say something that wasn't in his statement, something that would prove he was the CI. Maybe something that would prove that he was more than that.

Whitacre was almost shaking. Kennen thought he could see Whitacre's pulse in the vein popping out of his neck. And then he suddenly calmed down. He unclenched his hands and dropped his shoulders. His pasty complexion returned.

"You know what? You're just like your damn dad. I knew he was going to try and pin it on me back then. I was just convenient, right? Poor kid with no connections. It'd be easy; who cares if it was wrong? And you must be just the same way. I mean, it's pretty damn amazing you solve every case you investigate. Almost..." Whitacre squared his jaw and kept his eyes on Kennen's. "Almost unbelievable."

"It also looks pretty damn convenient that your 'volunteer' duties let you keep an eye on Tom Tilden here. Maybe you want to make sure he doesn't let something slip in his current state."

"Your asshole dad wanted to be the big hero. But I wasn't going to be the fall guy. Not for a cop's son." Whitacre waved a wild hand at Kennen. "Where were you that night, huh? You were out with Jesse? Bullshit. Jesse would always lie for his guys. Then you kept your mouth shut and Medina died for it!"

Whitacre was on the ground before Kennen even realized he had punched him.

MAY 1998

There was no school on Monday. Some sort of teacher professional development or something. Probably so they could have time to write even harder finals. Kennen sat down on his couch after lunch to call Leonie, both to fix things with her and to honor his promise to Alex.

"Hey." Leonie sounded tired.

"Hey."

"I'm sorry about prom," Kennen said.

"Yeah, me too," Leonie said.

"I was just being dumb."

"I should have been honest with you from the start."

Dead air.

"I just," Leonie went on, "I just have to get out of here. Away from my dad."

"I know, but it's only a few more months, then we'll be off to college." Kennen hoped she might bite at this. She still hadn't given any updates on her NYU status. The silence was getting too loud. "You still there?"

"Make me a deal, would you?"

"Sure."

"I'll promise to let you in on all of my schemes in the future if you promise you'll be my partner in crime. My wingman?"

"You do know Jim's a cop, right? I can't just run away to a life of robbing banks and selling drugs."

That got a soft laugh out of Leonie. "I promise to keep the schemes from being *too* illegal. Maybe some morally gray stuff, but no felonies."

"I can get behind that."

AUGUST 2017

Kennen was locked in a small room with piss-yellow walls and a mustiness to match. His right hand ached and was a bit puffy. Gemma couldn't stop the orderly from calling the police when she came in and saw Whitacre on the ground, spitting out what looked like blood and a tooth. Turned out it was actually just a crown; a little cement and his crooked smile would be back in business, but the damage was done.

Kennen couldn't help but worry that Jim had heard. He might be a grown man, but he couldn't completely ignore the nausea that was an almost nostalgic experience of teenage trouble. A shadow passed by the frosted window of the door followed by the sound of a key in the lock. An officer opened the door. Marty stepped in.

"Hello, Kennen," Marty said.

"How bad is it?" Kennen asked.

"Shouldn't you have some snarky remark about seeing the other guy?"

"That only works if the other guy fought back."

Marty sat and sucked in his lips. He seemed to be trying to find a place for his eyes to rest that didn't include Kennen, but the room was too small for that, so he finally settled them on Kennen's elbow.

"So, tell me. How bad is it?" Kennen asked again.

"Let's start with the good news." Marty leaned forward, massaging the palm of one hand with the opposite thumb. "Whitacre has decided not to press charges. Our lawyers have already contacted him. They're going to cover his dental work plus some walking around money."

"We're buying him off?" Kennen asked incredulously. "That won't do shit! He'll open his mouth for that dental work but he'll never shut it again!"

"That's what the producers thought as well. So they've made their decision."

"So, what are they going to do about it? What's the plan?"

"Kennen, I'm sorry," Marty said with a heavy sigh. "You're fired."

Finals were the week after next. Graduation was on the horizon. And Alex was the only one with any motivation left.

Leonie seemed to be okay with letting the next couple of weeks just happen, and Kennen wasn't one to argue with that sentiment, but Alex was insistent that they finish strong. They decided to hold a few study sessions at the library, but those started to make Leonie anxious.

"People can't keep their mouths shut. If my dad hears I'm meeting with Alex at the library, he won't let me leave the house at all."

So, they moved their meeting spot to Kennen's. Truth was, Kennen didn't regularly invite people over. Something about his stepdad being a police officer made his friends look over their shoulder, like Jim could just sniff the air and detect their sins. But Leonie and Alex had always been cool about it.

The night before, Jim got a call from Mr. Tilden. He was checking that Jim was okay with the session. At least that was what he claimed.

"What was that about?" Kennen asked when Jim got off the phone.

"Mr. Tilden wanted to make sure I knew Leonie was coming over tomorrow. Wanted to make sure she wasn't a bother."

Kennen sighed. He knew that wasn't it. Mr. Tilden was wondering if anyone else was invited to the session.

"Did you tell him Alex would be here?" Kennen asked, already dreading the answer.

"Did I ask you about who would be over?" Jim asked.

Kennen thought for a moment. He had just said "we" when asking if it was okay to host the group.

"I guess I didn't," Kennen said, almost as a question. What was Jim saying?

"So, clearly I could infer Leonie was part of your group since her father was calling me, but I have no evidence of anyone else." Jim gave a half smile and pulled open a newspaper.

Kennen walked away, smiling and slightly amazed.

A little before 7:00, Leonie leaned back. "That's it. That's all my brain can handle."

"We haven't even touched physics," Kennen complained. They had been going over vocab for the English final, and he wasn't worried one bit about that. Physics was another story entirely. The subject created its own black hole in Kennen's brain.

"You guys go on without me," she said. She stood and started packing her bag.

"You want someone to walk you home?" Alex asked. He flicked a glance Kennen's way.

Kennen straightened up. Alex was smoother than Kennen, but luckily he seemed to be okay with Kennen copying more than his Calc notes.

"Yeah, I could walk you home real quick," Kennen said.

"What's with all the chivalry? I got it. I can handle my way through the dangerous streets of Ashter. All six of them. I'll see you two tomorrow."

Kennen followed her to the door and closed it behind her as

she left. When he turned back, he saw Alex twisting his pencil back and forth between his thumb and forefinger, staring firmly into space. Kennen came back and sat across from him.

"Thanks for trying," Kennen said.

Alex sighed. "I'm worried about her. You're keeping an eye on her, right?"

"I mean, I guess." Kennen kept his eyes on Leonie a lot, but at that moment he wasn't sure how much he divined from the action.

"We've got to watch out for her, Kennen. We're all she's got."

"What are you talking about?"

Alex frowned and shook his head.

"What has she told you?"

Alex sighed and leaned back, putting the pencil down. "She hasn't said anything, but—" He stopped and ran his hand through his hair. "I know what it is like to have someone you love locked away from you."

"You mean your brother?"

"Yeah. I know the circumstances are completely different, but I think the frustration, the pain of it, is probably pretty similar."

Kennen nodded, unsure what to say.

"I guess it's just like, I can't relate to the fact that you lost your mom in a car wreck. I can't fully understand how devastating that must have been, but I'm sure if you knew someone else who had gone through the same thing, you could connect, you know? Understand each other better than even your closest friends would."

Kennen felt a wave of nausea rush over him. He did not expect this turn in the conversation. "I just don't think about it much."

"I think in that way you and Leonie are polar opposites. Her issues are all she can think about. They devour her."

"Maybe that's because of the difference between our two situations. For you and Leonie, your person is there, but you can't be with them. My mom isn't out there somewhere. My actual dad probably is, but you know, fuck that guy."

Alex gave him a small grin.

"But I guess you two both have hope." Kennen watched as Alex's smile vanished and his eyes dropped.

"I'm sorry, man, I didn't—"

"No," Kennen interrupted. "I didn't mean for that to sound like a good thing. I mean, yes, hope is a good thing, but that doesn't mean it doesn't come with painful consequences."

At this, Alex looked back up and nodded. "You know, however sucky my life happens to be at a certain moment, I've got my mom and my dad. I don't get to see my dad very often anymore, but I know that everything they do, every single thing, they do for me and my brother."

Kennen thought about Jim. When his mother passed, Jim kept telling him not to worry about anything, that Jim would take care of him. And without really thinking about it, Kennen had believed him.

"Like, I know what would happen if I got into serious trouble because I saw what my parents did when my brother got in trouble. What do you think Jim would do?"

"Kill me," Kennen said without missing a beat.

Alex laughed. "Yeah, I'll give you that, but afterward? Like what would he really do?"

Kennen hadn't ever really run any scenarios in his head, but he found he still had an immediate answer. "He'd try to help. Try to understand what happened."

"I think you're right. But what about Leonie?"

Kennen took another short moment to think. "He'd protect himself first."

"Exactly. He'd just want it to go away. And that's what I mean when I say that Leonie just has us. Both of us have someone that, when we get home, has our back. And Leonie has us."

243

Kennen gave a small tight nod, his stomach tensing as this realization sunk into his core.

"What was your mom like?" Alex was still leaning back, but now he looked actually relaxed. His shoulders had dropped and his eyes were placid.

They talked the rest of the evening until Alex needed to head home.

They never got back to physics.

AUGUST 2017

Kennen was being released. Marty had already left and Kennen was waiting to get his work bag back when Chief Nichols sauntered by.

"Stop by my office before you leave, would you?" Nichols asked.

Kennen nodded and turned back to Heather as she put his bag on the counter. He looked through it, then signed that everything was present. He slung his bag over his shoulder and turned to see Nichols hanging around outside of his office, waiting. He must have thought Kennen might try to just head out. Kennen couldn't blame him; it was what he wanted to do. But instead, he walked over to the chief, who ushered him into the office.

"You call that investigative technique?" Nichols asked with a little smirk as he closed the door behind them.

"Not my best moment. You're not going to call my stepdad, are you?" Kennen joked back.

Nichols gestured for Kennen to take a seat while he sat in an old office chair. Its faux leather material was peeling like some sort of lizard shedding its skin.

"In all seriousness, though, I know charges weren't formally made, but this puts us all in an awkward position."

"We had originally planned to come to you before approaching Whitacre," Kennen admitted.

"I wish you would have. People tell stories, and I've heard about how Whitacre was a bit of a mess as a kid, but he's been an upstanding member of this community for years now. He started volunteering with Caring Hearts, well, it must be about ten years ago now. It was just after his grandmother passed. She was out at Morton Hill as well, and she would tell him how sad it was that some of her neighbors never had any visitors. He's been committed to it ever since."

Ten years. Well before Tom Tilden was admitted. Fuck. How had they missed that when they were looking into Whitacre? Gemma never missed things like that. If she had done her damn job, they would have known not to go, not to chance running into Whitacre. Kennen would still have a job.

"All I'm saying is tread lightly, alright? I can't have you beating up citizens."

Kennen realized Nichols hadn't heard of his termination. He'd figure it out soon enough. Marty had told Kennen he had one more night, and then he needed to be out. Figure out a flight home. The show was cutting him off quick and cold.

This would be his last chance.

Kennen apologized again, standing slowly.

"I hate to do it considering, but I do have another favor to ask. While I'm here, could I take one last look at Leonie's planner?"

"Sure. What do you think you'll see that your partner didn't?"

"What do you mean?"

"Well, heck, Ms. James spent most of the morning on that before switching over to the diary."

That sent Kennen's head reeling. She hadn't mentioned looking at the planner, just the diary. Why not say anything?

Could she have also been holding back on her knowledge of Whitacre? Could he have been set up?

Kennen started replaying the last few weeks in his head. He had been with Gemma most of the time. There had been that day Marty, Greg, and Cora went to pick up the actors and the rest of the crew at the airport.

She had hung back to follow a lead, she said.

A lead that didn't pan out.

Could it be that she found something in the planner to pick up the trail again?

"I'll be quick. I just need to verify something."

Nichols shrugged and led him back to the evidence locker. Once Kennen had gloved up and got the planner, he settled at a desk, flipping through the pages rather quickly as there were so few entries. There were notes about their study group, college application dates, things she needed to take care of while her father was out. He flipped all the way through May. Nothing. He sat, looking at the first few weeks of May again. The only note was Study Session w/Kennen. He sighed. He was about to put it back when he looked at it again, trying to look at it like Gemma would. What could she have seen in all the blank spaces?

He stepped around the desk and called out to Heather. "Hey! Did you ever find that report on Medina?"

"No, I don't know what we've done, but I can't seem to find his name on any coroner's reports."

The shadow appeared just at the edge of his vision. It lifted its head. Kennen went back to the planner. Of course. Leonie didn't write Alex's name with the study sessions, just Kennen's. That would just be asking for her father to find them out. But there was nothing to prove that was the reason. Leonie had never mentioned in any of her writing that she was not to see Alex. All the team had was Kennen's word on that. So, Gemma had spent the morning looking at this, hoping to find an unassuming line, a clue, a pointed finger.

And the only name mentioned was Kennen's.

Greg and Cora shot up from the bench in the hotel lobby as Kennen stepped in the door. Clearly, they'd been waiting for him, but now they were just standing before him, looking sideways at each other.

"Hi, guys," Kennen said, breaking the awkward silence.

"Hey, Kennen," Greg finally said, letting it out like a sigh.

"We're so sorry," Cora said.

"No, I messed up in a spectacular way. The producers did the right thing. Lucky thing you hadn't started recording any spots with me yet, huh?" Kennen tried to give a short laugh, but it was more of a choke.

"Listen, when we get done shooting and we get back home, we'll give you a call, okay?" Greg asked.

"We can get together and grab a meal or something," Cora added.

"Yeah, that'll be great." Kennen believed that they would call him. But he didn't believe, at least at this point, that he would pick up.

Greg pulled him into a bumbling hug and Cora put a hand on his shoulder. He let go and saw Greg's eyes were red and watery. Then they started for the elevator, leaving Kennen alone in the lobby.

Kennen pulled his thoughts back together and called after them. "Where's Gemma?"

Cora, who had wrapped an arm around Greg's shoulders and was conducting him to the elevator looked back, then patted Greg's back in a silent cue to keep going. She returned and spoke softly.

"She took a camera down to the tracks. I think she's taking this pretty hard, too, but you know her. She buries herself in her work."

At that, the elevator door dinged and Cora walked away swiftly to catch Greg. The door opened to reveal Julia and Kyle, a.k.a. modern-day Leonie and Alex. They exited, heading for the conference room as Greg and Cora got on. Kennen watched them as they went. Julia made quite a show of not looking directly at Kennen while also holding a face that suggested she smelled sunbaked garbage. Leonie had never made such a face in her whole life. Kyle suffered him a glance and a weak half-smile. Kennen thought about calling after him. Those melancholy eyes he had just shown to Kennen?

Those would be perfect for his portrayal of Alex.

MAY 14TH, 1998

Kennen decided to take a quick shower after school. Leonie hadn't been at school, so as he wrapped a towel around his waist, he went to the phone, thinking he would call and check up on her. He was reaching for it when it rang.

"Hello?"

"Kennen?" It was Jesse. His voice sounded thick.

"Yeah? What's up?"

Jesse sighed. "It's Tracy." Tracy was Jesse's on-again-off-again girlfriend, though he rarely talked about her.

"What happened?"

"Found out she's been shacking up with Jeffie."

Kennen looked down at his math textbook sticking out of his backpack. It was bad enough to find out your girl was cheating. But to find out your girl was cheating on you with Jeffie? According to the transitive property, that equaled extra fucked up.

"Are you busy tonight?" Jesse asked.

Kennen had had plans with Leonie and Alex to study for the Calc final one last time before tomorrow. Leonie had volunteered her place because her dad was out of town. But Leonie was sick, so were they even still on? And it wasn't like Alex actually needed to study. And Jesse had been there for him on prom night.

"I'm free."

"I'll be by in fifteen," Jesse said.

Kennen hung up and went to change into some gym shorts and a t-shirt. He came back, again heading for the phone, this time to call Alex, when he heard the short honk from Jesse's dusty old Camry. It had been more like five minutes. It would be fine; Alex would figure it out.

Just as Kennen was headed for the door Jim opened it and stood in the doorway. An envelope fell to the floor. Probably another estimate from Rick's Roofing. They thought slipping free estimates into doors was a good way to drum up business. But Jim was well aware that the roof needed redoing, and these always just pissed him off. Kennen would have already trashed it, but he came in the back door and hadn't seen it.

"Who's that out front?" Jim asked.

"Jesse. We're just going out for a bit," Kennen said, stooping to grab the envelope and throw it on the living room table.

"Jesse? I thought you were studying with your friends tonight."

"It fell through."

"Shouldn't you still study?"

"Jesse has had a rough day. He needs me."

"Needs you," Jim said with a scoff. "What that kid needs is to get his shit together."

Kennen felt his face heat up. "You don't even know him."

Jim grunted. He had lots of grunts, but Kennen recognized this one as the you-don't-know-what-I-know variety. Which just pissed him off more.

"I know Jesse has a past, but I also know people can change."

Suddenly Jim looked tired. "Yeah. They sure do," he said. He almost looked sad, but Kennen wasn't going to fall for that tactic. The horn sounded again.

"I'm outta here." Kennen turned and pushed by Jim. When he

got down to the car, Jesse was stepping out from the driver's side.

"I'm not feeling great. Can you drive?" Jesse left the driver's door open and headed around to the passenger's side.

"Yeah," Kennen said.

As he rounded the door, he spotted a cooler already loaded in the backseat. He drove them to the river, where he parked in the parking lot near the boat ramp. Together they carried the cooler down to a well-used fishing spot. There, a large flat rock jutted out from the riverbank, creating a natural bench.

Kennen drank lightly, not interested in fighting a hangover during finals the next day. At first, Jesse drank fast and spoke little, but as the evening went on, he flipped. They talked about Carly for a bit, and how psycho girls seemed to be in general. Soon they moved on, talking about work, family, sports; just a little bit of everything. The sun sank, and the two street lights that lit the parking lot kicked on. The moon was bright, reflecting off of the river.

They were feeling good, laughing, when there was the sound of a truck nearby. Jesse was busy lighting a blunt, but Kennen stood to peer over the bank and see who was there. Kennen muttered *shit* under his breath, then looked to make sure Jesse hadn't heard him. It was Jeffie and some of his crew. They parked right at the edge of the boat ramp. Kennen watched as they pulled beers from the back of the truck. Someone turned on some music that just barely reached Kennen and Jesse's ledge, but it seemed they were going to stay up there. Kennen sat back down and Jesse offered him a hit. He passed. He was paranoid enough right now. What would Jesse do if he found out Jeffie was a matter of yards away? What would Jeffie do if he discovered Jesse? Kennen figured the best he could do was keep Jesse distracted and comfortable where they were. Maybe Jeffie's group wouldn't stay too long.

Things went well for about thirty minutes. That was apparently the amount of time it took one of the guys in Jeffie's group to get pretty buzzed and then decide it was a good idea to strip down to his boxers, run down the ramp, and jump in the river. Jesse turned to watch the commotion.

"Shit, it's cold!" the guy yelled climbing back up on the boat ramp. "My balls are up in my fucking armpits!"

Jeffie was quiet. Jesse, high and drunk, laughed way too loud. That was a mistake. The guy spotted Kennen and Jesse.

"What you laughing at, fags? Tired of sucking each other's cocks and want a taste of mine?" He grabbed his junk, or what was left of it, and shook it their way.

Jesse stood shakily and looked as if he might try to chuck his beer bottle at the guy.

"Hey, it's getting late, let's just get out of here," Kennen said, standing to block Jesse's view of the guy. But Jesse wasn't paying him any attention.

He had spotted Jeffie.

Jesse started scrambling up the path towards the truck. He was surprisingly fast, and Kennen struggled to keep up. Of course, Kennen was with it enough to still worry about falling headlong into the river. Jesse seemed to give no fucks.

"Hey!" Jesse called out when he was a few feet from the truck. Jeffie, who had been sitting on the passenger side seat with his feet hanging out the door, looked up. A beer bottle dangled from his hand. Kennen realized he was absolutely wasted, and that was strange. Jeffie partied, no doubt; but it suddenly occurred to Kennen that he had never seen Jeffie plastered. He always stayed in control. But right now he looked like a stiff breeze could throw him face down on the cement.

"Hey, you ... you fuck!" Jesse had clearly drunk and smoked away most of his words. Jeffie just stared at him, eyes glazed over, face drooping. He reminded Kennen of an elderly St. Bernard. Finally, Jeffie turned and looked behind him. Kennen followed his gaze, and in the low light saw that Calvin Travers was sitting behind the wheel, rocking slightly. He must have taken some kind of uppers. He looked ready to scratch his skin off.

"We need to get out of here," Jeffie slurred.

Calvin jerked his head towards Jeffie, then leaned out the door. "Get your dumbass up here and drive!" he yelled.

The river guy finished tugging his jeans on over his wet frame and ran the rest of the way up the ramp, carrying his shoes. The three of them folded themselves into the truck and pulled away.

Jesse yelled after them like he had won, but Kennen was just confused. Yeah, there seemed to be some long-standing truce between the two, but that was before one of them was sleeping with the other's girl. And Jeffie just backed down? Kennen steered Jesse to the car, got him in the passenger's side, then went back for the cooler. He drove them back into town and was headed for Jesse's place when Jesse spoke up.

"Just drive me to your house. I can get home from there."

"I don't think that's a good idea, man." Kennen had to admit, Jesse seemed to have suddenly sobered up on the drive home, but Kennen still didn't think he should be driving. Kennen tried to keep arguing his point, but Jesse was insistent. And it was his car after all. Finally, Kennen acquiesced and pulled up at the end of his street, which would make the drive about three blocks shorter for Jesse. He waved Jesse on and was pleased to see as Jesse pulled away that he did seem to be in control of the car. Kennen went up the street, planning to sneak in through the back. If he was lucky, Jim would already be asleep and he could lie about what time he got in. It was already 11:30, which was not going to go over well, especially considering their little fight earlier. But Jim wasn't home. Kennen went in and crawled into bed.

Kennen's last thought before nodding off for the night was about how lucky he was that Jim had been called out, and he hoped that Jesse had the same luck and got home without incident.

AUGUST 2017

Gemma was so focused on the viewfinder of the camera that she didn't react as Kennen came up behind her. Sunlight pierced the treetops, and the woods and tracks looked fake somehow, like a picture that had been heavily edited. She had set up directly at a switch point, the place where a train could be guided to one set of tracks or another, depending on the position of the switch.

"Gemma," he called.

She jumped and looked over her shoulder for a moment before turning back to look across the tracks. Kennen followed her gaze and thought he saw a shadow retreat.

"Goddammit!" she hissed, turning back to him. "What the fuck are you doing here?!" She was sweating and her curls were limp.

Kennen felt crippled under her gaze. He swallowed and tried to fight back his nerves. "Did you know Whitacre would be there?" He managed to keep his tone low and even.

There was a small flinch on Gemma's face, but she recovered quickly.

"Please don't put that on me."

"I'm not putting my actions on you. That is all on me. But did you set me up? Did you want to be there, to see what would happen if Whitacre and I were thrown together? Was this a little experiment of yours?"

"I was the one who said we should bring in the police before we interviewed Whitacre, remember?"

"But you want me to believe that you missed this? You never miss anything, Gemma. You don't make mistakes, not like this."

"I'm surprised you've noticed."

"What?"

"My work. Apparently, you are aware of it, all evidence to the contrary."

"Gemma, what are you talking about?"

Gemma turned, looking down the tracks. When she spoke, she didn't look back at Kennen. "You know, I was just so tired. I played the game right and I still couldn't win. I just..."

"Gemma, just tell me what this is about."

"Do you even know where I end up on the credits of the show?"

Kennen paused then sighed. "I can't say I do."

"Under crew. Generic label."

"I'm sorry about that. We should—"

"Last season, when we were going to start shooting, Marty suggested that maybe we show me conducting some of the interviews. Do you remember?"

"Yes."

"What did you say?"

Kennen had to dig. It wasn't a moment that had held much meaning for him. Clearly, it had for Gemma. "I said that I didn't think it was a good idea to have two people conducting interviews. I didn't want the audience missing key points because they were wondering who the woman asking questions was." Now that he said the words again, he realized how ridiculous he sounded, but at the time, those were his honest thoughts. "I didn't mean to slight you or your work. We really couldn't do this without you. I was really just thinking of the show."

Gemma turned back to him. Her eyes were damp, but it did nothing to soften her gaze. "You were just too happy to continue taking credit for everything. For all of my work."

Kennen felt his shoulders climb up his neck. "If you were so upset, why didn't you say something? I mean, Greg, Cora, Marty, they all do important work and you don't see them complaining." He knew that was a lame argument as soon as it left his lips, but he just didn't understand. What was the real issue here?

"Speak up? Do you really think it was Marty's idea? I suggested it, and he said he'd put it before the team. And you shot it down. Didn't even give it a second thought. Cora took me for a drink afterward to try and treat the sting, but you know, it just didn't work. It wasn't enough."

"Okay, I admit, that was a mistake on my part. I should have put more thought into it. But if it was such a big deal, why did you just ..." Kennen paused, waving his hands out to his side, "just keep going along? Hell, you could get a job anywhere."

"Oh, just leave? Why should that be the solution? Kennen, I care about the people we help with this show. I care about the people who make this show happen. They're my family. But you? It's the Kennen Clarke show at the end of the day. Never mind me, do you know anything about the other people around you? Do you know that Liza tells the best jokes? That Carlos is an amazing guitar player? That Ben and his wife are expecting and he is worried because the recording schedule reaches so close to their due date? Tell me one thing you know about a member of the crew that isn't one of us big five."

Kennen tried to hold her gaze but dropped it. If she had asked about anyone involved in any of the cases they had investigated, living or dead, he could have recalled their favorite restaurant and their astrological sign. But the people who rolled cords, who ran around working at the edges of a shot, who spent hours editing?

"You're right. I only see the job," he said to the rocks.

Gemma let out a short, dry laugh and threw her hands up. "Right, let's go into pity mode. Kennen was just doing his job."

"How the hell can you lecture me about making it all about me, about me not being part of the team, when clearly you think you are the MVP? Yeah, you know the crew better, but then you bitch about being listed next to them in the credits."

"We all have our jobs here. But as far as the show, the producers, the rest of the world is concerned, my work gets attributed to you." Gemma said the last words slowly, each landing like a steel billet.

"Okay, so you set me up against a person of interest, I fuck up, and voila, I'm gone and you can step in. You're right. You are clearly morally superior to me."

"This is not how I wanted things to play out. I never wanted anything like this."

"What do you mean by that?"

She reached up, rubbing her forehead. "If you could have just …" Gemma started. "If you could have just given me the room to grow, shared just a little of that space you occupy. It wouldn't have cost you a damn thing." She lowered her voice and looked away. "And now I've cost you everything." She shook her head. "God, how did this all get this fucked up?"

"Punching Whitacre is still on me," Kennen said, brushing his hair back.

Gemma bit her lip and looked to the woods. "It was selfish, I know. I just wanted a little … I wanted people to know what I did."

Kennen felt his eyes sting with the start of tears. "And you deserve that. I guess now they will. You're the obvious replacement for me." He found himself shaking his head, then nodding. "You'll be great." He started to turn.

"Kennen," Gemma started, then stopped to take a deep breath. Her tears finally broke through. "I told the producers."

"Gemma, you had to. If you didn't, Marty would have—"

"No, I'm not talking about what happened today. I told them about Leonie."

Kennen turned back around, trying to process what she just said. "What?"

"Didn't you ever wonder where the producers dug this up? Every time before, you and I had vetted an idea before it went before the producers."

"You—" Things weren't right. Maybe it was the heat, but the tracks didn't look quite solid anymore. They were nothing but light, reflected in neat straight lines. The rocks were abstractions, the trees imposters.

"I just thought–I wanted to believe–the producers would see more need for me on this one, for the integrity of the case. I thought I'd have a place right alongside you. But then they don't care about integrity. They care about drama that drums up ratings. And I truly am sorry, Kennen. I didn't know Whitacre would be there. I would never have done that to you—"

"So, you hadn't landed a spot in front of the camera," Kennen interrupted her, clenching his fist until his nails cut into his palm. "And you couldn't find enough dirt on me to get me forcefully pushed off the case, so you just decided to see what would happen if you put me up against Whitacre. See if I'd crack enough that you could slide in. Well, finally your experiment yielded the desired outcome. I have one question for you." Kennen paused. Gemma's eyes were round, deep. "Did you investigate me just for your own purposes? Because I know that's what you were doing. So, was it that, or did you actually think I was a murderer?"

Shock started at her eyes and pushed out across her face, rippling like a struck cymbal. "Is that what you thought I was doing? That I thought you were good for it?" She looked at the ground, and for a moment Kennen thought that she might be sick. Her curls let go to gravity, falling over her face. Finally, she threw them back and squared her shoulders. She looked at Kennen with those dark wells.

"You really don't know a damn thing about any of us, do you?"

She took her camera and left him standing there alone by the tracks.

JUNE 1998

Kennen heard the rumble of Jim's car out front, so he forced himself out of bed and went to shut his bedroom door. The door lock had been broken since they moved in, so this was the best he could do. He was back in his bed when he heard Jim unlocking the deadbolt on the front door.

Kennen's bedsheets desperately needed changing. So did his shirt and boxers. But he had another hour before he needed to hike out to Milton's for his shift, so he'd deal with it then. He had spent every minute not at work right here, in bed, since school had ended. It started when Jim wouldn't let him attend Leonie's funeral. Jim had threatened that if he showed up, Jim would drag him out himself. If he didn't want to ruin Leonie's funeral, he needed to stay away. So he did. And he also stayed away from Jim, shutting himself in his room if Jim was home. He stayed away from his graduation ceremony as well. At some point in his life, he might regret it, but for now, he was just happy to have pissed Jim off.

Kennen waited to hear Jim's heavy footfalls follow their regular pattern: go into the kitchen for a quick meal, go to the bathroom for an equally quick shower, and then, just like Kennen, disappear into his bedroom. The sound of shutting doors was becoming their primary form of communication. But Jim's footsteps started down the hall. Kennen tensed and sat up, waiting to hear if they would stop at Jim's room or the bathroom. As the steps kept coming, he looked at his closet. The sliding door was half open. He could slip in.

Kennen did recognize how stupid this thought was, how childish. But as the steps came to a stop outside of his door, he didn't care. Anything to not speak with Jim. Kennen stood silently, then stepped on discarded laundry to muffle the sounds of him crossing the room. He gently pressed back the clothes that hung in the closet and stepped in parallel to the sliding door, carefully guiding the clothes back in place without a sound.

"Kennen?"

Kennen sucked in his breath and held it. He heard the click of his door handle.

"Kennen?" This time it was clearer; Jim had to be peeking in the door. Kennen heard the door swing all the way open and Jim step into the room.

Kennen started to think of how he would explain the fact that he was standing in the closet. Jim had to know he was there. Why else would he come in?

Then Kennen heard a sound that made him boil. Jim was going through things on his bookshelf. What the hell was he doing? Jim had always respected his space, or at least he had thought so. But fuck, he was an investigator. He'd probably know exactly how to have a look around without leaving any evidence. Was this something he did regularly? Kennen clenched his fist, nails biting into his palms.

Jim moved on and Kennen heard the long zipper of his backpack. Kennen imagined turning, taking the door off of the roller tracks, and throwing it at Jim. But he didn't move. Despite his anger, he wanted to know what Jim was looking for. Next, he heard the creak of his bed and a soft grunt from Jim. It sounded like he was digging under the bed. Then all sounds stopped. Jim wasn't moving. He let out a strange sound. It was somewhere between a sigh and a moan, and, because of how painful it sounded, Kennen wondered if Jim had thrown out his bad knee.

This proved to not be the case though, because Jim stood and left quickly, shutting the door behind him. Kennen slid out quietly and tiptoed to his door, pressing his ear to the crack between the jamb and the door. He heard Jim close his own bedroom door.

Kennen dropped down by his bed. Had he actually found something? Or did he just give up, feeling guilty about searching his stepson's room? There wasn't much under there. He usually kicked his shoes off there. There was his little box of dumb treasures: movie stubs, baseball cards from a short stint of collecting when he was in seventh grade, stones from the time when cool-looking ones were schoolyard currency. Everything was still there. Kennen sat back, starting to relax. Jim hadn't found anything.

Then his heart skipped a beat. How could he have forgotten? He leaned over and ran his hands under the bed again, but it was no good. It was gone.

Jim had found the broken picture of Leonie. The one Kennen had never fixed.

What was Jim thinking right now? Kennen had spoken with Milner, Jim's partner, a few times since Leonie's murder. He had been with Jesse. Jesse had backed that up.

But what if Jim didn't believe it?

Kennen needed to get out of there. He threw on clothes and grabbed some shoes. He opened his door, slowly turning and releasing the knob so barely a click was heard. He got out and closed his door behind him, but now he needed to make it down the notoriously creaky hallway.

He took wide steps, hoping the less-trodden wood of the edges would be more forgiving. He made it past the bathroom door on the right and was about to pass Jim's door on his left when his foot landed on an old slat that squealed under his weight. Jim's door flew open before he could escape.

Jim stood there, red. "I didn't know you were home."

"I, uh, was in the bathroom," Kennen lied. He watched as Jim eyed the bathroom door. It stood partway open, as it usually did. Jim would have checked that before going into Kennen's room. He was caught.

"Didn't you hear me calling you?"

For some reason, Kennen kept playing along as well, giving a small pathetic head shake and shrugging his shoulders. He waited for Jim to say something more. Call him out. Say something about the picture.

"I need to ask you something."

Kennen braced himself.

"Tell me about Alex."

"What about him?"

Jim sighed heavily and looked at the floor. He started his next statement with his eyes closed. "There's been a change in the direction of the investigation. I shouldn't be telling you this, but we will be bringing him in to talk again. Tonight."

"Why?"

"Kennen, if there is anything you know—"

"Like it would make a damn difference. What are you going to tell the guys? 'My kid says Alex is innocent. We'll have to try something else.' You *know* Alex."

At this, Jim opened his mouth to argue, but Kennen wasn't having it. "You do! And if that isn't good enough, then anything I say won't be either. Stop pretending you care." Kennen stormed back down the hall to his room. He went to slam his door, but Jim had followed him, and he blocked it open with a strong hand.

"I do care. That is why I am asking."

"You know Alex isn't the type. Why bother bringing him in? Why 'the change' in direction?"

"Kennen, I just need you to trust me on this."

"Whatever. Why don't you just worry about doing your job *right*? That's all you care about anyway."

This time Jim let Kennen close the door. Kennen went back to his bed. He knew he'd gone too far, that he was raw from it all. But for fuck's sake, hassling Alex? They were so pathetic. So incompetent.

Kennen waited until he heard the front door close. He went to Jim's room to look for the picture but couldn't find it. Either Jim hid it well, or he took it with him. Kennen came out, defeated. Then his eyes fell on the phone.

Alex picked up on the third ring.

"Hello?"

"Hey, man, how are you doing?"

"I'm holding up. How about you?"

"About the same."

"We missed you at the funeral."

Kennen paused. "I was just calling because my asshole stepdad is coming to talk to you again. Just wanted to give you a heads up."

The other end of the line was completely silent.

"Alex, you still there?"

"Uh ... yeah." Alex's voice was thick, like he had just taken a slug from a bottle of syrup.

"You okay?"

"Thanks for letting me know."

Alex clicked off, leaving Kennen listening to silence.

AUGUST 2017

Kennen sat at the side of the tracks, avoiding the world beyond the two walls of woods on either side. Things were simpler here. There were two sets of tracks. One could take you left, the other right. Either way, it was a guaranteed trip out of this town. Had that been how Leonie saw it? Is that why she had wanted to meet here? If he had only found that note.

If he had only paid attention to what was happening to her, not what he wanted her to be.

And now he could say the same for Gemma. She was right. Not just about the show. Yes, Kennen had some serious shit in his past, but that didn't excuse how he treated people now.

It was a quiet night other than the rhythmic pulse of the insect songs. Finally, Kennen stood. He was surprised to find the night still so warm. A cool air rolled in along the ground, but a few feet above the ground the air was still thick with humidity. It was like standing up out of a cool stream. He waded his way back through the woods.

When he reached the hotel, he spotted one of the grips digging through the back of the van, most likely making sure everything was ready and charged for tomorrow.

"Hello," Kennen said as he came up behind the van.

"Oh! Uh, hi." The young man wore dusty jeans, a t-shirt, and a well-worn baseball cap.

"I need to borrow one of the cameras."

The techie froze. Kennen sighed.

"I'm not stealing it. I'll give it back tomorrow."

The young man still didn't move. Kennen could see the gears turning. Kennen had been in charge. Now he wasn't. The guy would be right to just tell him to fuck off, but it seemed he couldn't bring himself to do so.

Kennen made the choice for him. He reached in and grabbed a camcorder case and tripod. He didn't need anything particularly fancy for his purpose.

"I promise, you'll get it back. This is still for the show."

The brim of the baseball hat bobbed in silent acceptance.

Kennen turned and headed for the hotel. He had his hand on the door handle when he stopped.

"What's your name?" he called over his shoulder. The baseball cap popped out around the edge of the van.

"Ben."

"As in expecting-a-baby-soon Ben?"

"Uh, yeah."

"Congratulations."

Kennen had made a Hot Pocket before crashing back into bed. His shift at Milton's had been uneventful, but he still felt tired. He was always tired anymore. He woke up at about 4:00 am when his bladder forced him from his room.

After a stop by the bathroom, he headed to the kitchen, thinking of fetching a bag of chips. Instead, he found Jim sitting at the table. If that wasn't surprising enough, there was a bottle and a glass with a few fingers of amber liquid sitting in front of him. Kennen walked past silently to the cabinet, grabbed some potato chips and a glass of water, and started back when Jim pushed his chair out from the table, blocking Kennen's path.

"Sit down, Kennen."

Kennen looked around, evaluating his escape routes. He could try and hurdle the table, but he wasn't much for track and field. He could run out the back, but he had no pants. Damn.

"Please," Jim said.

Kennen sighed and pulled another chair out unnecessarily far from the table and sat. For the moment, Jim simply regarded his glass. Kennen decided to put his attention on his own, finishing his water in a few large gulps. He stretched forward and put the glass on the table, then leaned back, crossing his arms to wait. Then Jim did something that terrified Kennen. He unscrewed the lid of the bottle and put a couple of glugs of Scotch in Kennen's empty water glass.

"What's wrong? What happened?" Kennen demanded.

"We went to talk to Alex."

Kennen ran his fingers along the wood on the bottom of his chair seat. The outer edge, the part that was visible, was polished and smooth, but the inside edge was rough, unfinished. It tore at the pads of his fingers.

"He must have seen us coming," Jim continued, "because when we pulled up, he ran out the back. He was ready for us, had a backpack already packed up and ready to go. Milner was out of the car before I had it in park, giving chase."

Kennen snorted. "He couldn't have caught Alex." Milner lived up to the donut cop stereotype.

"No, he couldn't have. But he can yell. Sam Travers was out working in his shed and came out to see what all the commotion was about. Alex cut through his backyard. You see, Sam thought, with what he saw—"

"I know exactly what he thought he saw," Kennen muttered. He thought back to how Travers had behaved when Alex was crowned Homecoming King. He reached out for the drink Jim had poured him, letting the burn fight off the chill he felt creeping up his spine.

"Kennen, he had a gun in the shed with him."

Kennen carefully put the glass back on the table. "What are you saying?" he asked, his eyes still on the glass.

"Alex caught a bullet. Right along the side of his face here." Jim brushed the side of his cheek.

Kennen swallowed. "Is he…"

"He's at the hospital. If he makes it through the night, there's a chance, but… I'm going back over there soon. I wanted to tell you."

Kennen held tight to his chair. He willed for his head, his heart, for the universe, to stop spinning. But none of them would. So he stood and stumbled around Jim, who moved from his way. When he got to the hallway he stopped and looked back, hoping that maybe all of this had been a dream, but no. Jim leaned forward and finished off his glass. Kennen somehow made it back to his bed.

AUGUST 2017

Kennen set up the tripod across from the small table in his room. He unpacked the camcorder and mounted it, using the viewfinder to center the frame on one of the wooden chairs. He looked over the camera. There, in the corner behind the chair, was his shadow.

It was the most defined he had seen, all lean with curly hair on top.

"It's all right," Kennen said, preparing to hit the record button and step around to the chair. "I'm going to make it right this time."

The shade of Alex Medina nodded.

Kennen: In the end, I failed them all. I failed Leonie by refusing to see how she had changed right in front of me. The real Leonie no longer matched my fantasy version of her, if she ever had, and I just wouldn't see it. I have no proof, but I'm sure that night, alone on the tracks, she saw what she thought was her only way out and took it. And I think she was alone on those tracks.

I failed Jim, by not trusting the one man who had always taken care of me, of everything, when he needed my trust most. Jim would have given Alex a fair chance. He would have listened. Half the town might not have given him that chance, and I don't think Detective Milner would have, but Jim … Jim would have done it right.

I've since found out that Leonie sent me a note, just like the one found on Alex. The one that everyone pointed to as confirmation that he was the killer. I didn't know she had written me a note as well, but I had met Leonie near the tracks before. I could have said something. I could have stood up for the memory of my friend. But I didn't. I ran instead, leaving a lie to stand in my place. I've always known that Alex couldn't have been guilty.

Again, I have no proof, but I know Alex couldn't have been at the tracks that night. I know he went to her house earlier. Of course, he did. He was worried about her. He was the friend that she needed, that she deserved. And that's how I know he wasn't at the tracks. I don't know why he didn't make it, but if he had, they'd both be alive today. I'm sure of it.

Check-out for the hotel was at 11:00 am, and Kennen waited until the last minute to ensure everyone on the team was out working for the day before he made his final exit. He went down to the front desk, turned in his keycards, and left the camera, asking that they return it to Gemma when she got back with the message that she watch the recording saved on it.

When he stepped out of the Ashter Regal, Kennen spotted Jim's car across the street at the Red Dragon. Of course, it was Tuesday. Sweet and Sour Chicken day. He pulled his cap low and walked with his head down. He knew where he wanted to go, where he needed to go, before he left Ashter. Traveling on foot with his bags was going to take a while, but he wasn't going to try and get a ride. He needed to do this by himself.

It took him nearly an hour to get to the small cemetery that sat at the edge of town. He was sweaty and sticky by the time he arrived, but the clouds were starting to build up, breaking up the sun's unforgiving rays. The gate of the cemetery had one of those old metal signs that curved across the top, reading *Mansford Mound* in big block letters. He crossed back to the left toward a large oak tree. There stood a beautiful slate-colored stone with an engraving of three birds flying away. Someone had placed a bouquet of daisies at the base.

"Hey, Leonie," Kennen said softly. The only response was a gust of wind through the leaves of the old oak. A sting to his eyes hit quickly, his hand flying to his face.

"Thought I might find you here."

Kennen turned to see Jim.

"Still the investigator, huh?"

"Well, at least still lucky enough to get a break. I'm an old guy. I eat early. I saw you heading out with all of your bags," Jim said, nodding at the pile behind Kennen.

"Who do you think brought the flowers?" Kennen said, turning back to the stone.

Jim walked up to stand shoulder-to-shoulder with him. "Probably an old friend."

They stood in silence. A drop fell from the ever-darkening sky and ran down Leonie's stone like a single tear.

"What are you going to do now?"

Kennen wasn't surprised Jim had heard about it all.

"Well, I figured after visiting Leonie I'd go over and visit Alex. Past that, I haven't really thought about it yet."

Kennen looked across to the side where he knew Alex was buried. His stone was much smaller. No decorations other than the remnants of paint from graffiti declaring him a murderer, his stone defaced many times over the years. Kennen spotted two men walking in a nearby plot where the ground sloped off a bit. One held a large roll of paper that he consulted, then pointed to the ground. The other man was Hector Lopez.

"His sister passed yesterday."

"At least she'll get to be with Alex again." More drops started to fall around them.

After a long silence, Jim spoke. "So, you are done with the show? Completely?"

Kennen turned back to Jim. "Yeah." It was an odd change of

subject. He noticed Jim looking him over and then furrowing his brow, as if he was trying to settle something in his mind.

Finally he spoke.

"I'm assuming you are ready to get out of town?"

Kennen searched Jim's face. There was nothing ingenuine there. No passive-aggressive tone. Nothing to suggest Jim was upset about Kennen leaving him again. Just curiosity.

"Yeah."

"And you're free from a tight schedule for a bit?"

Kennen sighed and shook his head. "Yeah." He didn't know where Jim was going with all this, but the questions were slowly pecking away at his composure.

"And am I right that you probably would like to stay out of the public eye for a bit?"

Kennen would flat-out disappear for a while. Anyone looking to talk to him would be attracted to the smell of fresh blood from the carnage of his ruined career. "What are you getting at?"

"I might have a job for you." Jim was smirking, but then his face fell into seriousness. "There is something we can do about all this. You just have to trust me."

Kennen hesitated, not because he didn't trust Jim, but because he didn't know if he could trust himself. Jim apparently didn't interpret Kennen's hesitation that way.

"I know why that is hard. I know you left because you didn't trust me anymore."

"No!" Kennen was surprised at the force with which the word escaped from his mouth. "That was a gut reaction, a hurt-kid reaction, but I knew better." Kennen looked back at Leonie's stone. "I left because I couldn't face this. I couldn't face all that I had let fall apart. I ran from it all. Hell, I got a job where I figured out how to point the finger elsewhere, find out the guilt of others. But it never did anything to shift my own."

"Are you ready to do something real about it now?"

Kennen couldn't read what sat behind Jim's eyes.

"I think I can help you," Jim said.

"What are you talking about?"

"I need a favor. Your Ms. Jones and the rest of them are on top of things around here, and if I or one of the other witnesses they've talked with leave, it might cause them to perk up their ears. But you? You're supposed to leave. I guess the question I have is not if you are ready to leave but if you are ready to move on."

Kennen took a deep breath and put a hand on Leonie's grave. He closed his eyes, letting the cold stone warm slightly under his hand. He opened his eyes. "What is it that you need me to do?"

"Well, I need to confirm one more thing, but I'm assuming you are good for it as well."

"Yeah? And what's that?"

A slow but waggish smile grew on Jim's face. The rain was now breaking through the shelter of the tree.

"You aren't afraid of ghosts, are you?'

AUGUST 1998

Jim had offered to drive Kennen all the way to NYU one of the very few times they spoke that summer. But Kennen wasn't interested in being stuck in a car with Jim. So he bought his ticket for a train out of Chicago. He packed up his suitcase and two duffle bags. He was leaving a lot behind, and that suited him just fine.

He had planned to sneak out in the early morning hours. He had even checked that his suitcase would fit through his bedroom window. But the prep proved unnecessary; Jim was called out a little past 11 pm. So at 3 am, Kennen just walked out the front door and down the street to where Jesse was waiting to pick him up. They arrived at the train station in Chicago an hour before departure. Jesse helped Kennen with his bags, walking him to the platform. There they gave each other an awkward hug and promised to call now and then.

On the train, Kennen slid into a window seat, but he didn't look out at the first rays of light, slowly repainting the world with color. He looked at the empty gray seat next to him. The fabric was rough, worn. It should have held Leonie. Or Alex. Kennen closed his eyes. He imagined Leonie sitting there, smiling back at him. Alex sat across the aisle, leaning forward to wave at Kennen around Leonie.

The sound of someone clearing their throat made Kennen's eyes flash open. A shadow had passed over the seat. Kennen looked up to see a middle-aged man in a black polo with a small logo embroidered on the left of his chest.

"Is it okay if I sit here?" he asked slowly.

"Uh, yeah, of course. Sorry." Kennen turned around to look outside. There were more people milling about on the platform.

Not a single familiar face among them.

AUGUST 2017

Jim let Kennen throw his damp bags in the trunk before they both scrambled into the front seat of the car. The rain made Kennen's shirt stick to him, but it was still the most comfortable he'd felt since arriving at Ashter. The heat had broken.

Jim drove without speaking, but Kennen soon recognized the direction.

"Are we going to see Velma Warren?"

"Yes," Jim said with a heavy sigh. "But I have to warn you, that isn't the only person who will be there. It's ... it's going to be a shock. You should prepare yourself."

Kennen scrunched up his brow in confusion, but Jim said no more. When they pulled up in front of Warren's cabin, the rain had slackened. She sat on the covered porch, rocking in an old rocking chair. They parked and Kennen followed Jim up to the porch. Warren stood and as Jim came up to her, she put her hands up to his face, and he ducked in for a quick kiss. She turned and went inside the cabin. Jim waited for Kennen to catch up.

"That is pretty shocking," Kennen said.

Jim gave a short laugh. "That's just the start." He held the door for Kennen. Warren was taking a kettle from the stovetop.

"Have a seat," Jim said, pointing to the long table. Kennen went and sat, and that's when he saw there was someone in the corner. Someone hiding in the shadows.

"Who—" Kennen started, but Jim placed a firm hand on his shoulder, holding him in place. The man slowly stepped forward into the light from the small lamp. The low light actually helped Kennen recognize him. It had been dark when he saw him last.

"You're the man I saw that night on the tracks." Kennen could better see the old scar that still ripped across the man's cheek.

"Let me introduce you to Henry Alvarez," Jim said. "You knew him as Alex Medina."

All Kennen could do was breathe, and even that act seemed to take a lot of work. The man had his hair cropped short; there was only a hint of a wave. But the eyes were the same.

"Alex?" Kennen's voice was so faint, he wasn't sure if he had actually said it or just thought it.

"Hello, Kennen."

"I … I don't—" Kennen leaned away from Jim's hand and stood, knocking the chair back, barely missing Jim's shins. Kennen started to stumble backward but his legs went out from under him. He crumpled to the floor, his knees breaking against the boards. The man, Alex, started around the table to him. He seemed to tower over Kennen, large beyond reality.

"Oh," Warren let out, running to the chair as the two other men reached for Kennen's arms. "Let's get him back up in the chair."

Kennen couldn't even help as Jim and Alex lifted. Warren slid the chair to the back of his knees, and they lowered him carefully onto the seat. Jim started to take his hand away, but Kennen reached out with his other hand and held Jim's where it had been on his arm. Even in the chair, Kennen felt the world might buckle under him.

"Hold on, dear. I'll get you some tea. You're still damp." Warren went back to the kitchen. Jim kept his hand on Kennen but pulled another chair over and sat next to him. Alex backed around the table and took a seat. Warren came back with tea for all of them. She gently placed a small teacup in Kennen's hand. Kennen was thankful for it. He felt chilled to his soul.

Jim leaned back, removing his hand slowly. "Where would you like to start?"

Kennen opened his mouth, but he couldn't form words, never mind a coherent sentence.

"It's okay, sweetheart." Warren patted his shoulder, sitting down on the other side of him. "I know this is all overwhelming."

"You're not dead," Kennen said to the figure across the table from him. He was talking it out just like the team did when they were testing theories. "You're not dead," he repeated. The real truth was sitting there across from him, but the certainty of the belief he had carried for years was tenacious. The idea still seemed hypothetical.

"According to most of the world, I am," Alex said. "And, to be honest, Alex did die that night."

They all sat in silence for a moment. Kennen took a shaky sip and then sat the cup on the table. "How?"

Jim crossed his arms over his chest. "When I went back to the hospital that night, Henry was out of surgery and resting. His mother was there with Doc Rudy. She was a mess. Doc Rudy took me outside. He said the kid was going to be just fine. He'd have a nasty scar, but the bullet had only scraped along his cheekbone, nicked his ear. I asked why his mother was still so upset then, and Doc just looked at me." Jim paused and sighed. "I realized right away what a stupid question that was. Doc said a good prognosis meant nothing for what would happen the moment that kid left the hospital. So, Doc Rudy, Lily Medina, Velma, and I started hatching a plan."

"You were in on this?" Kennen asked Warren. She gave Kennen a sly smile. "Wait, then how long have you—" Kennen waved a finger back and forth between Jim and Warren. Jim just took a sip of tea and continued his story.

"We waited until shift change. Doc Rudy gave the story that they had missed a bullet fragment that had lodged in the brain. Alex Medina died of a brain bleed."

"But how? If there was no body—"

"Forged paperwork that his body was sent back to Chicago to be cremated. Then we just buried an empty box."

"Is that why there's no coroner's report?" Kennen asked.

"Luckily, no one was asking too many specific questions. Most people were just happy to have the whole business done."

"But—" Kennen threw his hands up. "People had to know. Had to suspect."

"You didn't," Jim pointed out with a smart-ass smirk.

"People at the hospital," Kennen said.

"Kennen," Warren said, "there were people who were suspicious. But what I don't think you know about this town is that there were people who knew Alex was a good kid. The people who worked at the hospital loved and respected his mother. They didn't want what was waiting for him. And all they had to do was keep their thoughts to themselves. That's all it took to help."

"And the people who weren't on his side? People like Whitacre? Like Travers?"

"They were happy with the story they were given," Jim said. "They were fine with Alex just becoming another ghost."

The man across from him had been silent during the retelling, looking into his cup of tea. "Where did you go?" Kennen asked him.

"Here. They brought me here." Alex reached a hand across to Warren who grasped it gently.

"Velma hid him here where Doc Rudy could check on him after his shift. When he was well enough, we took him back to Chicago," Jim said.

"And that's when I became Henry."

283

"Henry Alvarez, an immigrant from Mexico. He became his father's nephew instead of his son," Jim said.

"I'm a citizen. Again. That test is harder than you'd think," Alex said with a little laugh.

Kennen sat back. His mind was fractured, like puzzle pieces thrown on a table. He wasn't sure he could put it all together.

"Why did your mother stay in Ashter?"

"She never fully trusted the plan would work, so she stayed just to make sure if anyone started talking, she might hear it. And then she just never left."

"Was she able to visit you?"

"Yeah. That is until she got so sick. That's why I had to come back."

"Had you been back before?"

"Never."

"And of course, you had to show up, too. Talk about timing," Warren said with a little laugh, shaking her head.

"Shit," Kennen said. He'd nearly fucked it up for his friend again.

Alex said. "I walked in along the train tracks. I hoped to blend in with the other transients."

"But then we hyped up the ghost story—
"

"Hector was worried you would figure it out, so he came and let us know Henry was back to visit his mother," Jim said.

"But I had to come. I had to be here for her."

"Of course you did, Henry. But," Jim said, turning a half-smile on Kennen, "your team has made this all really challenging. They do pretty impressive work."

There was the sound of a car engine out front. Kennen jumped up in a panic, but Jim stood and raised his hand to signify everything was fine. He went to the door. Kennen watched, holding his breath.

"He's here. Time to go." But there was a challenge there. Everyone in the room looked at Kennen, and there was a tenseness constricting the air. Then the light bulb lit up in Kennen's mind: this was it. They had decided to trust him; Alex was trusting him with his entire life. But there was still a fear, and a reasonable one. This truth could also be Kennen's ticket back to his life. Forget the show, news people would be all over him. He could be on every morning and afternoon talk show with this story.

They waited. Kennen finally nodded. He made his choice. "Yes, it's time to go."

Jim went out on the porch. Alex and Warren went as well, Alex carrying a small satchel. Kennen followed. Hector Lopez stood in front of a beat-up old Pontiac. Lopez gave the hood a hefty pat.

"Been sitting out back of the shop for years, but I've got it working. At least for as far as you need her to go," Lopez said.

Jim started loading Kennen's bags from the back of his car into the Pontiac along with Alex's satchel.

"And where is that?" Kennen asked, grabbing a bag to help.

"Take the back road out of here and head towards Carmen. Then head back up to Chicago. It's an extra hour's drive, but it should keep you from running into any familiar faces on the way back in. Rent a car here." Jim passed Kennen a paper with an address scribbled on it.

"Leave the Pontiac there. We'll pick it up later," Lopez said.

"Then where?"

"I'll tell you when we are good and on our way," Alex said. He went over to have a few quiet words with his uncle.

Kennen turned back to Warren and Jim.

"So, he gave you the picture and note?"

Warren nodded. "I'm good at hiding things." She put her arm around Jim's waist and he pulled her in around her shoulders.

"To protect me?"

"And him," Warren said with a nod toward Alex. "I know it wasn't fair to Leonie, but she was already gone. We had to take care of what was left."

"If evidence surfaced that showed he might be innocent, people would get interested in the case again. We couldn't chance anyone finding Henry," Jim said.

"Okay," Lopez said loudly. Everyone turned.

Alex crawled into the back and lay down on the floor. Lopez and Jim pulled a blanket over him.

"Just until you get well outside of Ashter," Jim said.

Jim put out his hand. Kennen grabbed it, then pulled him in for a hug. Jim held on to him tight. Finally, they separated and Kennen crawled into the car.

Kennen drove all the way to Carmen trying to pretend like there wasn't someone hiding in the back of his car. It was easier than he would have thought, and he attributed that to the shadow that had followed him since he arrived. He'd been practicing for weeks, pretending Alex wasn't right there, right behind him. When they pulled out the far side of Carmen and started backtracking towards Chicago, the clouds finally broke away. He parked a block down from the rental place and left Alex while he filled out the paperwork.

As he was pulling back around in the rental, he felt his stomach sink when a thought hit him: what if Alex was already gone? But he was leaning there against the side of a building. He crawled in the passenger side.

"Where to?" Kennen asked.

"We're both going to New York. I'll tell you more as we get closer."

Kennen had fantasized about what he would say to Alex, to Leonie, if he had just five more minutes with them. It had become a game in college when he would be depressed or lonely, he would talk with them. Now he had hours to say what he needed to. But it took until the sun was falling behind them for him to dislodge it from his throat.

"Alex, if I had known what was going to happen, I would have never called."

"Please, it's Henry."

Kennen swallowed and looked sideways. Alex's–no Henry's–eyes met his.

"I wasn't thinking straight. I missed Leonie so much. I still do."

"I miss her too."

"She's not going to miraculously show up when we get to New York, is she?" Kennen asked with a pitiful laugh.

"No, Kennen. I'm sorry."

"That would be something, though, right?"

They rode in silence for a while.

"What do you think happened to her?" Kennen finally asked.

Kennen heard Henry shifting in his seat. Then Henry gave a loud sigh.

"Pull over."

"What? Why? Are you okay? Are you sick?" Kennen tried to find Henry's eyes again, but Henry was looking out the window.

"You need to pull over. I'll tell you what happened that night."

MAY 14TH, 1998

Alex looked at the note one more time before tucking it into his jacket and stepping out into the cool evening air. The sun was dropping and the shadows were long. He looked at his watch. He had plenty of time to make it, but he needed to do so quietly. Not mess up like he had earlier. He shook his head again. How could he have been so stupid? Someone must have seen him, beating on Leonie's door, peering in her windows. But he was so damned worried about her. First, she wasn't at school all day. Then, when he got home from baseball practice there was the note asking him to meet her in the clearing by the tracks that night. He had gone over when their study session had originally been planned, thinking she'd be there. He'd made a fuss when he couldn't find her and he wondered what the repercussions would be. What would Mr. Tilden do to her if he found out Alex had been around?

Dread, like a desperate bird, clawed at his stomach. He pulled his jacket close at the neck and walked quickly. When he got to the clearing there was hardly any light left, but he could see he was alone. He leaned against a tree and waited. He was about to leave when he heard the crunch of a branch. He carefully stepped back into the shadows, watching warily. This was a well-used spot; there was no guarantee it would be Leonie. But he caught the moonlight tipping her honey curls and stepped back out. She clicked on a flashlight and threw the light on his face.

"Oh, thank god, you got my note," she said, almost out of breath.

"Leonie, you're freaking me out. What is going on?"

"I have to leave. I have to leave tonight. I need you to cover for me."

"What are you talking about?"

"It's my dad."

"Leonie, please, let's talk this out. There is a lot on the line here. We've just got a week and then we'll be graduating. You've got college coming and—"

"No, I don't. I'm not going to college."

Alex shook his head, confused. "Why don't you want to go to college anymore?"

"It has nothing to do with wanting!" Leonie shouted. She gulped a breath. "I can't. My dad never sent any of my applications in."

"What?!"

"I can't stay–I gotta–I just—" Leonie's words were tumbling out faster than she could make a sentence.

Alex grabbed her and pulled her to his chest. She shuddered with a muffled sob. Alex rocked her gently, his face down in her curls. "Let's sit," he whispered. "Tell me what you know and then we'll figure this out." Alex waited, and finally, he felt her nod her head. He loosened his grasp, but kept his hands on her arms, guiding her over to a rock. They sat and he waited for her to go on.

"My dad has been having me help out with his work. Just paperwork mostly. But back just before spring break, I found a scrap of paper on the floor. It must have fallen out of the shredder bin when he emptied it. It was a piece of my NYU application. So I called. No one had seen my application. None of the schools had. So I went to see my mother. He found out and has watched me like a hawk ever since. This weekend is my only chance."

"Leonie, I just don't understand—"

"He's keeping me here. He hasn't let me out of his sight since spring break. He completely stopped going up to Chicago, but he couldn't get out of it this weekend. I knew this would be my only chance. Then a letter came in the mail today. He's signed me up at the tech institute for secretarial sciences." Leonie cut him off, shaking her head, lips pulled into a grimace. "He wants to keep me here, working for him. Keep me where he can always see me, control me."

Her words dripped with bile and burned into Alex's mind. He couldn't wrap his head around it. How could her father take all of that away from her? Her dreams? Her life?

"Okay, so you're leaving. But what's your plan?"

"He's had me run some checks to the bank before, so they are used to me coming in. I went in and asked for a balance on all of the accounts. I planned to just take the money from my college fund, but apparently, that isn't there anymore. So I just took $5000 from his savings, which turned out to be most of it." She opened her bag and pulled out an envelope full of hundred-dollar bills.

"They just let you withdraw that much?"

"I told them my dad needed me to withdraw it and bring it to him in Chicago for an emergency concerning one of his cases. The teller wilted under the threat of litigation."

"Where will you go?"

"I'm not telling you. I'm probably already getting you in enough trouble asking you to cover for me. My dad won't be back until Monday, so no one will even start looking until after that. Say that you saw me somewhere Sunday. It doesn't matter where."

"I don't know, Leonie. I want to help, but I'm worried—"

"Here. I don't need all this. Take $500. Just make them think I was still here until Sunday. I just need the time."

"Leonie, no, I don't want—"

"I'll give you some time." Calvin Travers stepped out from the treeline, flipping on a flashlight under his chin so he looked like some crazy from a horror flick. Jeffie followed.

"If it isn't the princess and the faggot," Jeffie sneered.

"Let's go," Alex said, standing and trying to pull Leonie up with him, but she was trying to stuff the envelope back in her bag and zip it.

"Why don't you offer me some?" Jeffie asked. "Then I won't have to let all this slip to your dad."

Alex stepped around Leonie. Jeffie came up and squared up with Alex. Jeffie faked and Alex fell for it, throwing the first punch. Even in the low light of the flashlights and moon, Jeffie was able to dodge, Alex's fist glancing off of his cheek. Jeffie took advantage of Alex's momentum, grabbing his arm on the follow-through and flipping him around. Jeffie pinned Alex's arm behind him, then grabbed him around the throat pulling him tight.

"Stop it!" Leonie cried.

"Make sure the bruises won't show," Jeffie said as Calvin stepped up front and center.

Calvin started rolling into Alex's defenseless torso like he was a punching bag. Alex collapsed forward, hanging from Jeffie's grip, his wallet and the note falling out of his jacket. Calvin was lining up to kick Alex in the side of the head when Leonie jumped on his back.

"You bitch!" Calvin growled, reaching behind and grabbing Leonie by her hair. He yanked her off his back. Alex looked over to see her fall, her mouth open, but her cry was distorted, deep. At first, he just thought it was the blood pulsing in his ears, but then he realized it wasn't that at all; instead, it was the rumble of the tracks. A train was coming.

"Grab the bag!" Jeffie screamed.

Alex scanned over and saw that the bag had been flung a few feet away. Alex didn't know where to run, to Leonie or to her bag, but it didn't matter. The sharp pains in his chest kept him grounded. Calvin got the bag and looked back at Jeffie.

"Come on!" Jeffie yelled, but Calvin hesitated. He heard the train as well. The train's light was just starting to reach them through the trees. Jeffie read the betrayal in Calvin's pause.

"You fucker!" exploded out of Jeffie as Calvin turned and ran towards the tracks. He had always been fast on the field and there was no way Jeffie, who was all bulk, could have caught him. Alex knew if Calvin got past those tracks before the train came, he'd be gone, the rest of them trapped on this side by a roaring wall of steel. But Alex was still having a hard time getting his feet underneath him.

But Leonie was up. She was running. And she was gaining! Alex started tumbling forward. He looked up to see her dive at Calvin. She grabbed the bag and her weight pulled Calvin down on his side, but he still had an arm through the strap. They both struggled to their feet, pulling the bag between them. Calvin found his footing and used the bag to fling her around onto the rock ballasts that held the tracks. She tumbled onto the rocks but didn't let go. There were about five feet between them and Alex.

Now three.

Leonie pushed herself up again and rushed at Calvin, shoving him and the bag toward Alex. Alex caught Calvin under the arms and Leonie was finally able to pull the bag from his grip. She turned.

And ran toward the tracks.

Alex tried to cry "No!" but his voice was lost in the train's horn. Would she make it? She was up on the rocks again.

She could make it.

But then Jeffie came up behind her.

He grabbed her by her collar and pulled her back like she was a rag doll. Alex let Calvin drop to the side. He saw the shock on her face as the train barreled past. She had missed her escape.

And she knew it.

Her face and shoulders dropped. Jeffie pulled the bag from her hands, but she didn't even fight it. He stared down at her, triumphant.

And she stepped backward.

Alex scrambled over Calvin. "Leonie!" he cried.

She stepped backward again, up onto the rocks. A confused look crossed Jeffie's face.

"Leonie, please!" He could almost reach her. The train shook the ground and it felt like the earth might just crumble away beneath his feet, but he kept pushing forward. His fingertips brushed the sleeve of her jacket.

And then time slowed.

And in the low light, Alex met her eyes. But they were empty. She dropped her arms away from his reach. He swore he saw her shake her head. Just slightly.

Alex blinked. There was a terrible sound.

When his eyes opened, she was gone.

There was only the train.

AUGUST 2017

Kennen sat still. They were on a quiet highway, sinking in the liminal darkness at the edge of two streetlight pools. There was a tickle on his cheek. When he reached up, his fingers came away wet with tears. How long had he been crying?

"What happened next?" Kennen asked, his voice thin.

"Calvin panicked. Jeffie had to grab him and hold onto him until the train had passed and it was quiet again. I just knelt there. I couldn't think. Finally, Jeffie started shaking me. He saw the note on the ground and asked what it was. He told me to take it with me, to get rid of it. He and Calvin would take the bag. And if I talked, they'd talk. And who would people believe, the kid with the football scholarship or the kid with the gangster brother?"

"So, they took her money?"

"I don't think they had it for long," Henry said.

"What do you mean?"

Henry shook his head. "The first time Milner and your dad interviewed me, Milner was yawning, couldn't be bothered. Then, the week before you called, I noticed him … around. Almost like he was tailing me. Then, the day they came, he was blocking anyway out to the south with the cop car and already had his hand on the gun. I have always wondered if they paid him off."

Milner's C.I., Sam Travers being ready with his gun close at hand. All of the coincidences started to collapse, leaving one reality behind.

"Why didn't you get rid of the letter?"

Henry looked down and shook his head. Kennen understood.

"I had a note too. I didn't know it. I would have gone, but I was out trying to cheer up Jesse, I—"

"I know, man, I know," Henry said, looking back at him. "Kennen, we need to get going again before someone notices a car pulled over. I can drive for a while."

Kennen felt the weight of exhaustion on his shoulders, bending his neck. They switched places and Henry pulled the car back onto the highway.

"Did you–do you–have a good life?" Kennen asked.

"Yeah, yeah I do," Henry said, smiling. "It wasn't the time-line I expected. I hung low for a number of years. As Henry, I had to earn my citizenship. I worked and put some money away. Got back to school after that. I work for an architecture firm now. I have a partner and two children."

Kennen found himself laughing in shock. "Do they know—"

"Oh, God no," Henry said, shaking his head. "Alex died that night. I'm Henry. I'm their father. Their husband. Not Alex."

"You live in New York?"

Henry nodded, but Kennen could feel a tension coming from him. "I'll go my own way when we get to Jamestown."

"We … we're not going to be able to just start over again, pick up from when we were teenagers, are we?"

Henry was quiet for a moment, rolling his palms over the wheel. He started to open his mouth, but Kennen put his hand up. "No, you're right. Alex is dead. I get it. You have to think of your family."

Henry let out a small sigh.

"I've got Jim to think about, too. And apparently Ms. Warren." They both laughed. "But we have this drive, right?"

"That we do," Henry said with a nod.

Kennen smiled.

"Then we'll just make the best of the time we've got."

ACKNOWLEDGMENTS

I am so lucky. I have so many people that have helped me get to this point. Thank you to my mother, Elizabeth Miller, and my grandparents Patricia (née Childers) and Ray Miller, for always reading or listening to whatever story I was writing. I can only imagine how much patience it took to bear the silly stories of a kindergartener. Thank you to my brother Kelly Davis, who not only was a beta reader, but also gave me feedback on the law enforcement aspects of this story. All mistakes are my own. Love you, Bro!

Thank you to my writing partner, Jenn Haskin, and all the members of our Monday night writing crew: Zach Drummond, Ethan Fitzgerald, Greg Gildersleeve, Berkay Karakurt, and Mark McGuiness. Thank you to all of the wonderful writers in Kansas Writers Inc., and especially the following, as they all have given feedback on this story at some point: Connie Beckett, Morgan Chilson, Romie Chavez, Leslie Galbraith, Tish (Bear) Glasson, Theresa Grennan, Shayne Huxtable, Angela Johnson, Billie-Renee Knight, Julie Nischan, and Anne Noble.

Thank you to my wonderful beta readers: Twyla Broadbent, Jessica Karns, and Kay Usrey. Their enthusiasm made me believe there could be a readership out there.

Thank you to Mark Ralston for the great headshots.

Shout out to the Topeka Shawnee County Public Library, which just happens to be the best library in the world. Thank you for providing an oasis in a crazy world.

Thank you to the wonderful people at Next Chapter for taking a chance on me.

Finally, thank you to my wonderful husband, Andrew Davis. No one else has to put up with my writer-weirdness as much as he does, and he still loves me at the end of the day. I couldn't have done this without his support.

ABOUT THE AUTHOR

A. D. Childers lives in Kansas where she enjoys a life full of teaching and writing. It helps pass the time while she waits for the next Tana French novel to come out. When not at work, she can be found hiking the local trails or hanging out at the library. She lives with her wonderful and bearded husband, a grumpy cat, and her sweet Kodi-beast-dog, who is her constant snuggle companion while writing.

To learn more about A. D. Childers and discover more Next Chapter authors, visit our website at www.nextchapter.pub.

The Switch Point
ISBN: 978-4-82418-932-5

Published by
Next Chapter
2-5-6 SANNO
SANNO BRIDGE
143-0023 Ota-Ku, Tokyo
+818035793528

9th December 2023

Printed in the USA
CPSIA information can be obtained
at www.ICGtesting.com
CBHW020703050224
3979CB00005B/4